THE NEPTUNE STORY

"That wonderful building must never be demolished
. . . our ghosts are still there."

— JOHN WOOD

THE NEPTUNE STORY

TWENTY-FIVE YEARS IN THE
LIFE OF A LEADING CANADIAN
THEATRE

RICHARD PERKYNS

Editorial and Research Associates
DOROTHY PERKYNS
BASIL DEAKIN

Editorial Consultatnt
DAVID RENTON

LANCELOT PRESS
HANTSPORT, NOVA SCOTIA

ISBN 0-88999-393-9
Cover design and
interior design: Joan Sinclair
Published 1989

Front cover photos, from top to bottom:
*Same Time Next Year, A Moon for the Misbegotten,
King Lear,* and *Private Lives.*
Back cover photos:
*The Caretaker, A Man for
All Seasons,* and *Reunion.*

LANCELOT PRESS LIMITED
Office and and production facilities located on Hwy. 1,
one-half mile east of Hantsport, Nova Scotia.

ACKNOWLEDGEMENT
This book has been published with the assistance of
The Nova Scotia Department of Tourism and Culture.

CONTENTS

This book is dedicated to the thousands
who have worked for Neptune Theatre
over twenty-five years
and in particular to the memory of
Neptune's first president, Arthur L. Murphy

also to the memory of my parents
Muriel and Charles Perkyns
great lovers of the arts

INTRODUCTION

The story that is about to unfold is a truly extraordinary one. It was a great act of vision and courage that started one of Canada's leading regional theatres a quarter of a century ago. If Neptune Theatre has never fully realized the ideals inspired by Leon Major in the early sixties, its artistic achievement has nevertheless been remarkable in the face of constant financial restraint.

This book is not principally, however, about fiscal problems and boardroom crises. While it would be unrealistic to ignore the difficulties and setbacks that any artistic director must face without limitless funds to mount one exciting and expensive production after another, this is above all an optimistic story, more about triumphs than disasters.

It is foremost about the artistic directors who have each in distinctive ways contributed their individual vision and leadership. But it is also about the multitude of personalities whose teamwork has created a company that has given immense pleasure to many thousands of people over twenty-five years. It is above all a very human story, with many tales that have become almost legendary: Neptune Theatre has begun to create its own mythology.

The tributes at the end of this book represent but a small cross-section of the thousands who have worked for Neptune Theatre since its inception, as part of the company or as volunteers. It was impossible to reach everyone, and some who were contacted have for various reasons not replied, but the enthusiasm of those who have written or recorded their impressions speaks also for the many who have been unable to do so. The most poignant letter was sent by Maxim Mazumdar from Buffalo where he was performing shortly before he died. But it was a letter that told of a happy experience, one that is recounted in Chapter 7. It was typical of this outstanding artist to make such a gesture at the end of a short life which gave so much inspiration and happiness to so many; he will be sorely missed. I would like to

Richard Perkyns

thank all of those who have helped to recreate the Neptune story, not least the artistic directors who gave generous time to record their ideas and feelings about something that was so close to them at a key period in each of their lives.

This volume is unique in that it records all the principal artists involved in mainstage and second stage productions over twenty-five years. For a small regional theatre the number of illustrious names that appear in these pages is astonishing: John Neville, Tony Randall, Roger Rees, Michael Gough, Odetta, Robin Phillips, to name only a few. Many who were unknown when they began at Neptune are now household theatrical names across Canada and beyond. Only lack of space precludes listing of Young Neptune or workshop presentations, or stage managers and other vital team members for all productions. Failure to mention them by no means diminishes their importance or denies recognition that no production can succeed without the essential role played by every member of a total ensemble.

The research required has been time-consuming, since over this lengthy period records have not always been kept in an orderly way. Much valuable documentation has disappeared somewhere between Neptune Theatre and Dalhousie Theatre Archives. Dr. Charles Armour and his staff at the Archives have been painstakingly diligent in seeking information for me, and I am grateful to my wife Dorothy and to Basil Deakin for research and editorial assistance. David Renton has been invaluable as a consultant in checking for factual errors or misleading statements, since people's memories can sometimes be unreliable! Every attempt has been made to verify all information. Lionel Simmons, Nicola Lipman and R.D. Reid have helped in finding elusive photographs. I should finally acknowledge the assistance and support given by Neptune's 25th Anniversary Committee, including chairman Edwin Rubin, Neptune president Allister Byrne, general manager Denise Rooney and especially public relations director Beverly West and artistic director Richard Ouzounian.

Some of the material in this book first appeared in an article "Two Decades of Neptune Theatre" in *Theatre History in*

Canada/Histoire du Théâtre au Canada, Vol. 6, No. 2, Fall 1985, though it has been extensively revised and expanded. All source material is annotated in that article. For subsequent sources I have made exclusive use of personal letters, taped interviews, or Neptune Theatre press releases. The book is published with the approval of the Canadian Actors' Equity Association and in accordance with the Canadian Theatre Agreement.

RICHARD PERKYNS
Halifax, December 1988

▲

*The opening production, **Major Barbara,** in rehearsal:*
the late Molly Williams, David Renton, Mavor Moore, Gary Krawford,
Joan (Gregson) Evans.

The origins of Neptune Theatre

WHEN LEON MAJOR asked his friend David Renton to join a new theatre company he was founding in Halifax, Nova Scotia, Renton's first reaction was, "You're kidding . . . Halifax?!" Who would be so mad as to start a professional repertory in such a drab, poor, neglected part of Canada? Yet when the dream became a reality, Renton jumped at the chance to become one of the fourteen core members of the original company, expecting to work fifty-two weeks of the year, in an experiment unique in Canada if not in North America.

Leon Major, already an experienced stage director before coming to Halifax, considers that Neptune owes its life to Peter Dwyer, executive director of Canada Council in 1957. One of the mandates of the newly formed Council was to encourage the growth of regional theatre in Canada by providing subsidies. The same year Major went to Europe to study the work of its most important theatre companies. After his return in 1959 he came to Halifax to adjudicate the regional finals of the Dominion Drama Festival and was impressed with the enthusiasm for theatre in the city. In particular he met the late Dr. Arthur Murphy and others who expressed the need for a theatre in Halifax.

It was still a time before the mushrooming of Canada's theatres; there was, of course, Stratford, and there were the Jupiter, Crest, New Play Society and other theatre companies in Toronto, but few comparable with these in the rest of Canada. Major decided that a small city like Halifax was the perfect place for theatre: he returned to Toronto "filled with ideals you have when you're twenty-nine years old and have been to Europe to see the Berliner Ensemble." He went to see Peter Dwyer, who found money for Major to go back to Halifax and write an outline of the ideal repertory theatre in Canada. With the assistance of Tom Patterson, founder of the Stratford Shakespeare Festival, and

Costume design sketch by Guido Tondino, 1978, for **Les Canadiens**

Costume sketch by Arthur
Penson, 1977-78, for Toby Tarnow
in **The Gingerbread Lady**

John (Jack) Gray, an experienced playwright who had studied in the U.K., he produced a report which favoured the establishment of such a theatre in Halifax.

The report to Canada Council was followed by a feasibility study that a committee chaired by Arthur Murphy prepared. The committee engaged a consulting firm to advise it on the financial and economic aspects of the project, as well as on means of getting the theatre started. Though the study was affirmative it was not produced without its authors facing indifference and even hostility, covert if not overt, from some members of the community, especially the élite and even the newspaper publisher. According to Major, "One person said, with his feet on the desk, *What do you need a theatre here for, when you can go to New York or London?* My answer was, *What about the people who cannot afford to go to New York or London?* He replied, *Well, they don't need a theatre!*"

The study said "everyone wants a theatre", but, says Major, it was a concealed lie: any feasibility study can prove what you want to prove. He was determined to have a theatre in Halifax, and was supported by a handful of enthusiasts like Arthur Murphy, George Hawkins, and his father-in-law Robert Strand. They said, "Let's have it! Let's do it!" Major won the support of John Lloyd, then Mayor of Halifax, who saw the proposal as a spur for city redevelopment, increased tourist spending, and the attraction of new industry in the way that Stratford had done. The Professional Repertory Theatre Project advocated a professional company with a strong permanent body of performers.

According to Lloyd Newman, a former president, Neptune would probably not have been born without Bob Strand, a man of drive, energy and wit: "After an unsuccessful attempt to create a free port in Halifax, Bob hit upon the idea of a theatre here to emulate the just-born Stratford Festival in Ontario, where Leon was an assistant director. He brought his son-in-law to Halifax to address a parlour meeting of interested citizens. Leon and the interested attendees hit it off." Later Strand became Neptune's part-time publicist.

The ideals were realized, in spite of pockets of opposition. It was not, after all, a totally unsuitable place to establish such a theatre, or to name it "Neptune". The traditions were there. Nova Scotia could boast the first French-language theatrical presentation ever seen in the New World, Marc Lescarbot's *Le Théâtre de Neptune en la Nouvelle-France*: this pageant expressing loyalty to the French Crown was enacted on the shore and in the water at the fort of Port Royal in Acadia, at what is now Lower Granville, near Annapolis Royal, in 1606. The earliest known theatrical performance in Halifax was in 1768, by soldiers manning the garrisons; just six years later they produced the first known English-Canadian play, *Acadius; or, Love in a Calm*. Halifax was a major part of call for the theatrical and vaudeville ensembles that visited in the heyday of touring companies, during the nineteenth and early twentieth centuries.

When the new Neptune Theatre Foundation first met in July 1962, Arthur Murphy was elected president and Laird Fairn vice-president. Murphy was not only a surgeon but a playwright for stage, radio and television, and a well known figure in local community theatre. The following month the Neptune board voted to open the first repertory season in July 1963. But they needed a building. Apart from the Capitol, the only theatre in Halifax with a stage was the Garrick on Sackville Street, which had opened as a vaudeville house in 1915, but in 1928, redecorated after a fire, it was used as a repertory theatre for about five years. After the Depression it operated mainly as a cinema until the new Neptune company took over.

The projected cost of $60,000 included leasing and renovating the Garrick Theatre. Arthur Murphy and George Hawkins prevailed upon Colonel Sidney Oland to buy the building from the Odeon chain on behalf of Neptune for $100,000. Within twenty-four hours a deal was struck, and Oland with several other prominent citizens guaranteed the mortgage on the asset through Canada Permanent Trust Company. There was still no company, still no clear concept of how it would work, no certainty of how much money could be raised. But idealism and enthusiasm carried the day. Without the Oland family's generosity, says Lloyd Newman, we would not have had twenty-

▲
The late Dr. Arthur L. Murphy, first president of Neptune Theatre Foundation

When the building was still a cinema: the Garrick, shortly before renovation in 1963.

five years' use of what Nathan Cohen called "a jewel box of a theatre." "My own memories of Neptune are intertwined with my memories of the Oland family," says Newman. "I remember vividly the theatre's opening night. It was July 1, 1963, and Colonel Oland was attired — quite unaccountably — in a velvet-collared overcoat. As we walked down the aisle, he turned to me (we had never met), handed me a telegram he was holding in his hand, and said, *Look after that.* I — quite unaccountably — did."

Fairn's architectural firm undertook the renovations of the Garrick, under the direction of Toronto stage designer Les Lawrence, who was to become resident designer with the first Neptune company. Leon Major, appointed artistic director in September 1962, found himself part of the crew, shovelling dirt and clearing up the old theatre. Joan Gregson, a member of the first company, remembers going into the gutted building and seeing the new theatre develop: "I tried to visualize how it was going to be, and it turned out to be a beautiful, beautiful little theatre." Every attempt was made to refurbish and preserve the architecture: much of the former ornate rococo design was uncovered from layers of plaster; a fake ceiling was removed and the original high-arched ceiling restored. A thrust stage was built out an additional eight feet, and to the proscenium were added flanking balconies with detachable stairs. The entire balcony was renovated and new seating installed. Though additions were made to the cramped basement dressing-room area, and some adjacent office, storage, and workshop room was found, to this day lack of wing, backstage and general working space has remained a perpetual problem. Despite several fund-raising campaigns, including those by the Neptune ladies' auxiliary, the Tridents, and a pledge of $25,000 from the Nova Scotia government, costs and credit rose alarmingly. Renovation costs alone, originally estimated at $20,000, rose to $200,000 before the alterations were complete.

Robert Doyle, the company's first costume designer, explains some of the difficulties: "I don't think it had crossed anyone's mind the expense of a regional theatre; certainly no thought had been given to workshop space. I was offered Leon

▲

Announcing the gala opening, 1963.

◄

Neptune Theatre under construction: aerial view from Sackville Street. "Johnnies" is still on the corner of Argyle Street.

Planning the first season:
Mavor Moore, Leon Major,
Robert Dexter, Arthur Murphy.

Major's office for two hours per day to get the costumes ready for the first season. Not accepting it, I did manage to obtain what is now part of the actors' green room, a space 14' x 16' to create the clothes for the first seasons. Shopping in Halifax in those days left a good deal to be desired; for instance, Goodman Textiles at that time were still wrapping their bolts of cloth in brown paper to protect them for shelf soiling, something like the early 19th century drapers. On the other hand, there existed here shops like Colwell Bros. that carried the most extensive line of gentlemen's accessories, i.e. white gloves, white silk scarves, collar studs, bowler hats, straw boaters — you name it and they probably had it. Neptune Theatre inherited their old rental stock of evening clothes, tuxedos, evening suits, directors' suits, frock coats, top hats — much of which still exists. Shaw's Men's Wear on Barrington Street was another such mine of wonderful pre-war clothing."

John Blackmore also recalls that period: "The production manager, in the summer of 1963, was Bob Dexter and he couldn't find anybody in Halifax who had any knowledge of scenery, so he went to the CBC. The carpenters at CBC said *No way! We don't want any extra work.* I happened to be working there part time, so they said, *Get Blackmore!*" At that time John and his brother William were building at home. Leon Major and Arthur Murphy came out to the house one night and put pressure on them. "They put it in such a way we couldn't turn them down." The Blackmores agreed to do one set, and twenty-five years later they're still doing the sets: "It's interesting; that's why we're still here."

Something of the backstage drama, the behind-the-scenes struggle, is described by David Renton. He comments on how costly the renovations were. The fly gallery was old, the timbers had shrunk, and there was little support between the beams holding the pulleys. Actors' Equity said the structure was not safe and the grid was dangerous. Temporary measures had to be taken to make it secure for the first year.

In its early years Neptune was beset by constant problems. Financial woes were the greatest of the worries, but it was not the

▲
The interior of the new theatre

only time in Neptune's history that mounting debts threatened to close the theatre. Harry Bruce's *Happy Birthday, Dear Neptune,* published on the Foundation's tenth anniversary, analyzes many of these troubles, including stormy board meetings and clashes of personality. But that great act of faith, the vision of what Neptune could become, surmounted all crises. Major still speaks very highly of Neptune's first board of directors, of their courage and of the risks they took. "Neptune is a dream that realized half of its potential," he says.

Setbacks were constant. Major recalls now with amusement

► Master carpenters William and John Blackmore at work on the sets.

— though it was far from funny at the time — how during renovations to enlarge the dressing-room area fuel tanks had been disconnected. The oil company had not been notified, and on April 2, 1963 an oil truck (Harry Bruce suggests it might have been sent on April Fool's Day) pumped 900 gallons of oil which spread to a depth of fourteen inches over the basement floor. This was only one of many calamities. Yet the race to finish preparations for the opening on July 1 was won by a great act of faith, excitement, zeal, and desperately hard work on the part of the founders and the new company.

▲

Mavor Moore, on his way to rehearsal, stops to look at the advertisement outside the theatre for Neptune's opening season.

◄

Front of Neptune theatre just before the doors opened, July 1963.

one

LEON MAJOR

artistic director
1963 - 1968

"It is very hard for me to believe that Neptune is twenty years old. I know it factually but it seems only yesterday that we started rehearsals for *Major Barbara* and *Mary, Mary*."

(Leon Major in a letter, April 27, 1983)

LEON MAJOR saw the challenge of Neptune as a unique experiment. His model was the great European theatres, such as the Moscow Art Theatre or the Abbey in Dublin; when he told Ria Mooney, administrator of the Abbey, that he wanted to start such a theatre in Canada, she replied, "Then get the hell back and start it." He wanted to see playwrights attached permanently to the theatre. He hoped regional legends about farmers, miners and fishermen would find expression on the stage. To this end John (Jack) Gray was appointed resident playwright as well as administrator. Gray summarized the aims of Neptune in this way: "The Neptune Theatre is an attempt to establish a fully professional regional theatre presenting plays in repertory, based on the assumption that the theatre in Canada must be subsidized, both to open and to continue in operation. Its repertory season will include the best plays of the past in balance with new plays, Canadian wherever possible, but new."

Major never had any qualms about the risks he was taking, and about the fact that he and the board were allowing the theatre to go into debt. Although he believes he could not be accused of overspending or doing lavish shows, he knew the money was not there to meet the basic needs of the company. Yet the job *had* to be done; the end justified the means. In the first place it was a "viable project." Moreover there was no reason, in his judgment, why the Maritimes should not have a theatre, why it should not have the best actors available, or why it should just follow a Broadway tradition.

▲

The final scene of Shaw's **Major Barbara,** the opening production at Neptune: Joan (Gregson) Evans, David Renton, Gary Krawford, Molly Williams, Mavor Moore, Ted Follows, Dawn Greenhalgh.

◄

Joan (Gregson) Evans in the first of several two-handers in which she was to star, here with Bernard Behrens in **The Fourposter.**

MARY, MARY

by Jean Kerr
directed by Leon Major
settings designed by Les Lawrence
costumes designed by Robert Doyle
lighting by Wallace Russell

Bob McKellaway / TED FOLLOWS
Tiffany Richards / DIANA LEBLANC
Oscar Nelson / BERNARD BEHRENS
Dirk Winston / GEORGE SPERDAKOS
Mary McKellaway / DAWN GREENHALGH

ANTIGONE

by Jean Anouilh
adapted by Lewis Galantiere
directed by Leon Major
stage settings and costumes
designed by Les Lawrence
special music for "Antigone"
composed by John Fenwick

Chorus / TED FOLLOWS
Antigone / DIANA LEBLANC
Nurse / MARY McMURRAY
Ismene / DAWN GREENHALGH
Haemon / DAVID RENTON, GARY KRAWFORD
Creon / NORMAN WELSH
First Guard / GEORGE SPERDAKOS
Second Guard / JOHN HOBDAY
Third Guard / STEPHEN WILBAND
Messenger / GARY KRAWFORD,
DAVID RENTON
Page / PETER WRIGHT
Eurydice / UNA WAY

DIAL "M" FOR MURDER

by Frederick Knott
directed by Mavor Moore
settings designed by Les Lawrence

Margot Wendice / DAWN GREENHALGH
Max Halliday / GARY KRAWFORD
Tony Wendice / DAVID RENTON
Captain Lesgate / BERNARD BEHRENS
Inspector Hubbard / NORMAN WELSH
Policeman / STEPHEN WILBAND

Major contrasts the needs of regional theatre with those of the large theatre centres. A regional theatre must be part of the community and direct its work to the needs of the people. Broadway theatre, he notes, doesn't care about the community of New York, even though New York depends on the existence of Broadway. The moment you go to Seattle or Halifax, however, the theatre has to be involved in the life of the community. He still maintains that Neptune should have a permanent company, be a fifty-two week theatre, have its own school, develop the entire Maritimes as an acting school, and "forget the rest of Canada."

Some members of the first company have had long service with Neptune. Robert Doyle, for example, has frequently been praised over the years for his ingenious and colourful costume and stage designs. John Blackmore, now 62, has given twenty-five years' continuous service as Neptune's master carpenter; his brother William, now 83, still works on sets part-time. "When we started on the summer repertory in June 1963," says John, "it was terrible, it was so hot. In those days they had no subscribers; they depended on people walking in off the street. And there was no advertising, except a little thing in the paper. In that first season we didn't even put the set together; it was picked up and that's the last I saw of it until I went to the opening night. It went on like that for at least five years. They had no storage, so every morning we had to take the truck, pick up enough material to work that day, and do the same thing the next morning. At that time we didn't have Johnnie's." Johnnie's was the little corner shop at the intersection of Argyle and Sackville streets, within the Neptune Theatre block, which was run by a Chinese Canadian.

"For I don't know how many years," adds Blackmore, "we had a shed on the back of the Neptune building, next to the City Club, and that was good. When we first moved into the carpenter's shop, in the basement backstage, we built benches and tables for our work. We decided to paint them green; it was a horrible green but the only colour we had. Leon Major walked in and he was horrified. He told us to paint it some other colour at once. He hated green paint backstage." John says that they were always faced with lack of storage until a working space was found for them on Creighton Street in August 1987, twenty-four years after they started. "There was no paint in the shop backstage. A lot of people don't know how hard it was even to keep the theatre going, not money-wise but physically. It was just terrible."

Some players who joined the first company made the province their home, and have likewise given long service. Major brought in actors like David Renton, who had originally come from Australia, and Mary McMurray, a trained singer who came, says Major, "from the cornfields of Iowa to the east coast of Canada" via a production of *Rigoletto* he had directed in Toronto. After twenty-five years Joan Gregson, Mary McMurray and David Renton are still actively serving the community and performing, sometimes at Neptune Theatre itself.

Ted Follows and his wife Dawn Greenhalgh brought their first two children (before the now-famous daughter Megan was born) to settle in remote Halifax, away from the comparative safety of Upper Canada. The actors, in fact the whole company, took "incredible risks" according to Major. Others in the first company included Diana Leblanc, George Sperdakos, Bernard Behrens, Gary Krawford, and the late Molly Williams. Mavor Moore, already a major figure in Canadian theatre, played Undershaft in the production of Shaw's *Major Barbara,* which, under the direction of George McCowan, was chosen for the theatre's gala opening. Norman Welsh, one of the most experienced players in the company, took over the role of Undershaft when Moore was committed elsewhere. In order to participate in opening night he appeared as the butler, a role normally played by Stephen Wilband; this was a gesture which symbolized the ideal of repertory. The aim was to develop a resident acting company. The members were given an almost unheard-of 52-week contract, with a paid vacation; Neptune became the first fully year-round theatre in the country.

The core of company members consisted of those who already lived in Nova Scotia. Some of the first group of actors had been well known amateurs working with such companies as the Theatre Arts Guild. Performers such as Joan Gregson

ROMANOFF AND JULIET

by Peter Ustinov
directed by Leon Major
assisted by Ted Follows
settings designed by Christopher Adeney
costumes designed by Robert Doyle

First Soldier / JOHN HOBDAY
Second Soldier / DAVID RENTON
The General / NORMAN WELSH
Hooper Moulsworth / BERNARD BEHRENS
Vadim Romanoff / GEORGE SPERDAKOS
Igor Romanoff / GARY KRAWFORD
Juliet Moulsworth / DIANA LEBLANC
The Spy / GAVIN DOUGLAS
Beulah Moulsworth / MARY McMURRAY
Evdokia Romanoff / DEBORAH CASS
Capt. Marfa Zlotochienko / DAWN GREENHALGH
Freddie Vanderstuyt / DAVID BROWN
The Archbishop / TED FOLLOWS

ARMS AND THE MAN

by George Bernard Shaw
directed by Norman Welsh
settings designed by Christopher Adeney
costumes designed by Robert Doyle

Catherine / MARY McMURRAY
Raina / JOAN EVANS
Louka / DEBORAH CASS
Blunchli / TED FOLLOWS
Officer / GARY KRAWFORD
Nicola / GAVIN DOUGLAS
Major Petkoff / GEORGE SPERDAKOS
Sergius / DAVID RENTON

SLEEPING BEAUTY

by Chris Wiggins
directed by Norman Welsh
sets and costumes designed
by Les Lawrence
music by John Fenwick

The Apprentice / DIANA LEBLANC
Mother Pink / MARY McMURRAY
General Fitztwiddle / TED FOLLOWS
The Purple Witch / MILO RINGHAM
The King / NORMAN WELSH
The Queen / MOLLY WILLIAMS
Briar Rose / JOAN EVANS
The Prince / GAVIN DOUGLAS
The Knight / TED FOLLOWS

DIARY OF A SCOUNDREL

by Alexander Ostrovsky
directed by Leon Major
sets designed by Les Lawrence
costumes designed by Robert Doyle

James Sterling / DAVID RENTON
Gladys Sterling / MOLLY WILLIAMS
Musset / BERNARD BEHRENS
Harvey Wright / GARY KRAWFORD
Alexander Dube / GAVIN DOUGLAS
Mme. DeWolfe / JOAN EVANS
Manservant / DAVID BROWN
William Armstrong / TED FOLLOWS
Gen. Blackadar / NORMAN WELSH
Caroline Armstrong / DEBORAH CASS
Lewis Thompson / GEORGE SPERDAKOS
Mary Anne / MILO RINGHAM
Charlotte / DAWN GREENHALGH
Sophie Langille / MARY McMURRAY
Cecilia / DIANA LEBLANC
Joseph / DAVID BROWN

THE FANTASTICKS

book and lyrics by Tom Jones
music by Harvey Schmidt
directed by Leon Major
musical director John Fenwick
sets designed by Les Lawrence
costumes designed by Robert Doyle

The mute / DEBORAH CASS
The narrator / ROSS LAIDLEY
The girl (Luisa) / LORO FARELL
The boy (Matt) / GARY KRAWFORD
The girl's father / BERNARD BEHRENS
The boy's father / DAVID MURRAY
The old actor / GEORGE SPERDAKOS
The man who dies / DAVID RENTON

DESIRE UNDER THE EMS

by Eugene O'Neill
directed by Leon Major
sets designed by Chris Adeney
costumes designed by Robert Doyle

Ephraim Cabot / BERNARD BEHRENS
Simeon Cabot / TED FOLLOWS
Peter Cabot / GAVIN DOUGLAS
Eben Cabot / GEORGE SPERDAKOS
Abbie Putnam / DAWN GREENHALGH

(known at first under her married name, Joan Evans), David Brown, Ed Rubin and David Murray learned much from colleagues who had had longer professional training. There was much give and take from the beginning: actors were generous with sharing their knowledge in the early years; the community as a whole was kind in its reception of actors from Toronto. Mary McMurray mentions particularly Norman Welsh, Bernard Behrens and Ted Follows, who were willing at any time to help those who were less experienced; they were helpful and generous with their time. "Working with people like David Renton, who was so accomplished yet so generous on stage, enabled you to do your best."

Several members of the that first company refer to it as a "family," with Leon Major as a firm but kindly father. Among people Mary says should never be forgotten were Judith Major, who gave Leon "terrific support": she was "wonderful" to the company, cheering them all on, even lending Mary maternity clothes. Another who gave great support to the company was Moira Dexter. The Ladies' Auxiliary, the Tridents, headed by Nancy Norwood, gave valuable help, refurnishing the green room, setting up a kitchen for the actors. David Renton remembers especially the help given by Wynn Chisholm, the first wardrobe mistress; Mavor Moore's daughter Tedde was on the wardrobe staff. Another dresser, Gloria Barrett, was a great personality, soothing everyone's nerves. Ted Follows was very wise and so modest about his abilities, according to Mary. He always asserted that rehearsal time was the best time: if only they could have rehearsed six weeks instead of three!

The stories that are told about those first years are legion. When Mary McMurray married David Pigot at the Courthouse, just down the street from Neptune, the whole company came tearing down in their costumes afer a matinee of *Cinderella,* and after the wedding reception there were some unusually colourful performances at the theatre that night, with George Sperdakos, as the legend goes, making an unscheduled exit in the middle of *The Glass Menagerie.* Another wedding of Neptune family members, Jimmy Beggs and Anna Hagen, took place on the rocks

▲

*Nova Scotian history was featured in **Louisbourg,** by Neptune's first resident playwright, Jack Gray. Looking from the ship's helm are Bernard Behrens, David Brown and Norman Welsh among the entire company that participated in this production.*

BUS STOP

by William Inge
directed by Leon Major
sets designed by Chris Adeney
costumes designed by Robert Doyle

Elma Duckworth / DIANA LEBLANC
Grace Hoylard / MARY McMURRAY
Will Masters / GAVIN DOUGLAS
Cherie / MILO RINGHAM
Dr. Gerald Lyman / NORMAN WELSH
Carl / DAVID RENTON
Virgil Blessing / TED FOLLOWS
Bo Decker / GARY KRAWFORD

LOUISBOURG

by John Gray
directed by Leon Major
sets designed by Les Lawrence
costumes designed by Robert Doyle
special music composed by John Fenwick

The entire Neptune Theatre took part in this production. Each member of the company played several roles.

► 2nd SEASON

June 1964-April 1965

COME BLOW YOUR HORN

by Neil Simon
directed by Leon Major
settings designed by Chris Adeney
costumes designed by Robert Doyle

Alan Baker / DAVID RENTON
Peggy Evans / MILO RINGHAM
Buddy Baker / DAVID BROWN
Mr. Baker / BERNARD BEHRENS
Connie Dayton / ROBERTA MAXWELL
Mrs. Baker / MARY McMURRAY
A Visitor / MURIEL WHITE

▲

George Sperdakos on his bike, this time on Quinpool Road, no doubt reciting lines!

CINDERELLA

a special play for children adapted by Gavin Douglas directed by Eddie Gilbert

Cinderella / DIANA LEBLANC
Clock / JOCK FERGUSON
Stepmother / DAVID MURRAY
Gretchen / DAWN GREENHALGH
Drusilla / ROBERTA MAXWELL
Mouse / GEORGE SPERDAKOS
Turnip / JAMES BEGGS
Prince / DAVID RENTON
Flavius Flunkey / JAMES CRAIG
Grand Vizier / GAVIN DOUGLAS
Fairy Mother / MURIEL WHITE

at Duncan's Cove. Monique Gusset played the organ, which was carried out over planks to an adjacent rock, while a captain in the Salvation Army performed the ceremony. David Renton believes it was Bob Strand who observed, "A marriage which starts on the rocks has nowhere to go but up!" Robert Doyle remembers George Sperdakos riding his bike down Barrington Street, reciting his lines from *Henry IV*, not watching where he was going. George himself tells how once when he was moving house to Duncan's Cove his old Morris Minor disintegrated: "the car's body fell to the wayside, books were scattered, records smashed, clothes were strewn all over." A little later a man drove by, got out, looked at the mess, and said, "Sperdakos, there's nothing you won't do for a special effect!" It was his colleague and friend David Renton. Sperdakos writes of the "grand times" with "generous, wonderful people." But he doesn't mention how Dawn Greenhalgh, with a face sore from the beard that George wouldn't shave during a production of *Desire Under the Elms*, threatened to throw a jar of cold cream at him during a tour in P.E.I.; "he withdrew like a dog in a kennel," says Mary McMurray, who shared Dawn's dressing-room.

Many of the productions are still memorable to Major. Among them were new Canadian plays, some written specially for the company. These were moments when Neptune came close to living up to the early idealism. The first season ended with Jack Gray's historical drama *Louisbourg*. The first seven seasons also saw three world premières of plays by Neptune's first president, Arthur Murphy: *The Sleeping Bag, Charlie,* and *Tiger! Tiger!* Of these Major remembers *The Sleeping Bag* with particular affection. Two of its three actors were those stalwarts of Neptune, Joan Gregson and David Renton. It was a popular play, right for its time, performed in two consecutive seasons; the second time, along with O'Casey's *Juno and the Paycock,* it toured Canada for the 1967 Centennial and Expo celebrations.

Another particular favourite of Major's was *The Wooden World,* written by a member of the company, (John) Gavin Douglas. This dramatized history of Nova Scotia, colourfully staged by Leon Major, was, surprisingly for a dramatic reading, a

▲
*The dance scene from Eugene O'Neill's **Desire under the Elms:**
seated are old Ephraim Cabot (Bernard Behrens) with his voluptuous
young wife Abbie (Dawn Greenhalgh). Others present include Mary
McMurray, Gavin Douglas, Milo Ringham, Gary Krawford, David Renton
and Diana Leblanc.*

THE GLASS MENAGERIE

by Tennessee Williams
directed by Curt Reis
settings designed by Tom Spaulding
costumes designed by Robert Doyle

Tom Wingfield / GEORGE SPERDAKOS
Amanda Wingfield / DAWN GREENHALGH
Laura Wingfield / DIANA LEBLANC
The Gentleman Caller / GAVIN DOUGLAS

TWO FOR THE SEESAW

by William Gibson
directed by Curt Reis
designed by Les Lawrence

Jerry Ryan / TED FOLLOWS
Gittel Mosca / ROBERTA MAXWELL

TWELFTH NIGHT

by William Shakespeare
directed by Leon Major
settings designed by Les Lawrence
costumes designed by Robert Doyle

Orsino / GAVIN DOUGLAS
Valentine / EDWIN RUBIN
Curio / JOCK FERGUSON
A Lord / DAVID PIGOT
Viola / DAWN GREENHALGH
Sea Captain / JAMES BEGGS
Sir Toby Belch / BERNARD BEHRENS
Maria / MARY McMURRAY
Sir Andrew Aguecheek / TED FOLLOWS
Feste / DAVID RENTON
Olivia / ROBERTA MAXWELL
Malvolio / GEORGE SPERDAKOS
Fabian / JAMES BEGGS
Antonio / DAVID MURRAY
Sebastian / DAVID BROWN
Constables / FRED ALLEN, JAMES CRAIG
A Priest / ROSS HILL
Gentlewomen / DIANA LEBLANC,
MILO RINGHAM

▲
*David Renton (centre) as Feste in Leon Major's highly praised production of Shakespeare's **Twelfth Night**. Also featured are Roberta Maxwell, James Beggs, Anna Hagen and Diana Leblanc.*

▲

*Mary McMurray took over the "huge part" of Madame Rosepettle in Arthur Kopit's black comedy **Oh Dad, Poor Dad . . .**; with her is Bernard Behrens.*

THE PRIVATE EAR AND THE PUBLIC EYE

two plays by Peter Shaffer
directed by Curt Reis
designed by Chris Adeney

The Private Ear:
Bob / WILLIAM ARMSTRONG
Ted / DAVID RENTON
Doreen / DAWN GREENHALGH

The Public Eye:
Julian / DAVID RENTON
Charles / GAVIN DOUGLAS
Belinda / DAWN GREENHALGH

UNDER THE YUM-YUM TREE

by Lawrence Roman
directed by Leon Major
designed by Fred Allen

Irene Wilson / JOAN EVANS
Robin Austin / MILO RINGHAM
David Manning / DAVID BROWN
Hogan / TED FOLLOWS
A Milkman / ROSS HILL
A Cabdriver / LEN DONCHEFF

OH DAD, POOR DAD, MAMMA'S HUNG YOU IN THE CLOSET AND I'M FEELIN' SO SAD

by Arthur L. Kopit
directed by Ted Follows
settings designed by Tom Spaulding
costumes designed by Robert Doyle

Madame Rosepettle / MARY McMURRAY
Jonathan / DAVID BROWN
Head Bellboy / EDWIN RUBIN
Bellboys / JAMES CRAIG,
JOCK FERGUSON, ROSS HILL
Rosalie / MILO RINGHAM
Commodore Roseabove / BERNARD BEHRENS

JOHN A. BEATS THE DEVIL

by Tommy Tweed
directed by Leon Major
settings designed by Chris Adeney
costumes designed by Robert Doyle
music composed by John Fenwick
voice coaching by Mary McMurray

Belial Burns / GEORGE SPERDAKOS
Newsboy / ROSS HILL
Newsboy / JAMES CRAIG
Newsboy / FRED ALLEN
Agnes MacDonald / DAWN GREENHALGH
Bridgit (the maid) / MARY McMURRAY
John A. Macdonald / TED FOLLOWS
The Governor General / GAVIN DOUGLAS
Bates / EDWIN RUBIN
Telegraph Boy / ROSS HILL
Pierre / DAVID RENTON
Henry / JAMES BEGGS
Patrick Buckley / BERNARD BEHRENS
Charles Tupper MP / DAVID BROWN
Donald Smith MP / DAVID MURRAY
Mrs. Bernard / MURIEL WHITE
William MacDougall MP / GAVIN DOUGLAS
Alf Brown / DAVID RENTON
In addition to the above, the following appeared
in the picnic scene: Diana Leblanc, Roberta
Maxwell and Milo Ringham.

THE SCHOOL FOR WIVES

by Molière
newly translated and adapted by
Gavin Douglas
original music composed by
John Fenwick
designed by Les Lawrence
costumes courtesy of Stratford
Shakespearean Festival
directed by Leon Major

Arnolphe / TED FOLLOWS
Chrysalde / GAVIN DOUGLAS
Alain / DAVID RENTON
Georgette / DAWN GREENHALGH,
ROBERTA MAXWELL
Agnes / DIANA LEBLANC, MILO RINGHAM
Horace / MALCOLM ARMSTRONG
Oronte / LEN DONCHEFF
A Notary, Enrique / EDWIN RUBIN

hit which won standing ovations for two years running; even a hardened critic like Nathan Cohen was moved by the potent emotional impact of this "richly edited collage". D. Ray Pierce, then a junior member of the company, recalls John Douglas as one of the most creative people who ever trod the stage at Neptune: he had the good of the theatre in the broader sense at heart, and had a strong influence on the younger actors. Another Canadian play, Tommy Tweed's *John A. Beats the Devil,* which opened on tour at the new Confederation Centre, Charlottetown, was considered an entertaining way of presenting history, but produced shock waves among some P.E.I. clergy when Canada's first prime minister was presented as a drunkard!

From its inception Neptune began the practice of taking two plays a season on an extensive Maritime tour, sometimes including the additional trip to Newfoundland. As more regional theatres developed, the tour was restricted to Nova Scotia, but Neptune has to this day maintained an unbroken touring tradition. In the early seasons major, expensive productions often went on the road, leading up to the ambitious nation-wide tour of 1967. Looking back to the early years Major still finds them amazing: an Atlantic tour with two full-scale plays (*Major Barbara* and *Antigone*) was an "extraordinary feat" for a theatre in its first year.

The national tour was one of the first times a regular theatre company had ever toured the country; it gave Neptune a much broader exposure and erased any notions that it was solely a regional theatre. The tour went as far west as Swift Current, Saskatchewan. The company ended up rescuing a woman and her son on the prairies in the midst of a winter storm. The tour bus passed the stranded car when no other traffic was around. After the company had played for ten days at the Port Royal Theatre in Montreal they were royally treated to Expo — the first company to visit the exhibit. Ray Pierce remembers that it was a great cultural experience, as all the visiting arts companies were mixed in the residences.

John Blackmore's most embarrassing moment occurred at this time. The scenery for *The Sleeping Bag* was notable for some

▲
A not always flattering portrait of Canada's first prime minister!
Ted Follows, Diana Leblanc, Roberta Maxwell, Milo Ringham, Dawn
Greenhalgh, Bernard Behrens, Mary McMurray, and David Renton in
Tommy Tweed's **John A. Beats the Devil.**

Chorus leader Ted Follows in Jean Anouilh's **Antigone**, flanked by Una Way as Eurydice, Mary McMurray as Nurse and Diana Leblanc as Antigone. The guards are Stephen Wilband, John Hobday and George Sperdakos. Gary Krawford as Haemon is r.

Les Lawrence's highly detailed set for **Mary, Mary** highlights Ted Follows, Diana Leblanc, Dawn Greenhalgh, George Sperdakos and Bernard Behrens.

*Planning one of the Neptune productions to tour Canada in 1967, O'Casey's **Juno and the Paycock**, are director Leon Major (seated centre) with members of the company.*

large "rocks" near which the characters had to "sleep" in sleeping bags. The Blackmores constructed the rocks out of welded tubular steel covered by papier maché. "All was ready, and the van was at the Neptune side door at about midnight, ready to load up the rocks and other items of the set," says John. "Then, to our horror, we found that the crate containing the rocks would not go through either the door from the carpenter's shop, or the door out of the theatre. We had made it too big! The only thing we could do was to uncrate the rocks and cut them in two, which we did. Eventually we were able to load the van, and the tour was able to start off on its journey west. It certainly taught us a lesson we never forgot! We probably wouldn't have been able to unload it at some of the even smaller theatres and schools at which the company was playing on the tour."

Some choices of play were bold but they did not succeed in bringing in audiences. Major still recalls with pride his production of Anouilh's *Antigone,* though it was a box-office disaster, despite a striking performance by twenty-year-old Diana Leblanc in the leading role. Not the least of the company's troubles was the smell from a waterfront fish-curing factory

3rd SEASON

June 1965-August 1966

TUNNEL OF LOVE

by Joseph Fields and Peter de Vries directed by Ted Follows set and costume design by Fred Allen

Augie Poole / ERIC DONKIN
Isolde Poole / ROBERTA MAXWELL
Dick Pepper / DAVID RENTON
Alice Pepper / MILO RINGHAM
Estelle Novick / JOAN GREGSON
Miss McCracken / MURIEL WHITE

MARY, MARY

revived with same cast as in 1963, except Oscar Nelson was played by David Murray

THE CRUCIBLE

by Arthur Miller
directed by Curt Reis
settings designed by Les Lawrence
costumes designed by Suzanne Mess

Betty Parris / GILLIAN MacINTOSH
Rev. Samuel Parris / JACK MEDLEY
Tituba / JUNE BUNDY
Abigail Williams / RUTH LIVINGSTON
Susanna Walcott / DEBORAH ALLEN
Mrs. Ann Putnam / MARY McMURRAY
Thomas Putnam / MALCOLM ARMSTRONG
Mercy Lewis / JOAN GREGSON
Mary Warren / VICTORIA MITCHELL
John Proctor / PAUL MASSIE
Rebecca Nurse / PHYLLIS MALCOLM
STEWART
Giles Corey / DAVID BROWN
Rev. John Hale / DONALD MEYERS
Elizabeth Proctor / LAURINDA BARRETT
Francis Nurse / GAVIN DOUGLAS
Ezekiel Cheever / BRUCE ARMSTRONG
John Willard / RAY PIERCE
Guard / ROBERT CARLEY
Judge Hathorne / DAVID RENTON
Deputy-Governor Danforth / RON HASTINGS

EPITAPH FOR GEORGE DILLON

by John Osborne and Anthony Creighton
directed by Leon Major
settings and costumes designed by
Fred Allen

Josie Elliot / ROBERTA MAXWELL
Ruth Gray / JOAN GREGSON
Mrs. Elliot / PHYLLIS MALCOLM STEWART
Norah Elliot / MILO RINGHAM
Percy Elliot / RON HASTINGS
George Dillon / DAVID RENTON
Geoffrey Colwyn-Stewart / MALCOLM
ARMSTRONG
Mr. Webb / DAVID MURRAY
Barney Evans / ED RUBIN

▲
Playing during a forty-inch snowstorm did not deter the cast of **The Fantasticks**, *featuring Deborah Cass, Bernard Behrens, Loro Farrell, Gary Krawford, David Murray and Ross Laidley.*

▲

Ron Hastings as Le Beau tells of the impending wrestling match in **As You Like It**: *listening are Touchstone (Ted Follows), Celia (Roberta Maxwell), Rosalind (Dawn Greenhalgh), with Gentlewomen Diana Leblanc and Milo Ringham*

AS YOU LIKE IT

by William Shakespeare
directed by Leon Major
set designed by Les Lawrence
costumes designed by Suzanne Mess
and Les Lawrence
Music played by Phyllis Ensher - Harp
and Frank Peters - Oboe/English Horn
wrestling coached by Bill Taylor

Orlando / DAVID RENTON
Adam / ERIC DONKIN
Oliver / MALCOLM ARMSTRONG
Dennis / EDWIN RUBIN
Charles / LEN DONCHEFF
Celia / ROBERTA MAXWELL
Rosalind / DAWN GREENHALGH
Touchstone / TED FOLLOWS
Le Beau / RON HASTINGS
Frederick / GAVIN DOUGLAS
Duke Sr. / DAVID MURRAY
Amiens / LEN DONCHEFF
Forester / JOAN GREGSON
Corin / EDWIN RUBIN
Silvius / RON HASTINGS
Jaques / GEORGE SPERDAKOS
Audrey / DIANA LEBLANC
Martext / GAVIN DOUGLAS
Phebe / MILO RINGHAM
William / ERIC DONKIN
J. de Boys / GAVIN DOUGLAS
Gentlewomen, Lords, Attendants, Foresters /
DIANA LEBLANC, MILO RINGHAM, JOANNE
HANCOCK, DAVID HELLYER, ERSKINE
SMITH, KEITH WOOD and others

A SHOT IN THE DARK

by Marcel Achard
directed by Leon Major
settings designed by Chris Adeney
costumesd designed by Helen Campbell

Paul Sevigne / PAUL MASSIE
Morestan / MALCOLM ARMSTRONG
Lablache / GAVIN DOUGLAS
Antoinette Sevigne / VICTORIA MITCHELL
Josefa Lantenay / RUTH LIVINGSTON
Dominique Beaurevers / LAURINDA BARRETT
Benjamin Beaurevers / JACK MEDLEY
Guard / DOUGLAS FRENCH

UNCLE VANYA

by Anton Chekhov
translation by Ann Dunnigan with
special reference to Constance Garnett
directed by Curt Reis
settings by Chris Adeney
costumes by Suzanne Mess
guitar instruction by Walter Purcell

Marina Timofeyevna / HELEN ROBERTS
Astrov, Mikhail Lvovich / GEORGE
SPERDAKOS
Voinitsky, Ivan Petrovich (Vanya) / TED
FOLLOWS
Serebryakov, Aleksandr / ERIC DONKIN
Telyegin, Ilya Ilyich / GAVIN DOUGLAS
Sofya Aleksandrovna (Sonya) / DIANA
LEBLANC
Elena Andreyevna / DAWN GREENHALGH
Voinitskaya, Maria Vasilyevna / MURIEL WHITE
A workman / LEN DONCHEFF

THE PHYSICISTS

by Friedrich Dürrenmatt
translated by James Kirkup
directed by Curt Reis
settings by Marie Day
costumes by Robert Doyle

Police Doctor / JOSEPH RUTTEN
Guhl / BRUCE ARMSTRONG
Blocher / ROBERT CARLEY
A Policeman / CHRIS BROOKS
Police Inspector Richard Voss / JACK MEDLEY
Marta Boll, the matron / MARY McMURRAY
Herbert Georg Beutler / MALCOLM
ARMSTRONG
Fraulein Doktor Mathilde von Zahnd /
LAURINDA BARRETT
Ernst Heinrich Ernesti / PAUL MASSIE
Frau Lina Rose / RUTH LIVINGSTON
Oskar Rose / DONALD MEYERS
Adolf-Friedrich / DOUGLAS FRENCH
Wilfried-Kaspar / PETER WRIGHT
Jorg-Lukas / RAY PIERCE
Johann Wilhelm Mobius / ROLAND HEWGILL
Monika Stettler / VICTORIA MITCHELL
Uwe Sievers / RONALD HASTINGS
McArthur / WILLIAM CLARK
Murillo / ED RUBIN

blown by offshore winds into the theatre's air-exchange fan system. Not all the audience may have been imaginative enough to accept the suggestion of a Toronto *Daily Star* critic that the action in Thebes was sickened by the smell of a rotting corpse outside the wall. On the other hand, a popular comedy, *Mary, Mary*, starring Dawn Greenhalgh, was a sell-out two years running; the author, Jean Kerr, had taken the unusual step of making a gift of the play to Leon Major while it was still running on Broadway. The gift was expedited as Leon Major and Jean Kerr both had the same agent in New York; Arthur Murphy also said that his old friend, film director and Glace Bay native Dan Petrie, had a hand as intercessor.

In spite of mounting debts and boardroom crises, the company managed to survive with a mixture of plays from the classical repertoire and popular comedies. Attempts at Shakespeare varied in success. Some aspects of *Twelfth Night*, directed by Major in 1964, so impressed Michael Langham that he used them as the basis for his Stratford production: Langham was particularly interested in David Renton's interpretation of Feste as an elderly retainer, suggesting a harsher underlying theme. This production was also cited as a model by Clifford Leech, the Shakespearean scholar, who was in Halifax at the time giving lectures arranged jointly by Dalhousie Theatre Department and Neptune (others who came in successive years included dramatist J.B. Priestley and actress Barbara Jefford).

Dawn Greenhalgh and Roberta Maxwell were highly praised for their roles in *As You Like It*. Major remembers too with affection *The Taming of the Shrew* and *Henry IV, Part I*. He recalls that one actor in the latter had such an emotional response in a dress rehearsal that he fainted each time he saw the bare blade of a knife. The wardrobe mistress, Helen Campbell, was fortunately also a registered nurse, who soon got him back on his feet in time for performance. Ray Pierce, who played three or four small roles in that production, says he lost three to five pounds a night: there was then no air conditioning in the theatre, and they were playing in the summer in Suzanne Mess's beautifully authentic but heavy costumes.

▲

Prince Hal (Paul Massie, c.) with tavern friends Mistress Quickly (Phyllis Malcolm Stewart), Poins (Malcolm Armstrong), Peto (David Brown), Gadshill (Ron Hastings) and Bardolph (the late Donald Meyers) in Shakespeare's **King Henry IV, Part I.**

HENRY IV, PART I

by William Shakespeare
directed by Leon Major
settings designed by Les Lawrence
costumes designed by Suzanne Mess
incidental music by John Fenwick
music performed by David Woods,
trumpet; Marius Kraal, trombone;
Max Ball, percussion
fencing coached by Coleman Day
Welsh text coached by Alun Jones

King Henry IV / ROLAND HEWGILL
Prince John of Lancaster / D. RAY PIERCE
Earl of Westmoreland / GAVIN DOUGLAS
Sir Walter Blunt / EDWIN RUBIN
Henry, Prince of Wales / PAUL MASSIE
Sir John Falstaff / RONALD BISHOP
Poins / MALCOLM ARMSTRONG
Thomas Percy / JACK MEDLEY
Henry Percy, Earl of Northumberland /
JOSEPH RUTTEN
Henry Percy, "Hotspur", son to the Earl /
DAVID RENTON
1st Carrier / BRUCE ARMSTRONG
2nd Carrier / ROBERT CARLEY
Gadshill / RON HASTINGS
Chamberlain / EDWIN RUBIN
Peto / DAVID BROWN
Bardolph / DONALD MEYERS
Lady Percy / RUTH LIVINGSTON,
VICTORIA MITCHELL
Francis / D. RAY PIERCE
Vintner / EDWIN RUBIN
Mistress Quickly / PHYLLIS MALCOLM
STEWART
Sheriff / GAVIN DOUGLAS
Edmund Mortimer / DAVID BROWN
Owen Glendower / JOSEPH RUTTEN
Lady Mortimer / LAURINDA BARRETT
Archibald / RON HASTINGS
Sir Richard Vernon / MALCOLM ARMSTRONG
Lords, Pages, Servants, Travellers, Henry's
Soldiers, Hotspur's Soldiers / DEBORAH
ALLEN, BRUCE ARMSTRONG, BARBARA
BLACKMORE, CHRIS ROOKS, DAVID BROWN,
ROBERT CARLEY, TOM DUNPHY, DOUGLAS
FRENCH, MARGARET PALMER

ARSENIC AND OLD LACE

by Joseph Kesselring
directed by Curt Reis
settings designed by Chris Adeney
costumes designed by Robert Doyle

Abby Brewster / PHYLLIS MALCOLM STEWART
Rev. Harper / ROLAND HEWGILL
Teddy Brewster / DONALD MEYERS
Officer Brophy / ROBERT CARLEY
Officer Klein / JOSEPH RUTTEN
Martha Brewster / MARY McMURRAY
Elaine Harper / JOAN GREGSON
Mortimer Brewster / DAVID BROWN
Mr. Gibbs / BRUCE ARMSTRONG
Johnathan Brewster / RON HASTINGS
Dr. Einstein / DAVID RENTON
Officer O'Hara / RAY PIERCE
Lieutenant Rooney / BRUCE ARMSTRONG
Mr. Witherspoon / ED RUBIN

THE SLEEPING BAG

by Arthur L. Murphy
directed by Leon Major
settings designed by Fred Allen
costumes designed by Robert Doyle

DuBaie Johnston / RONALD BISHOP
Arnold Wamsley / DAVID RENTON
Venise Smith / JOAN GREGSON

▲
The Sleeping Bag by Neptune's first president, Arthur L. Murphy, was chosen to tour Canada for Expo in 1967. This revival starred David Renton, Joan Gregson and Ron Hastings.

Pierce remembers what a wonderful director Kurt Reis was: his production of *Arsenic and Old Lace* brought a fresh approach to a hackneyed play. He says what a great treat it was to work with David Brown: in this production he broke up every night when on stage with David. Brown himself recalls that after one performance of the same play Ed Rubin, "instead of walking into the wings, walked off the front of the stage. As the rest of the cast came out for their curtain call, to see Ed's contorted body sprawled across the laps of two astonished ladies was a sight to collapse all of us." Pierce also tells of Ron Hastings as the punner of the Neptune family: claiming to be able to make a pun on any subject, he was challenged by David Brown one night to make a pun on the Queen; he replied, "The Queen is not a subject." Pierce also says that Reis' production of *The Crucible* was one of Neptune's best-ever shows, but tragically performed in the summer to very small audiences.

David Renton recalls many other memorable moments of the early days. *The Fantasticks,* directed with tremendous skill by Leon Major, was greeted by a forty-inch snowfall for its opening; the city could hardly move for a week. *The Diary of a Scoundrel,* adapted by Arthur Murphy, gave Renton his first leading role and was set in a military garrison city like 19th century Haliax. Renton remembers with affection the wonderful personality of the late David Murray, who had his own radio show on opera, and was an ugly sister (with Dawn Greenhalgh) in Gavin Douglas's version of *Cinderella.* Mary McMurray got her first big role when Molly Williams refused the part in Kopit's black comedy *O Dad, Poor Dad . . .* because in those days she thought it distasteful: Mary loved playing that "huge part".

How was it that Leon Major managed to mount up to thirteen plays in a repertory season, with the constant changes of set required, in a small theatre with minimal wing and backstage space, while no artistic director who followed him could do so? In the first place, "We worked much harder," he explains. The enthusiasm and energy were implicit in the vision. It was an "unbelievable" first company. But changes had to come; they could not go on living a dream forever.

4th SEASON

March-September 1967

JUNO AND THE PAYCOCK

by Sean O'Casey
directed by Leon Major
settings designed by Fred Allen
costumes designed by Robert Doyle

'Captain' Jack Boyle / ROLAND HEWGILL
Juno Boyle / MAUREEN FITZGERALD
Johnny Boyle / MALCOLM ARMSTRONG
Mary Boyle / YVONNE ADALIAN
'Joxer' Daly / DAVID RENTON
Mrs. Maisie Madigan / PHYLLIS MALCOLM STEWART
'Needle' Nugent / DONALD MEYERS
Mrs. Tancred / JOAN GREGSON
Jerry Devine / RON HASTINGS
Charles Bentham / JACK MEDLEY
An Irregular Mobilizer / D. RAY PIERCE
An Irregular / DAVID CLEMENT
A Coal Block Vendor / LIONEL SIMMONS
A Sewing Machine Man / D. RAY PIERCE
Furniture Removal Men / LIONEL SIMMONS, RON RAYNOR
Two Neighbors / DEBORAH ALLEN, TRIXIE LEDERER

WAIT UNTIL DARK

by Frederick Knott
directed by Heinar Piller
settings designed by Fred Allen
costumes designed by Helen Campbell

Mike Talman / DONALD MEYERS
Sgt. Carlino / RON HASTINGS
Harry Roat / DAVID RENTON
Susy Hendrix / JOAN GREGSON
Sam Hendrix / JAMES BRADFORD
Gloria / PAT LANE
Two Policemen / D. RAY PIERCE, EWAN S. CLARK

PRIVATE LIVES

by Noël Coward
directed by Denny Spence
settings designed by Fred Allen
costumes designed by Helen Campbell

Sibyl Chase / YVONNE ADALIAN
Elyot Chase / JACK MEDLEY
Victor Prynne / MALCOLM ARMSTRONG
Amanda Prynne / SUSAN CHAPPLE
Louise / KELLY ROSS

BAREFOOT IN THE PARK

by Neil Simon
directed by Leon Major
settings designed by Fred Allen
costumes designed by Robert Doyle

Corie Bratter / DIANA LEBLANC
Telephone Repair Man / DAVID MURRAY
Delivery Man / LIONEL SIMMONS
Paul Bratter / DAVID BROWN
Corie's Mother / PHYLLIS MALCOLM
STEWART
Victor Velasco / ROLAND HEWGILL

CHARLIE

by Arthur L. Murphy
directed by Frank Canino
settings designed by Fred Allen
costumes designed by Robert Doyle

Sam Kluzac / MALCOLM ARMSTRONG
Jerry Deveau / JAMES BRADFORD
Albert MacLean / DAVID CLEMENT
Joe Morello / RON HASTINGS
Charlie MacLean / ROLAND HEWGILL
Terry Doyle / DONALD MEYERS
Jimmy MacLean / D. RAY PIERCE
Phil Latter / EDWIN RUBIN
Mike Petrie / LIONEL SIMMONS
Martha MacLean / MAUREEN FITZGERALD
Frances MacLean / KELLY ROSS
Miners / IVAN BLAKE, EWAN S. CLARK,
MARK DeWOLF, PHIL PHELAN

▲
*More Atlantic history in **The Wooden World** by company member (John) Gavin Douglas: the players are Jack Medley, Harry Jackson, the late David Murray, David Renton, Yvonne Adalian, Ron Hastings and Don Allison, foreground.*

▲
*Katherina (Mary McMurray) battles with Bianca (Susan Chapple)
in Shakespeare's **Taming of the Shrew** while servants Phil Phelan,
Ewan Clark, Ivan Blake and Mark DeWolf look up in consternation.*

THE WOODEN WORLD

*assembled by Gavin Douglas
directed by Leon Major
sets designed by Fred Allen
costumes co-ordinated by Robert Doyle*

*music arranged and played by
Harry Jackson*

Cast / DAVID BROWN, SUSAN CHAPPLE,
JOHN HORTON, JACK MEDLEY, DAVID
MURRAY, DAVID RENTON

THE TAMING OF THE SHREW

*by William Shakespeare
directed by Leon Major
settings designed by Les Lawrence
costumes designed by Robert Doyle
incidental music by Kenneth Elloway*

Christopher Sly / DAVID RENTON
Hostess of an Ale House / YVONNE ADALIAN
A Lord / JAMES BRADFORD
Huntsmen and Servants of the Lord /
DAVID CLEMENT, D. RAY PIERCE, EDWIN
RUBIN, LIONEL SIMMONS
Bartholomew / ROBERT HAWKINS
Tranio / JACK MEDLEY
Lucentio / MALCOLM ARMSTRONG
Hortensio / DONALD MEYERS
Gremio / DAVID MURRAY
Bianca / SUSAN CHAPPLE
Katherina / MARY McMURRAY
Baptista Minola / RON HASTINGS
Biondello / DAVID CLEMENT
Petruchio / JOHN HORTON
Grumio / DAVID BROWN
Curtis / D. RAY PIERCE
A Pedant / LIONEL SIMMONS
A Tailor / JAMES BRADFORD
Vincentio of Pisa / EDWIN RUBIN
A Widow / KELLY ROSS
Apprentices to the Players serving as Haberdasher,
Messengers, etc. / DEBORAH ALLEN, IVAN BLAKE
EWAN S. CLARKE, MARK DeWOLF, PHIL PHELAN
The musicians / HENRY MAX BALL, KENNETH
ELLOWAY, ERNO RETI, DAVID WOODS

**HE DONE HER WRONG, or,
WEDDED BUT NO WIFE**

by Anita Bell
*a special Centennial project, performed in
Halifax Public Gardens on June 21, 1967*
directed by Heinar Piller
settings designed by Fred Allen
costumes designed by Robert Doyle

Miss Hyacinth Haven / DIANA LEBLANC
Mrs. Octavia Moneycracker / PHYLLIS
MALCOLM STEWART
Miss Alvina Moneycracker / K. ROSS
Miss Linettenor Darwood / Y. ADALIAN
Mr. Fleetwood Dashaway / DAVID RENTON
Master Fitzjohn Oliphant / J. BRADFORD

A Revival
THE SLEEPING BAG

by Arthur L. Murphy
directed by Leon Major
settings designed by Fred Allen
costumes designed by Robert Doyle

DuBaie Johnston / RON HASTINGS
Arnold Wamsley / DAVID RENTON
Venise Smith / JOAN GREGSON

5th SEASON

February-September 1968

THE ODD COUPLE

by Neil Simon
directed by Heinar Piller
settings designed by Fred Allen
costumes designed by Robert Doyle

Speed / DAVID RENTON
Murray / EDWIN RUBIN
Roy / RAFE MacPHERSON
Vinnie / DONALD MEYERS
Oscar Madison / DAVID MURRAY
Felix Ungar / JACK MEDLEY
Gwendolyn Pigeon / JOAN KARASEVICH
Cecily Pigeon / YVONNE ADALIAN

For one thing, the image of Neptune was still uncertain. In February 1965 Leon said, "We're still searching — after two years — to find out how important the theatre is to the community." He commented on the potentially wide range of the audience and on the need for new, especially Canadian works. After three years Nathan Cohen took stock of the company's achievement. The première performance, he noted, invoked the image of Neptune as the property of the very rich, professional class, and intellectuals; it was still a false image, yet remained an albatross. He blamed the still modest 50% audience average on administrative incompetence. It was still not a grassroots theatre, still had no distinctive style nor authentic individual voice, but it had the makings of a solid, interesting acting company. "Still an experiment," he concluded, "it is no longer an alien luxury."

"What mistakes did I make?" asked Major in 1968. "Do you have a week to listen?" Costs had been wildly underestimated, and audiences were less consistent in attendance than expected. In the spring of 1966 the provincial government had given the lion's share in contributions of over $250,000 to wipe out accumulating debts. To protect the province's interest, Robert Stanfield appointed the late Charles L. Beazley, Q.C., to the newly formed Executive Committee. According to Lloyd Newman, "It was because of Beazley's keen interest, kindly nature (sometimes hidden beneath a prickly facade), and meticulous attention to detail that Neptune survived and thrived. My fondest memory of Charles, among dozens of memories, was of him at one of the Executive Committee meetings we attended every Monday afternoon. We all had in front of us the Theatre's interim financial statement. Our helpless manager was being interrogated about the statement and giving vague, unsatisfactory answers.Exasperated, Charles pulled down his reading glasses, glared at the perspiring fellow, and drawled, *Tell me, young man, what do you do there at Neptune? Why don't you pick a typical day, start at 9:00 a.m., and tell me what you do all day long?"*

It was only in this way that the theatre was surviving what Harry Bruce called "the financial high wire act". With the help of American expert Daniel Newman the first formal charter subscription series campaign was started for the 1967 season. Newman analyzed the reasons why people want to go to the theatre, and they had nothing to do with quality. "Subscriptions are the only proven and successful marketing tool there is to fill your houses," says Heinar Piller, who became Major's associate director in 1968. By the 1966 summer season attendance had sunk to 48.3% average. But from 1967 the worst attendance was 74.2% (in the summer of 1968), and the winter figure consistently averaged over 85%. But ideally Major feels that the moment you start subscriptions you are looking at X number of weeks, and it leads to a "slowly eroding integrity."

Another matter on which Major and Piller continue to agree philosophically and artistically, but which they agree has to be compromised in the face of reality, is the year-round repertory. The system that Leon started and Heinar continued was to begin a season with one "biggie" for the whole company, but simultaneously split the company into two halves which do plays two and three. The first year Piller was there *Henry IV, Part I* was the "biggie" while *Arsenic and Old Lace* and *A Shot in the Dark* were the "small" ones. Then plays four and five would go into rehearsal, and so on. But the pressures of repertory became harder to cope with. The system demanded three rehearsal spaces, but there was no room at the theatre, no backstage space, no storage. The directors had to be ingenious to keep the plays constantly moving on Neptune's tiny stage.

Moreover, Canadian theatre was now growing across the country. With it came the strengthening of the Canadian Actors' Equity Association. Pay rates, which had often been deplorable, were now improving, but it became more difficult to keep a large and united company together. Once a season was played in stock, there was no longer reason for actors to take an interest in the community: it was "a job: next week, Vancouver," says Piller.

One of Major's greatest achievements was to change the "black tie and limousine" image that Neptune acquired from the first fund-raising dinner and the gala opening, to make inroads into public indifference and the assumption that Neptune was merely a coterie or an art club. As Piller testifies, it took years to

MY THREE ANGELS

by Sam and Bella Spewak
directed by Heinar Piller
settings designed by Fred Allen
costumes designed by Robert Doyle

Felix Ducotel / DONALD MEYERS
Emilie Ducotel / FAITH WARD
Marie Louise Ducotel / JOAN KARASEVICH
Mme. Parole / YVONNE ADALIAN
Joseph / DAVID RENTON
Jules / DAVID MURRAY
Alfred / RON HASTINGS
Henri Trochard / JACK MEDLEY
Paul / RAFE MacPHERSON
Lieutenant / DON ALLISON

THE SUBJECT WAS ROSES

by Frank D. Gilroy
directed by William Davis
settings designed by Fred Allen
costumes designed by Robert Doyle

John Cleary / RON HASTINGS
Nettie Cleary / MARY McMURRAY
Timmy Cleary / DON ALLISON

A MAN FOR ALL SEASONS

by Robert Bolt
directed by Heinar Piller
sets designed by Fred Allen
costumes designed by Robert Doyle

The Common Man / JONATHAN WHITE
Sir Thomas More / JACK MEDLEY
Master Richard Rich / DONALD MEYERS
Duke of Norfolk / EDWIN RUBIN
Lady Alice More / FAITH WARD
Lady Margaret More / SYLVIA FEIGEL
Cardinal Wolsey / RON HASTINGS
Thomas Cromwell / DAVID RENTON
Signor Chapuys / DAVID MURRAY
Chapuys' attendant / RAFE MacPHERSON
William Roper / DON ALLISON
Henry VIII / RICHARD DAVIDSON
A Woman / YVONNE ADALIAN
Thomas Cranmer / RON HASTINGS

A SLEEP OF PRISONERS

by Christopher Fry
performed in St. Paul's Church
directed by Heinar Piller

Private David King / RICHARD DAVIDSON
Private Peter Abel / DON ALLISON
Corporal Joseph Adams / RON HASTINGS
Private Tim Meadows / JONATHAN WHITE

◄

The support of Petrofina in the 1960s anticipates more regular sponsorship of productions by the late 1970s.

▼

Fund-raising: Neptune staff soliciting and filing subscriptions.

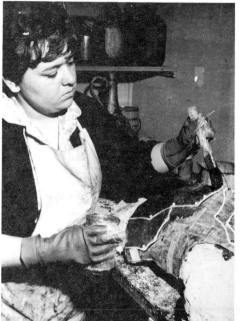

At work backstage:

◄

In the props department, Barbara Howatt making a suit of armour from fibreglass moulding.

▼

In the wardrobe department, Louise Muir with assistant Leslie McKinnon.

A Revival
THE WOODEN WORLD

assembled by Gavin Douglas
directed by Leon Major
sets designed by Fred Allen
costumes designed by Robert Doyle
music arranged and played
by Harry Jackson

Cast / DAVID BROWN, YVONNE ADALIAN,
RON HASTINGS, JACK MEDLEY,
DAVID RENTON, DAVID MURRAY

BLACK COMEDY AND WHITE LIES

by Peter Shaffer
directed by Penny Spence
costumes by Robert Doyle
sets by Fred Allen
lighting by David Hignell

White Lies
Sophie / MARGARET MacLEOD
Frank / JACK MEDLEY
Tom / DONALD MEYERS

Black Comedy
Brindsley Miller / DAVID BROWN
Carol Melkett / YVONNE ADALIAN
Miss Furnival / MARGARET MacLEOD
Colonel Melkett / GAVIN PAYNE
Harold Gorringe / JACK MEDLEY
Schuppanzigh / DAVID RENTON
Clea / LINDA LIVINGSTON
Georg Bamberger / DONALD MEYERS

THE RAINMAKER

by N. Richard Nash
directed by Leon Major
costumes by Fred Allen
sets by Fred Allen
lighting by David Hignell

H.C. Curry / EDWIN RUBIN
Noah Curry / RON HASTINGS
Jim Curry / DON ALLISON
Lizzie Curry / MARY McMURRAY
File / REX SOUTHGATE
Sheriff Thomas / RAFE MacPHERSON
Bill Starbuck / AUGUST SCHELLENBERG

ONDINE

by Jean Giraudoux
adapted by Maurice Valency
directed by Heinar Piller
costumes by Robert Doyle
sets by Robert Doyle
lighting by David Hignell

Auguste / REX SOUTHGATE
Eugenie / MARGARET MacLEOD
Ritter Hans / DON ALLISON
Ondine / LINDA LIVINGSTON
The Ondines / RUTH DANSON, VICKI
WARREN, JAN HENDERSON
Old One / RON HASTINGS
Lord Chamberlain / JACK MEDLEY
Superintendent of the Theatre / GAVIN PAYNE
Trainer of Seals / RAFE MacPHERSON
Bertha / LYN WRIGHT
Bertram / AUGUST SCHELLENBERG
Violante / YVONNE ADALIAN
Angelique / VICKI WARREN
Matho / DAVID BROWN
Salammbo / MARY McMURRAY
The King / DONALD MEYERS
Page / HANS BÖGGILD
A Servant / GAVIN PAYNE
First Fisherman / DAVID BROWN
First Judge / DAVID RENTON
Second Judge / EDWIN RUBIN
Executioner / RAFE MacPHERSON
Kitchen Maid / YVONNE ADALIAN

SUMMER OF THE SEVENTEENTH DOLL

by Ray Lawler
directed by Denny Spence
costumes by Robert Doyle
sets by Fred Allen
lighting by William Severin

Pearl Cunningham / MARGARET MacLEOD
Bubba Ryan / VICKI WARREN
Olive Leech / LYN WRIGHT
Emma Leech / YVONNE ADALIAN
Barney Ibbot / DAVID RENTON
Roo Webber / REX SOUTHGATE
Johnnie Dowd / DON ALLISON

break down the prejudice, to convince people that "it's all right to come in a T-shirt in the summer." Perhaps the most telling tribute Heinar makes to reveal the fruits of Leon's labours is his account of that change in acceptance which was wonderful to see in the Neptune audience. He tells of the time when he came as stage manager and saw the high-school kids being dragged in to see Shakespeare — the *last* thing they wanted to do. At one point David Renton had to stop the show for the coke bottles and paper clips thrown onto the stage: it was "panic time" says Piller. He wondered at that point, "What are we trying to do here?" A few years later he saw some of the same teenagers, "now with a date in tow," coming voluntarily to Neptune. They had got the taste for it. Seeing the audiences grow made it all worthwhile.

In 1968 Leon Major had much confidence in handing over the reins at Neptune to Piller, while he took up his new post as director of productions at the Graduate Centre for the Study of Drama, University of Toronto, though he continued to act as consultant and occasional guest director. "I could not have taken Neptune through that next phase if Leon had not stuck to his guns and established a repertory company according to his ideals and philosophy," declares Piller. "That's the only reason it survived. Otherwise it would have been a continuation of Theatre Arts Guild, with everyone getting Equity wages the only difference. They would have continued to do the latest Broadway comedy, with the odd art classic thrown in to appease the more intellectual members of the audience, the only difference being it would have been more professionally designed and mounted . . . What Leon made was a very bold statement: he created something unique in Canada at the time." Mary McMurray remembers that *Ondine* was the last production when Leon was around: "We were sitting in the green room. No one else seemed to feel as acutely as I did that it was the passing of an era."

two

HEINAR PILLER

artistic director
1969 - 1971

CACTUS FLOWER

by Abe Burrows
based on a play by Pierre Barillet
and Jean-Pierre Gredy
directed by Heinar Piller
costumes by Maurice Strike
sets by Maurice Strike
lighting by Tom Saunders

Toni Simmons / NANCY WATT
Igor Sullivan / RICHARD DONAT
Stephanie Dickinson / FAITH WARD
Mrs. Dixon Durant / MARGARET MacLEOD
Dr. Julian Winston / JACK MEDLEY
Harvey Greenfield / DAVID BROWN
Senor Arturo Sanchez / DONALD MEYERS
Boticelli's Springtime / SUSAN CHAPPLE
Waiters, cab driver / MARCEL MAILLARD,
KEN McBANE, MARK DeWOLF

WHO'S AFRAID OF
VIRGINIA WOOLF?

by Edward Albee
directed by Marigold Charlesworth
costumes by Ken McBane
sets by Maurice Strike
lighting by Tom Saunders

Martha / LYNNE GORMAN
George / RON HASTINGS
Honey / LINDA LIVINGSTON
Nick / DON ALLISON

BY 1968 LEON MAJOR, who was frequently away with play or opera productions in Toronto, left Neptune more and more in the hands of Heinar Piller. Piller, who joined the theatre as stage and company manager in 1966, stayed on to become first associate and then full artistic director in 1968-69. The style of theatre on which Major had modelled Neptune was one with which Piller had grown up in his native Austria; he knew no other. He has great respect for what Leon and the first company accomplished, against all odds. Heinar's task was to let the roots that Leon planted reach further and further, and identify the theatre within the community: "He put out more roots in the community than I ever did," asserts Major. One of the primary ways he did this was to take over responsibility for all the tours, including the national one for Expo.

Another experiment to strike roots in the community was the occasional special performance, such as Anita Bell's *He Done Her Wrong; or, Wedded but No Wife* in the Public Gardens, or Christopher Fry's *A Sleep of Prisoners* in St. Paul's Church, both directed by Piller. The players were nearly thrown out of the church when one of its officials heard a member of the company uttering a four-letter word! One of the real highlights for Piller was his 1968 production of *A Man for All Seasons,* for which newly appointed business manager John Hobday "had to set the world in motion" to obtain rights for the first production of the play in North America while the film version was still running. Heinar was in a panic — could they still do it? Then he couldn"t

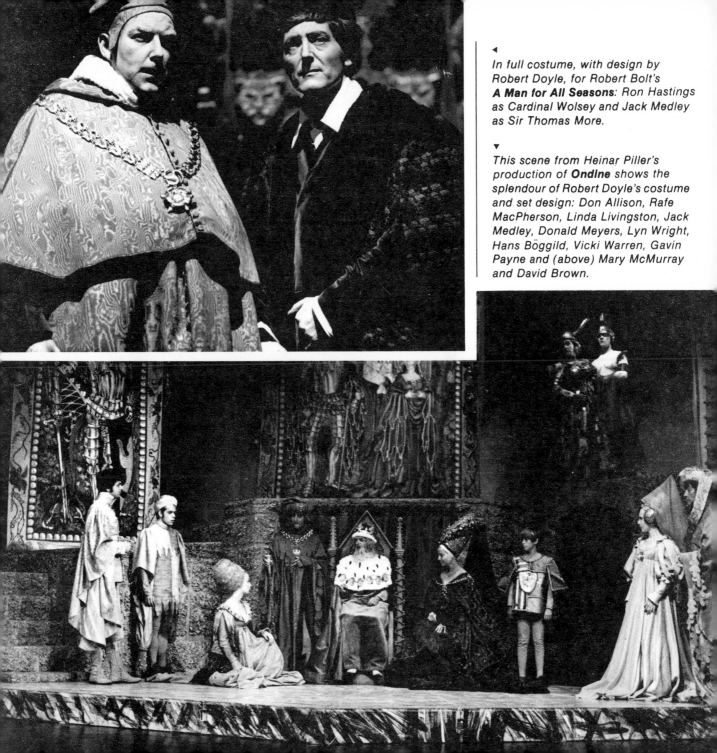

◄

In full costume, with design by Robert Doyle, for Robert Bolt's **A Man for All Seasons**: Ron Hastings as Cardinal Wolsey and Jack Medley as Sir Thomas More.

▼

This scene from Heinar Piller's production of **Ondine** shows the splendour of Robert Doyle's costume and set design: Don Allison, Rafe MacPherson, Linda Livingston, Jack Medley, Donald Meyers, Lyn Wright, Hans Böggild, Vicki Warren, Gavin Payne and (above) Mary McMurray and David Brown.

PYGMALION

by George Bernard Shaw
directed by Marigold Charlesworth
costumes by Maurice Strike
sets by Maurice Strike
lighting by Tom Saunders

Prof. Henry Higgins / JACK MEDLEY
Col. Pickering / DENNIS THATCHER
Freddy Eynsford-Hill / DON ALLISON
Alfred Doolittle / DONALD MEYERS
Eliza Doolittle / LINDA LIVINGSTON
Mrs. Eynsford-Hill / YVONNE ADALIAN
Clara Eynsford-Hill / SUSAN CHAPPLE
Mrs. Higgins / FAITH WARD
Mrs. Pearce / MARGARET MacLEOD
Parlour Maid / MARGOT SWEENY
Bystanders / RICHARD DONAT, RON
HASTINGS, MARGOT SWEENY, MARCEL
MAILLARD, HANS BÖGGILD

THE BOY FRIEND

by Sandy Wilson
co-ordinated by Heinar Piller
choreographed by June Sampson
musical direction by John de Main
sets and costumes by Maurice Strike
lighting by Tom Saunders

Hortense / SUSAN CHAPPLE
Maisie / JUNE SAMPSON
Dulcie / LINDA LIVINGSTON
Fay / KATHRYN WATT
Nancy / MARGOT SWEENY
Polly Browne / YVONNE ADALIAN
Madame Dubonnet / FAITH WARD
Bobby Van Husen / FRED GRADES
Percival Browne / JACK MEDLEY
Tony / DAVID BROWN
Lord Brockhurst / DENNIS THATCHER
Lady Brockhurst / MARGARET MacLEOD
Marcel / RON HASTINGS
Pierre / RICHARD DONAT
Alphonse / MARCEL MAILLARD
Policeman/Waiter / KEN McBANE
Lolita / JUNE SAMPSON
Pepe / MICHAEL TABBITT

▲
Ray Lawler's Australian play **Summer of the Seventeenth Doll***: Margaret MacLeod, David Renton, Rex Southgate, Lyn Wright and Yvonne Adalian.*

find an actor for Sir Thomas More, until he realized that the answer was right under his nose: Jack Medley, better known for lighter roles, who had been dying to play More, was given his chance and was a spectacular success in the part.

"Among the sets we built," says John Blackmore, "*A Man for All Seasons* stands out. It was a lovely set [designed by Fred Allen]. We had winding stairs with a great platform and on stage right another platform with big columns and it was all black. There was a big throne centre stage and the costumes [designed by Robert Doyle] were so beautiful. One thing that stands out in my mind was the robe, a beautiful maroon robe."

It became the thing for actors such as Jack Medley, Denise Fergusson or Douglas Chamberlain to remain from season to season. "They were stars within our own little world," recalls Piller. "People would come to see a show because Duggie or Denise was in it." This was still consistent with the idea of repertory, because the actors were able to make the essential contact with the community, which was impossible if they came for a single production. Although there were still pockets who felt "those Upper Canadians are coming down to teach us what theatre's all about," most actors were accepted with pleasure and hospitality into the community. New members of the company such as Don Allison and Faith Ward have performed regularly, even in recent years, while others such as Eric Donkin, Ron Hastings and Linda Livingston appeared many times with great success.

Other highlights at this time included Lynne Gorman as a forceful Martha in *Who's Afraid of Virginia Woolf?* directed by Marigold Charlesworth, and Linda Livingston dazzling in Piller's production of Giraudoux's *Ondine*. On the opening night of *Ondine* the medieval set caught fire and Hugh Jones, the technical director, strode onto the stage with a fire extinguisher, "while the actors and audience never missed a beat," according to Don Allison. Don also recalls his feet slipping when he was supposed to stride on the stage as the hero of Arbuzov's *The Promise,* and sliding down a fifteen-foot ramp to centre stage, more like a clown.

THE PROMISE

by Alexei Arbuzov
directed by Heinar Piller
sets and costumes by Maurice Strike
lighting by Tom Saunders

Marat / DON ALLISON
Lika / PATRICIA LUDWICK
Leonidik / DAVID FOSTER

LILIOM

by Ferenc Molnar
directed by Heinar Piller
costumes and sets by Maurice Strike
lighting by Tom Saunders

Marie / LINDA LIVINGSTON
Julie / PATRICIA LUDWICK
Mrs. Muskat / MARGARET MacLEOD
Liliom / LEON POWNALL
Servant Girls / YVONNE ADALIAN,
KATHRYN WATT
First Plainclothes Man,
First Mounted Policeman,
First Heavenly Policeman / DON ALLISON
Second Plainclothes Man,
Second Mounted Policeman,
Second Heavenly Policeman / RICHARD DONAT
Mother Hollunder / JOAN ORENSTEIN
Ficsur / DAVID RENTON
Wolf Beifeld / RON HASTINGS
Young Hollunder / DAVID FOSTER
Suburban Policeman / JAMES HURDLE
Linzman / EDWIN RUBIN
The Doctor / ALAN BLEVISS
The Carpenter / EDWIN RUBIN
The Rich Man / JACK MEDLEY
The Poor Man / LIONEL SIMMONS
The Old Guard / ALAN BLEVISS
The Magistrate / JAMES HURDLE
Louise / KATHRYN WATT
Peasants, townspeople, etc. / HANS BÖGGILD,
CHRIS CHRISTAKOS, SUSAN DEVEAU,
RHONA GOLD, MICHAEL HAWKINS, SEAN
HAWKINS, NICKI HUBBARD, ALAN JOLLI-
MORE, KEVIN JOLLIMORE, PAT JOLLIMORE,
ALEX JONES, BIANCA LANG, MARIA LANG,
MARCEL MAILLARD, CECILIA ORENSTEIN,
RUTH ORENSTEIN, SARAH ORENSTEIN,
RICHARD POCHINKO, JANE RISLEY,
SARAH STEVENS, IAN WALLACE

▲

Artistic director Heinar Piller, right, discusses contract arrangements in 1970 with Jack Medley, left and Ron Hastings.

CHARLEY'S AUNT

by Brandon Thomas
directd by Heinar Piller
costumes by Ken McBane
sets by Maurice Strike
lighting by Tom Saunders

Stephen Spettigue / LIONEL SIMMONS
Col. Sir Francis Chesney / RON HASTINGS
Jack Chesney / DON ALLISON
Charles Wykeham / DAVID FOSTER
Lord Fancourt Babberley / JACK MEDLEY
Brassett / RICHARD DONAT
Donna Lucia / MARGARET MacLEOD
Amy Spettigue / LINDA LIVINGSTON
Kitty Verdun / PATRICIA LUDWICK
Ela Delahay / KATHRYN WATT

Lloyd Newman remembers that when he was president, and hosting the Canada Council Board at Neptune, he attended a performance of *Ondine* with newly installed Lieutenant Governor Victor Oland, son of the Colonel: "I escorted him to his seat and stood at nervous attention by his side, waiting for *God Save the Queen*. Somehow, I don't know how, the staff had loaded the tape backwards. As the unfathomable music went on, a gentleman next to me began to laugh hysterically. I pulled myself to my full height of pompous dignity, and said, 'Please! Show some respect. We're playing *The Queen* for the Lieutenant Governor.' 'I know,' he replied, 'I'm his son.' "

Joan Gregson gave a riveting performance as the blind girl in *Wait Until Dark*. She says that one of the finest and most moving compliments she ever received was from a man suffering from glaucoma who was going blind. At the end of the play he turned to his companion and said, "Well, if she can do it, so can I." Faith Ward remembers that she was dogged by misfortune over a quick costume change in *Cactus Flower*. At dress rehearsal she rushed backstage, cutting both shins on an unmarked platform in the dark, with blood streaming everywhere. At one performance her zipper broke and she had to tell David Brown not to expose her back to the audience. When she was playing in *The Killing of Sister George* she was accosted by a loud-voiced woman in a small bank on Robie Street: "She asked what I was doing in such a filthy play and how I could justify doing that kind of character. Everyone in the bank turned and looked at me. Because I was angry I defended the play more than I would otherwise have done."

Internationally known artists joined the company for the 1970 season. Two of Eastern Europe's most prominent designers, Antony and Olga Dimitrov, who had fled from their native Czechoslovakia after the 1968 Russian invasion, stayed for two seasons. Libby Day, public relations director at the time, remembers asking Olga, still new to Canada and the English language, to explain to a "relatively proper group" on a tour of the theatre what she was doing when she was cutting out a large shirt; "with her wide and wonderful smile she replied, 'I make a big shit.' " There'were also many stories about Michael Gough, well known for performances in countless stage plays and films, and a member of the National Theatre Company of Great Britian later in the seventies, who headed Neptune's acting company that season. On one occasion when he was in *Tiger! Tiger!* he couldn't remember the traditional Scottish names of members of the Hunter family who had died, and he had to improvise, leaving the whole company in stitches as he recalled "Clara and Pedro and Simon and Roy . . ." Other notable members of that company included Lynne Gorman, Douglas Chamberlain and Kenneth Pogue. Music for another production in this season, *The Lion in Winter,* was provided by a local group, April Wine, which later became known internationally: rock-band music was skilfully integrated with the medieval sound of Gregorian chant, pointing the way to a comparable idea with the *Medea* eleven years later.

Piller also instituted Neptune's Studio Theatre for experimental works, performed in an auditorium in the basement of King's College in 1969. He had himself tried out some workshop productions of avant-garde plays by Strindberg, Pinter and Beckett two years previously, and now handed over to other directors to present Beckett's *Waiting for Godot,* N.F. Simpson's *A Resounding Tinkle* and Mrozek's *The Police.* He also found funding for and directed a high-school touring company with *Four Aloud* in 1968. This company had first been proposed, conceived and organized by David Renton the previous year, with actors Hamilton McClymont, Diana Leblanc, Ron Hastings and Renton himself contributing long hours of voluntary time, driving, loading and unloading, and set-constructing as well as performing from a script by Harry Whittier based on Homer and Shakespeare. This was the true pioneering start of Neptune's educational role in going out to the schools, which was to develop at stages in the years to follow, frequently under Renton's guidance. Renton also compiled an entertainment called *Now the Buffalo's Gone* on the still topical subject of the treaties between the Canadian government and its native peoples. He directed it for a special performance during the 1969 Canada Games in Halifax.

The touring of plays was a manifestation of Piller's commitment to the theatre as part of the community. It was

BOEING BOEING

by Marc Camoletti & Beverley Cross
directed by Heinar Piller
costumes and sets by Maurice Strike
lighting by Tom Saunders

Bernard / JAMES HURDLE
Janet / KATHRYN WATT
Bertha / MARGARET MacLEOD
Robert / EDWIN RUBIN
Jacqueline / YVONNE ADALIAN
Judith / LINDA LIVINGSTON

STUDIO NEPTUNE
at King's College

A RESOUNDING TINKLE

by N.F. Simpson
directed by Alex Jones

Middie / JOAN ORENSTEIN
Bro. / RON HASTINGS
Uncle Ted / PATRICIA LUDWICK

THE POLICE

by Slawomir Mrozek
directed by Clarke Rogers

The Chief of Police / JACK MEDLEY
The Prisoner / LIONEL SIMMONS
The Police Sergeant / RON HASTINGS
The Sergeant's Wife / JOAN ORENSTEIN
The General / RICHARD DONAT
A Policeman / DAVID FOSTER

WAITING FOR GODOT

by Samuel Beckett
directed by Harry Whittier
lighting by Rod Olafson

Estragon / DAVID RENTON
Vladimir / LEON POWNALL
Lucky / JAMES HURDLE
Pozzo / ALAN BLEVISS
A Boy / HANS BÖGGILD

YOU KNOW I CAN'T HEAR YOU WHEN THE WATER'S RUNNING

by Robert Anderson
directed by Keith Turnbull
costumes by Olga Dimitrov
sets by Lawrence Schafer
lighting by David Hinks

Jack Barnstable / SANDY WEBSTER
Herb Miller / KENNETH POGUE
Dorothy / YVONNE-ADALIAN
Richard Pawling / DOUGLAS CHAMBERLAIN
Salesman / SANDY WEBSTER
Harriet / MARGARET MacLEOD
George / KENNETH POGUE
Jill / YVONNE ADALIAN
Chuck / SANDY WEBSTER
Edith / MARGARET MacLEOD
Clarice / YVONNE ADALIAN
Herbert / SANDY WEBSTER
Muriel / MARGARET MacLEOD

THE LION IN WINTER

by James Goldman
directed by Heinar Piller
sets by Antony Dimitrov
costumes by Olga Dimitrov
lighting by David Hinks

music composed and played by April Wine

Henry II / MICHAEL GOUGH
Alais / YVONNE ADALIAN
John / DAVID FOSTER
Geoffrey / DOUGLAS CHAMBERLAIN
Richard Lionheart / KENNETH POGUE
Eleanor / LYNNE GORMAN
Philip / TERRY JUDD

◄

The battle of the sexes rages in Edward Albee's **Who's Afraid of Virginia Woolf?** *: Lynne Gorman, Don Allison, Linda Livingston and Ron Hastings*

▶

Jack Medley as Professor Higgins and Linda Livingston as Eliza Doolittle, centre, surrounded by bystanders Margot Sweeny, Richard Donat, Marcel Maillard, Ron Hastings, Hans Böggild and Susan Chapple in the opening scene of Shaw's **Pygmalion**.

▼

Another classic comedy: Linda Livingston, Jack Medley, Patricia Ludwick, Margaret MacLeod and Kathryn Watt in **Charley's Aunt**.

THE KILLING OF SISTER GEORGE

by Frank Marcus
directed by David Renton
sets by Antony Dimitrov
costumes by Olga Dimitrov
lighting by David Hinks

June Buckridge / LYNNE GORMAN
Alice "Childie" McNaught / TERRY TWEED
Mrs. Mercy Croft / FAITH WARD
Madame Xenia / MARGARET MacLEOD

TIGER! TIGER!

by Arthur L. Murphy
directed by Heinar Piller
sets by Antony Dimitrov
costumes by Olga Dimitrov
lighting by David Hinks

John Hunter / KENNETH POGUE
Agnes Hunter / MARGARET MacLEOD
William Hunter / MICHAEL GOUGH
Dr. Samuel Johnson / LIONEL SIMMONS
Top Hat / DOUGLAS CHAMBERLAIN
Joey / KENNETH WICKES
George Selwyn / DAVID RENTON
Nurse / YVONNE ADALIAN
Francis Tomkins / CLAUDE BEDE
Robert Home / SANDY WEBSTER
Anne Home / TERRY TWEED
Matthew Baillie / DAVID FOSTER
Thomas Spence / EDWIN RUBIN
Joseph Banks / TERRY JUDD
A Whore / YVONNE ADALIAN
A Patient / MARCEL MAILLARD
Students, guests, etc. / YVONNE ADALIAN,
MAUREEN E. ALLAN, HANS BÖGGILD,
LESLEIGH GRICE, PETER GUILDFORD,
GEORGE JORDAN, TERRY JUDD,
MARCEL MAILLARD
Voice of Oxford Professor / DR. M. USMIANI

◄

*Frank Marcus' **The Killing of Sister George** shocked at least one audience member by touching on the subject of lesbianism: Lynne Gorman, Terry Tweed and Faith Ward.*

►

*David Foster, Patricia Ludwick and Don Allison in Heinar Piller's production of Alexei Arbuzov's drama **The Promise**.*

▼

*Heinar Piller's spectacular production of Molnar's **Liliom** features Richard Pochinko, Patricia Ludwick, Hans Böggild, Joan Orenstein, Jane Risley, Ron Hastings, Linda Livingston, David Foster and Leon Pownall (foreground) in the title role.*

A FLEA IN HER EAR

*by Georges Feydeau
directed by Heinar Piller
assistant director David Foster
sets by Antony Dimitrov
costumes by Olga Dimitrov
lighting by David Hinks*

Camille Chandebise / DOUGLAS CHAMBERLAIN
Antoinette Plucheux / YVONNE ADALIAN
Etienne Plucheux / KENNETH WICKES
Dr. Finache / SANDY WEBSTER
Lucienne / LINDA LIVINGSTON
Raymond Chandebise / MARGARET MacLEOD
Victor Chandebise / MICHAEL GOUGH
Romain Tournel / DAVID RENTON
Carlos / KENNETH POGUE
Eugenie / TERRY TWEED
Augustin Feraillon / CLAUDE BEDE
Olympe / FAITH WARD
Baptistin / TERRY JUDD
Herr Schwartz / HEINAR PILLER
Poche / MICHAEL GOUGH
Guests at the Hotel Coq d'Or / GEORGE JORDAN, LESLEIGH GRICE

DEATH OF A SALESMAN

*by Arthur Miller
directed by Keith Turnbull
sets by Antony Dimitrov
costumes by Olga Dimitrov
lighting by David Hinks*

Willy Loman / SANDY WEBSTER
Linda / MARGARET MacLEOD
Biff / KENNETH POGUE
Happy / JERRY FRANKEN
Bernard / KENNETH WICKES
The Woman / LIZA CREIGHTON
Charley / DAVID RENTON
Uncle Ben / RON HASTINGS
Howard Wagner / JACK MEDLEY
Jenny / TERRY TWEED
Stanley / BARRY WALSH
Miss Forsythe / ROSEMARY RADCLIFFE
Letta / PATRICIA LUDWICK

▶
*Anthony Dimitrov's extraordinary set design for Feydeau's **A Flea In Her Ear**.*

THE EGG

*by Felicien Marceau
adapted by Patricia Moyes
directed by Keith Turnbull
sets by Antony Dimitrov
costumes by Olga Dimitrov
lighting by David Hinks*

Magis / HEINAR PILLER
Doctor / SANDY WEBSTER
Barbedart / KENNETH POGUE
Tanson / KENNETH WICKES
1st Woman / TERRY TWEED
2nd Woman / LIZA CREIGHTON
3rd Woman / MARGARET MacLEOD
Young Girl / ROSEMARY RADCLIFFE
Mlle. Durant / MARGARET MacLEOD
Customer / RON HASTINGS
Duffiquet / JACK MEDLEY
Justine / TERRY TWEED

(continued on next page)

therefore disappointing to him that the touring could not be kept up on the scale that it was at the beginning. The first time he took over a Maritimes tour the company travelled with twenty-four actors, and a crew of eight or ten. In his last season, 1971, he could not use more than eleven players in a large-cast play. The situation forced him to compromise all the way: "Never mind what you wanted to do," he says, "never mind what was current and had to be brought to Halifax because it just became the hottest property, never mind the token gesture to the classics, never mind the new play you wanted to commission and do ... All these considerations went out of the window." He was almost reduced to looking into French's catalogue to find a play with eleven or fewer characters.

Piller recalls that when he first joined Neptune it was "just after that initial dream Leon started with was evaporating in the

face of reality, the pressure of financing, the danger of weekly collapse. Can we meet the payroll? Can we not?" The answer was in the appointment of John Hobday as business administrator in December 1967. Hobday had been an actor with the first Neptune company and then administrator at the Confederation Centre in Charlottetown. After the 1968 winter season he was able to report that public hostility and suspicion had been replaced by "an enormous amount of goodwill towards Neptune," through a combination of increased sales of subscription tickets and a prudent choice of plays. A year later subscriptions rose to more than 4,000. Hobday was appointed executive director of Neptune early in 1970, but gave up after the 1971 season, having accepted the post of national director of the Canadian Conference of the Arts. The 1970 winter season saw a surplus of just $397, with 86% of ticket sales from subscriptions. By now the Canada Council

ANY WEDNESDAY

by Muriel Resnick
directed by Heinar Piller
sets by Fred Allen
costumes by Olga Dimitrov
lighting by David Hinks

Ellen / ROSEMARY RADCLIFFE
John / JACK MEDLEY
Dorothy / FAITH WARD
Cass / RON HASTINGS

8th SEASON

December 1970-August 1971

RUMPLE STILTSKIN

book, music, lyrics by
Ronald Chudley & Diane Stapley
directed by Heinar Piller
musical direction by Monique Gusset
sets by Antony Dimitrov
costumes by Olga Dimitrov
lighting by David Hinks

Rumple Stiltskin / KENNETH WICKES
Wrinkle Stiltskin / DAVID RENTON
The Miller / LIONEL SIMMONS
Melinda / GRACIE FINLEY
The Prince / GEORGE JORDAN
The Queen / BARBARA BRYNE

THE CARETAKER

by Harold Pinter
directed by Eric Salmon
sets by Antony Dimitrov
costumes by Olga Dimitrov
lighting by David Hinks

Mick / KENNETH POGUE
Aston / DAVID RENTON
Davies / PATRICK BOXILL

▲
Arthur Murphy's **Tiger! Tiger!**, *with costumes by Olga Dimitrov,*
featured David Renton, Lionel Simmons, and internationally known
star Michael Gough.

grant had risen to $130,000, still short of what was applied for, while both provincial and city grants were frozen at $80,000 and $25,000 respectively.

More than anything else it was the compromising of ideals that led Piller to hand in his resignation in 1971. Times were changing. It was now virtually impossible to get top players to move to the regions for several months. Why should they leave Toronto? They would lose out if they moved for even one show. The Stratford and Shaw Festivals were waiting to snap up the leading actors. At the time he left Major said, "Heinar Piller, my successor, will be a much better administrator than I ever was." "The success of Heinar," he says today, "(He wouldn't say it, but I would) is that he recognized that it was time for retrenchment in terms of spending." Major says that he himself had recognized rightly that the theatre had to be there if they could afford it or not. But Piller shifted the theatre to accommodate its needs at the time he took over.

In retrospect Piller's work for Neptune was of incalculable importance. When Robert Sherrin took over in 1971 he found a season already prepared and a theatre company established with integrity and with its finances in good order. And the magic of Neptune has remained with Piller in spite of the compromise. "Neptune is now twenty-five years old, which I cannot believe," he says. "It's still very close to me, no matter how many years come between."

A MIDSUMMER NIGHT'S DREAM

by William Shakespeare
directed by Heinar Piller
assistant director David Renton
set by Antony Dimitrov
costumes by Olga Dimitrov
lighting by David Hinks
music composed & arranged by
Ken Elloway

Theseus / KENNETH POGUE
Egeus / PETER STURGESS
Lysander / DON ALLISON
Demetrius / BRIAIN PETCHEY
Philostrate / PETER ELLIOTT
Peter Quince / DAVID RENTON
Nick Bottom / DOUGLAS CHAMBERLAIN
Francis Flute / KENNETH WICKES
Tom Snout / LAWRENCE BENEDICT
Snug / JACK NORTHMORE
Robin Starveling / LIONEL SIMMONS
Hippolyta / DIANA BARRINGTON
Hermia / CAROLYN YOUNGER
Helena / DENISE FERGUSSON
Oberon / KENNETH POGUE
Titania / DIANA BARRINGTON
Puck / MARGOT SWEENY
Peaseblossom / JOHN DUNSWORTH
Cobweb / IAN DEAKIN
Moth / STUART DUNSWORTH
Mustardseed / DUNCAN HOLT
Other fairies attending Oberon and Titania; attendants on Theseus and Hippolyta / HANS BØGGILD, WANDA GRAHAM, LESLEIGH GRICE, NICKI HUBBARD, SHELLEY MATTHEWS, SUSAN SADLER

LONG DAY'S JOURNEY INTO NIGHT

directed by William Davis
sets by Antony Dimitrov
costumes by Olga Dimitrov
lighting by David Hinks

James Tyrone / DAVID DODIMEAD
Mary Cavan Tyrone / LYNNE GORMAN
James Tyrone Jr. / KENNETH POGUE
Edmund Tyrone / BRIAIN PETCHEY
Cathleen / PATRICIA LUDWICK

THE FANTASTICKS

by Tom Jones & Harvey Schmidt
directed & choreographed by Alan Lund
music directed by Errol Gay
sets by Antony Dimitrov
costumes by Olga Dimitrov
lighting by David Hinks

The Mute / BOB AINSLIE
The Narrator / BILL COLE
The Girl / BETH ANNE COLE
The Boy / JEFF HYSLOP
The Girl's Father / DOUGLAS CHAMBERLAIN
The Boy's Father / JACK NORTHMORE
The Old Actor / DAVID RENTON
The Man Who Dies / KENNETH WICKES

BLITHE SPIRIT

by Noël Coward
directed by Robert Sherrin
set by Antony Dimitrov
costumes by Olga Dimitrov
lighting by David Hinks

Edith / DAPHNE GIBSON
Ruth / FERN SLOAN
Charles / JACK MEDLEY
Dr. Bradman / DAVID RENTON
Mrs. Bradman / PATRICIA HAMILTON
Madame Arcati / MADELEINE CHRISTIE
Elvira / DENISE FERGUSSON

THE IMPORTANCE OF BEING EARNEST

by Oscar Wilde
directed by Robert Sherrin
set by Antony Dimitrov
costumes by Olga Dimitrov
lighting by David Hinks

Lane / LESLIE CARLSON
Algernon / COLIN FOX
John Worthing / JACK MEDLEY
Lady Bracknell / MADELEINE CHRISTIE
Hon. Gwendolen Fairfax / DENISE FERGUSSON
Miss Prism / PATRICIA HAMILTON
Cecily Cardew / FERN SLOAN
Rev. Canon Chasuble / DAVID RENTON
Merriman / LESLIE CARLSON

▲
Heinar Piller's final production at Neptune, **A Midsummer Night's Dream**, opened the 1971 season. Kenneth Pogue as Theseus, and Diana Barringston as Hippolyta, who also doubled as Oberon and Titania, are centre.

▲

Administrative staff and company of Neptune Theatre 1969-70.
Artistic director Heinar Piller is on the far left.

THE STAR-SPANGLED GIRL

by Neil Simon
directed by Henry Kaplan
set by Antony Dimitrov
costumes by Olga Dimitrov
lighting by David Hinks

Andy Hobart / COLIN FOX
Norman Cornell / LESLIE CARLSON
Sophie Rauschmeyer / CAROL SCHLANGER

three

ROBERT
SHERRIN

artistic director
1971 - 1974

THE DANDY LION

by Pat Patterson and Dodi Robb
directed by Robert Sherrin
designed by Aristides Gazetas

Andrew / JIMMY MacNEIL
Dalton the Lion Tamer / DON ALLISON
The Lion / LIONEL SIMMONS
Clifford the Clown / DAVID MILLER
Bareback Rider / MARGO SWEENEY
Tightrope Walker / KATHLEEN FLAHERTY
Ringo the Ringmaster / DAVID RENTON
Musicans / DON LePAGE (drums),
MONIQUE GUSSET (piano)

A DAY IN THE DEATH OF JOE EGG

by Peter Nichols
directed by Joseph Shaw
designed by Aristides Gazetas

Bri / COLIN FOX
Sheila / ANNE BUTLER
Joe / ELIZABETH THOMSON
Freddie / DAVID RENTON
Pam / IRENE BALSER
Grace / DORA DAINTON
Musician / DON LePAGE

THERE WAS A SMOOTH TRANSITION when Robert Sherrin began his tenure as artistic director in 1971. Piller had already planned the winter season, though Sherrin had a hand in casting and other details. Guest director William Davis mounted an absorbing *Long Day's Journey into Night*. Eric Salmon's splendid production of Pinter's *The Caretaker* provided David Renton as Anton with possibly the finest of his more than one hundred roles for Neptune, with Patrick Boxill and Ken Pogue co-starring superbly.

Sherrin acknowledges that he came at a change period for the company. The early idealism of permanent repertory had gone. Neptune was already becoming a stock company when Piller left: it was the only way it could survive. Sherrin is not philosophically opposed to repertory, but in contrast to the national situation in the theatre just a few years previously, you simply couldn't attract the best actors by getting them to stay for a long period of time in Halifax. "By the time I came along," says Sherrin, "two things were important:

"1) to bring back year-round quality in the theatre, which I did — so that virtually we hardly ever closed; we could employ the very best back-stage people and give them some kind of security so that they could live in Halifax, work there, and didn't have to go away and find work in between; they could literally stay the season round, therefore we kept our key people throughout that period;

Mick (Kenneth Pogue, c.) teases Davies (the late Patrick Boxill, r.) in the title role of Harold Pinter's **The Caretaker** while Mick's brother Aston (David Renton) looks on.

"In vino veritas": James Tyrone (David Dodimead, right), faces family truth with his sons Edmund (Brian Petchey) and Jamie (Kenneth Pogue) in Eugene O'Neill's autobiographical drama **Long Day's Journey Into Night**

THE SERVANT OF TWO MASTERS

by Carlo Goldoni
directed by Robert Sherrin
designed by Robert Doyle
lighting by Rae Ackerman

Dr. Lombardi / TONY VAN BRIDGE
Pantalone / JAMES VALENTINE
Smeraldina / NICOLA LIPMAN
Silvio / BRIAN McKAY
Brighella / GRANT COWAN
Clarice / SUSAN HOGAN
Truffaldino / DOUGLAS CHAMBERLAIN
Beatrice of Turin / TEDDE MOORE,
JOAN GREGSON
Florindo Aretusi / DAVID RENTON
A musician / ALAN TOROK
Porters and waiters / MICHAEL HOGAN,
LIONEL SIMMONS

I DO! I DO!

by Tom Jones & Harvey Schmidt
directed by Robert Sherrin
choreographed by Walter Burgess
designed by Maurice Strike
music directed by Barbara Spence
lighting by Rae Ackerman

Michael / MARK ALDEN
Agnes / EVELYNE ANDERSON
Musicans:
1st piano / BARBARA SPENCE
2nd piano / MONIQUE GUSSET
percussion / DON LePAGE

THE PRICE

by Arthur Miller
directed by Kurt Reis
designed by Aristides Gazetas

Victor Franz / EDWARD BINNS
Esther Franz / LUDI CLAIRE
Gregory Solomon / ALBERT M. OTTENHEIMER
Walter Franz / LAURENCE HUGO

"2) to have as wide a range of activity as possible so that we could discover and keep local talent: Joan Orenstein and Flo Paterson, for example, now work spectacularly all over the place. People who are now well known came from that period. It was a process of exploring what people were available to us locally so that through a whole explosion of activity — two stages, children's and schools' programmes — I was enabled from time to time to populate the main stage with members of a young company, while bringing in [well known] actors for particular plays."

Moreover, as money was very tight, the theatre couldn't afford to have major actors playing small parts. A better design quality was possible if you didn't have to strike a set and change it every night. There were no facilities or room at the theatre to play repertory and give the kind of standards that were expected. Sherrin was keen to raise the standards of acting and design, even if, as he admits, he didn't always achieve what he aimed for. Accordingly he made changes in policy from the fall of 1971. Since August 1966 the theatre had been dark between September and February, with the exception of 1970-71, when the season began with the Christmas play. Now seasons would revert to the almost year-round activity, running from November to August. The single season made planning easier, and more economical with one subscription campaign. Patrons could subscribe for either the whole season, including summer plays, or just for the winter portion.

Another major innovation was the establishment of Neptune's Second Stage, aided by L.I.P. grants. Over three seasons Second Stage mounted an impressive array of chamber or experimental works, many by Canadian authors. Second Stage was a training ground for many players such as Susan and Michael Hogan, Blair Brown or Richard Donat, who have since become nationally known artists. Others included Nick Mancuso in Whitehead's *The Foursome*, Joan Orenstein imperious in Beverly Simons' *Crabdance* and pairing strongly with Joseph Rutten in Michel Tremblay's *Forever Yours, Marie-Lou*, Terrence G. Ross with a virtuoso solo in Samuel Beckett's *Krapp's Last Tape*, and Jerry Franken in Michael Ondaatje's *The Col-*

lected Works of Billy the Kid. With the support of Neptune, James Reaney conducted at Second Stage his famous children's workshops on the Donnellys and began his association with Keith Turnbull; hence the formation of the NDWT company, which returned to Neptune in triumph with the full *Donnellys* trilogy on its fall tour of 1975.

Richard Donat recalls how the youthful Second Stage company, in adapting the film script of Ingmar Bergman's *The Seventh Seal* to the stage, failed to contact Bergman for the rights until the last moment. "We sent a telegram and he sent one back saying we would not be allowed to put on his play. Shortly before opening we sent a night letter to Faro Island off the coast of Sweden, explaining that we were a small group in a fifty-seat theatre and were on the verge of opening. We got a telegram back saying we could do the show only in Second Stage for the two weeks we had specified. The show went on to good response."

R.D. Reid, who directed James Nichol's *Sweet Home Sweet* for Second Stage, tells how "the 'Black Panthers' from California were in town and making everyone nervous. Since the play was the first incidence of black people taking a major role in a professional play on Neptune's stages, we were concerned about being used politically. No problem. They sent us two dozen roses before opening, attended en masse and cheered the house down, which was the kind of violence we appreciated." This production was to anticipate others prominently featuring black performers, by John Wood in 1977 and by Richard Ouzounian in 1988.

According to Bob Sherrin, "Designers [of Second Stage] were generally a collective of whoever was available at the time. Also the running of Second Stage was a very informal affair . . . I merely asked Don [Allison], then Keith [Turnbull] and finally Michael [Mawson] if they would run the place, under my general supervision. The Board was not invovled and it was a very loose arrangement." Two different spaces were used: 1588 Barrington Street, January-May 1972; and 1667 Argyle Street, June 1972-August 1974. "We were constantly expending enormous energy fixing up the space we were moving into," Sherrin recalls. "Part of the excitement was in the doing of it, and no one minded, but it wasn't something the same people could do year after year."

THE MATCHMAKER

by Thornton Wilder
directed by Robert Sherrin
set designed by Aristides Gazetas
costumes by Hilary Corbett

Horace Vandergelder / SANDY WEBSTER
Ambrose Kemper / DON ALLISON
Joe Scanlon / LIONEL SIMMONS
Gertrude / PHYLLIS MALCOLM STEWART
Cornelius Hackl / DEAN REGAN
Ermengarde / JENNIFER MORROW
Malachi Stack / DAVID RENTON
Mrs. Dolly Levi / HELENE WINSTON
Barnaby Tucker / BRIAN McKAY
Mrs. Irene Molloy / PATRICIA HAMILTON
Minnie Fay / BETH ANNE COLE
A cabman / JOHN CRIPTON
Rudolph / BRUCE ARMSTRONG
August / IAN DEAKIN
Miss Flora van Huysen / PHYLLIS MALCOLM STEWART
Miss Van Huysen's cook / JOAN STEBBINGS

THE MISER

by Molière
directed by Jean-Louis Roux
designed by Mark Negin
lighting by Rae Ackerman

Elise / DIANE D'AQUILA
Valere / DAVID RENTON
Cleante / DEAN HARRIS
La Fleche / JERRY FRANKEN
Harpagon / DAVID DODIMEAD
Master Simon / LIONEL SIMMONS
Frosine / DENISE PELLETIER
Brindavoine / BOB REID
La Merluche / TOM CELLI
Dame Claude / FLORENCE PATERSON
Master Jacques / ERIC HOUSE
Mariane / BARBARA KYLE
A Commissioner of Police / LIONEL SIMMONS
His Clerk / BOB REID
Anselme / TERRENCE G. ROSS

WHAT THE BUTLER SAW

by Joe Orton
directed by Robert Sherrin
designed by Mark Negin
lighting by Jane Boland

Dr. Prentice / ERIC HOUSE
Geraldine Barclay / PEGGY MAHON
Mrs. Prentice / ANN MORRISH
Nicholas Beckett / JERRY FRANKEN
Dr. Rance / DAVID RENTON
Sergeant Match / TOM CELLI

SECOND STAGE

CREEPS

by David Freeman
directed by David Renton

Michael / IAN DEAKIN
Pete / LIONEL SIMMONS
Tom / KEITH MADDOCK
Sam / DON ALLISON
Jim / DAVID MILLER
Miss Saunders / FLORA MONTGOMERY
Thelma, Miss C.P. / DIANNE LeDUC
Shriner / ERNEST FLEET
Shriner / BRIAN CROCKER
Mr. Carson / DAVID RENTON

STONEHENGE

by Douglas Bankson
directed by Don Allison
assisted by Stephan Regina-Thon
set by Hugh Jones
lighting by Jane Boland
costumes, properties by Barbara Joudrey

The Ancients / BRUCE ARMSTRONG,
PHYLLIS MALCOLM-STEWART, JOAN
STEBBINGS, FLORA MONTGOMERY-MOORE
Helga Helmgrin / KAREN MARGINSON
Chester / KEITH MADDOCK
Dorothy / NICOLA LIPMAN
Wanda Weaver-Cartlidge / FLO PATERSON
Dr. Tom Suture / BOB REID
Gelda Pratt / JOAN ORENSTEIN
Frank Pratt / LIONEL SIMMONS

▶
*Florence Paterson and Vernon Cain in an early Second Stage production, James Nichol's **Sweet Home Sweet**, 1972.*

▼
*Robert Sherrin directed Joe Orton's hilarious farce **What the Butler Saw**, with expert comic timing by, L-R, Jerry Franken, Ann Morrish, Peggy Mahon, Tom Celli, David Renton, Eric House.*

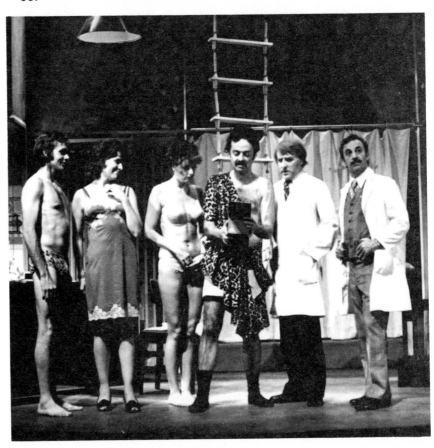

THE NEPTUNE STORY 73

SWEET HOME SWEET

by James Nichol
directed by Robert Reid
set by Phil Phalen &
Geoff LeBoutelier
lighting by Jane Boland
costume, properties by Barbara Jou'drey

Billy Brown / BRUCE WILSON
Marcey / HEATHER CHANDLER
Ruth Brown / FLO PATERSON
Abraham Lincoln Brown / VERNON CAIN

THE ST. FRANCIS XAVIER
PERFORMING GROUP:

THE MAN WITH SEVEN TOES (1)

by Michael Ondaatje
directed by John Rapsey
costumes by Robert Doyle
lighting by Jane Boland
sounds by Denise Golemblaski

Narrator / DAVID MILLER
Lady / CECILE O'CONNOR
Convict / BARRY REYNOLDS
Dancers / GILE BOURASSA, ALLAN MEUSE
Musician / BRIAN FURLOTT

BABEL (2)

a collective work,
directed by John Rapsey
costumes by Candy Sweet
lighting by Jane Boland
Song: lyrics by J. Rapsey,
music by Brian Furlott, Luke
Wintermans and Urban Bree

Performers:
DENISE GOLEMBLASKI
MARY TRAMLEY
PATRICK DUNNE
ALLAN MEUSE
BARRY REYNOLDS
Musician / BRIAN FURLOTT

KRAPP'S LAST TAPE (3)

by Samuel Beckett
directed and performed by
Terrence G. Ross

CRABDANCE (4)

by Beverley Simons
directed by Michael Mawson
lighting by Jane Boland

Sadie Golden / JOAN ORENSTEIN
Mowchuck / BARRY MINSHULL
Dickens / JOHN GARRETT
Highrise / HOWARD D'ARCY

GORILLA QUEEN

by Ronald Tavel
directed by Keith Turnbull
original music composed by
John Roby and John-Paul Ellis
choreography by Jaqueline Moriarty

Brute / BILL GRANCHELLI
Glitz Ionas / NINA HVOSLEF, WINSTON
MacDONALD, KAREN MARGINSON, ALLAN
MEUSE, PETER MUSHKAT, FLORENCE
PATERSON, SUZANNE TURNBULL
Mais Oui / ELLEN McGINN
Clyde Batty / BOB MARTYN
Karma Miranda / MARGOT SWEENY
Taharahnugi White Woman / BRUCE WILSON
Chimney Sweep / DAVID MILLER
Venus Fly Trap / PATRICIA LUDWICK
Sister Carries / ROBERT REID
Paulet Colbert / DIANE D'AQUILA
Queen Kong / EWAN SUTHERLAND
Clinic Intern / BARRY REYNOLDS
Musicians / JOHN-PAUL ELLIS, JOHN ROBY,
TIM COHOON, with BRUCE WILSON,
DIANE D'AQUILA

◄

Mâitre Jacques (Eric House) shares a joke with Harpagon (David Dodimead) and Valère (David Renton) in Molière's famous comedy **The Miser.**

▼

Another Orton black farce, **Loot,** *was directed by Christopher Newton and starred Bob Cartland, David Renton, Tom Carew, Dean Harris and Patricia Ludwick.*

3000 RED ANTS

by Lawrence Ferlinghetti
directed by Michael Mawson

Cast:
LIONEL SIMMONS
MARGOT SWEENY

ONE MAN MASQUE

by James Reaney
directed by Michael Mawson

Cast:
IAN DEAKIN, JOHN DUNSWORTH,
PATRICIA LUDWICK, ALLAN MEUSE,
SUZANNE TURNBULL

THE DEATH OF FIELDING

by Tom Lackey
directed by Keith Turnbull

Charlie Anderson / HANS BÖGGILD
Bill Travaskiss / DEAN SMITH
George Jones / RICHARD DONAT
Johnny Hazelton / R.D. REID
Captain Fielding / MICHAEL HARTLEY-
ROBINSON

10th SEASON

November 1972-August 1973

LOOT

by Joe Orton
directed by Christopher Newton
designed by Maurice Strike
lighting by Hugh Jones

McLeavy / BOB CARTLAND
Fay / PATRICIA LUDWICK
Hal / DEAN HARRIS
Dennis / TOM CAREW
Truscott / DAVID RENTON
Meadows / ROBERT D. REID

COLOUR THE FLESH
THE COLOUR OF DUST

by Michael Cook
directed by Robert Sherrin
music composed by Alan Laing
designed by Robert Doyle
lighting by Rae Ackerman

Willie / DEAN HARRIS
Ben / PETER ROGAN
Sean / R.D. REID
Lieutenant Mannon / JAMES HURDLE
Marie / DIANE D'AQUILA
A biddy / JOAN ORENSTEIN
Another biddy / JOAN HURLEY
James Tupper / ERIC HOUSE
A boy / IAN DEAKIN
Mrs. McDonald / FLORENCE PATERSON
Magistrate Neal / DAVID RENTON
A spokesman / DON ALLISON
Patrick / GREG WANLESS
Michael / BRUCE ARMSTRONG
Kevin / DEAN SMITH
Lawrence / LIONEL SIMMONS
Gert / MARGOT SWEENY
Captain Gross / ROWLAND DAVIES
A fisherman / DONALD MEYERS
A French officer / R.D. REID
A French soldier / GEORGE HENDERSON
An English officer / R.D. REID
An English soldier / GEORGE HENDERSON
A percussionist / BRIAN FURLOTT
A fiddler / LEO DOUBLET

THE MAGICAL GUITAR

by Janet MacEachen
directed by Robert Sherrin
set and costumes by Robert Daniels
songs by Janet MacEachen, arranged
by Steven Freygood

Molly / MARGOT SWEENY
Nora / FLORENCE PATERSON
Leo / DAVID RENTON
Linda Librarian / NICOLA LIPMAN
Cowboys / LIONEL SIMMONS, DON ALLISON
GREG WANLESS
Pianist / MONIQUE GUSSET

When L.I.P. grants were withdrawn, Second Stage disappeared.

Robert Sherrin attracted many major directors, designers and performers to Neptune. As well as his Second Stage work, Keith Turnbull brought great imagination and energy to such large-scale productions as Reaney's *Listen to the Wind,* and his own colourful adaptation of *The Good Soldier Schweik,* which received a great response as it was set in Halifax during the Second World War. Bob was particularly pleased with the productions of the Joe Orton black farces *What the Butler Saw* which he himself directed and *Loot* directed by Christopher Newton; David Renton showed a new brilliance in comedy performance in these plays, while in the former Eric House gave a portrayal of masterly comic timing as Dr. Prentice. The irreverent Orton plays showed how much people love to be shocked.

House was also outstanding as Maître Jacques in Molière's *The Miser,* directed by Jean-Louis Roux. On the night I saw this production, a small boy in the audience commented audibly on Maître Jacques' behaviour, and House, while remaining in character, fixed him with such a look as to win a loud round of delighted applause — one of those rare moments of spontaneous theatre. The production also marked one of the last performances of the notable French-Canadian actress Denise Pelletier, who died shortly afterwards. David Renton found playing a supporting role in Peter Nichols' *A Day in the Death of Joe Egg,* at the same time as planning a production of David Freeman's *Creeps* which he was directing at Second Stage, both of which concern the victims of cerebral palsy, an extraordinarily moving experience, especially as his youngest child was born the first week of the run.

Andrew Downie brought with him from the English Royal Shakespeare company a young, then unknown actor named Roger Rees, who gave an electrifying performance as Marchbanks in his production of Shaw's *Candida;* Rees has since won international acclaim in the title role of the Royal Shakespeare Company's *Nicholas Nickleby.* Sherrin considers this production of *Candida,* which also starred Joan Gregson and David Renton, the best he has ever seen. The tenth season at

▲
In Keith Turnbull's colourful staging of James Reaney's **Listen to the Wind**, the children provide a chorus while the play-within-a-play is enacted around the sick bed of the child Owen. L-R: Stephen Jeans, Robert Davidson, Susan MacNeill, Emilie Hujdic, Lynda Jeans, Diana Sheffield, Kenneth Kempster, and Cecile O'Connor.

LISTEN TO THE WIND

by James Reaney
with poems by Charlotte & Emily Bronte
directed by Keith Turnbull
design co-ordination by Nancy Pankiw
lighting by Bennet Averyt

Cast:
JERRY FRANKEN, NICOLA LIPMAN,
NANCY BEATTY, BLAIR BROWN,
TOM CAREW, BRYAN STANION,
EDGAR WREFORD, JOAN ORENSTEIN,
ROWLAND DAVIES, DIANE D'AQUILA

Chorus:
JENNIEFER BOYANOWSKY, ALEX BRUCE,
ROBERT DAVIDSION, EMILIE HUJDIC,
LYNDA JEANS, STEPHEN JEANS,
KENNETH KEMPSTER, SHELAGH McNAB,
SUSAN MacNEILL, CECILE O'CONNOR,
ANTHONY SALTER, DIANA SHEFFIELD,
NEIL THOMPSON, WADE WINN

Fiddler / JIM DANSON

LEAVING HOME

by David French
directed by Robert Sherrin
designed by Fred Allen
lighting by Hugh Jones

Mary Mercer / FLORENCE PATERSON
Ben Mercer / ASHELEIGH MOORHOUSE
Billy Mercer / RICHARD KELLEY
Jacob Mercer / GERARD PARKES
Kathy Jackson / MARY LONG
Minnie Jackson / LIZA CREIGHTON
Harold / ROBERT D. REID

PEER GYNT

by Henrik Ibsen
translated by Norman Ginsbury
directed by Robert Sherrin
designed by Robert Doyle
lighting by Robert C. Reinholdt
music composed by Milan Kymlicka
movement by Don Himes

Peer Gynt / HEATH LAMBERTS
Aase / FLORENCE PATERSON
Aslak / DON ALLISON
Fiddler / JIM DANSON
Steward / PETER ELLIOTT
Wedding Guests / GERALD BOWEN,
ALEX BRUCE, DAVID FERRY, GILLIAN
HANNANT, DEAN HARRIS, R.D. REID,
PATRICIA LUDWICK, CECILE O'CONNOR,
LIONEL SIMMONS, SUZANNE TURNBULL
Mads Moen / JERRY FRANKEN
Bridegroom's Mother / ELIZABETH
SHEPHERD
Bridegroom's Father / MACON McCALMAN
Solveig's Father / DAVID RENTON
Solveig's Mother / IRENE BALSER
Solveig / MARTI MARADEN
Helga / ELIZABETH THOMSON
The Farmer / COLIN FOX
Ingrid / NICOLA LIPMAN
Cowherd Girls / GILLIAN HANNANT,
NICOLA LIPMAN, PATRICIA LUDWICK
The Woman in Green / ELIZABETH SHEPHERD
Troll King / MACON McCALMAN
Troll Courtiers / DAVID RENTON, R.D. REID,
Boyg / HEATH LAMBERTS

(continued on next page)

Neptune was the most remarkable in the theatre's history. Several productions were of plays by Canadian dramatists of such eminence as Reaney, Tremblay, Cook and French. When local actress Florence Paterson played Mary Mercer in Sherrin's production of *Leaving Home,* David French knew that this was the definitive performance, and she was the obvious choice for the role in the sequel, *Of the Fields, Lately,* both at the Tarragon in Toronto and at Neptune. *An Italian Straw Hat* and *Peer Gynt* were enterprising choices for a summer season. Sherrin considers the part of Peer Gynt was tailor-made for Heath Lamberts, his friend for many years. One night in that production Don Allison and David Ferry switched roles and nobody noticed except the stage manager.

The ninth and tenth seasons each began with a tour which included a visit to the National Arts Centre, Ottawa. During the first of these trips the company was invited to lunch in a private parliamentary dining room by the Rt. Hon. Robert Stanfield, then leader of the opposition. According to tour manager Bruce Blakemore, their arrival on Parliament Hill happened to coincide with that of Mr. Kosygin, who was on a state visit from the U.S.S.R.: "It took some convincing of RCMP and security personnel that we were not part of the demonstrators but hungry actors." Tony van Bridge, who also gave his one-man show on G.K. Chesterton at Neptune, appeared as Dr. Lombardi in Goldoni's *The Servant of Two Masters.* On the opening night of this play at Neptune following the tour, leading lady Tedde Moore collapsed on stage and had to be taken to hospital. Bruce Blakemore recalls: "I had to read her part for the second act. I was appallingly bad but the audience was very kind. Probably they were totally befuddled. An actress named Tedde was replaced by a female stage manager named Bruce in the part of a woman who was disguised as a man. I had on my opening-night clothes of a lace blouse and leather skirt so when I referred to them as *my brother's clothes,* it brought down the house." Bob Sherrin remembers how at intermission he went into the audience and pressed Joan Gregson to take over the part for the rest of the run; she went on the next night with the part half learned.

The world première of Michael Cook's *Colour the Flesh the*

▲

*Robert Sherrin chose Henrik Ibsen's great epic drama **Peer Gynt** for Neptune's tenth anniversary production. Here Heath Lamberts in the title role becomes crowned 'King of Self' among lunatics in an asylum.*

Trolls / DON ALLISON, IRENE BALSER, GERALD BOWEN, ALEX BRUCE, PETER ELLIOTT, DAVID FERRY, JERRY FRANKEN, GILLIAN HANNANT, DEAN HARRIS, NICOLA LIPMAN, PATRICIA LUDWICK, CECILE O'CONNOR, LIONEL SIMMONS, SUZANNE TURNBULL
The Birds / NICOLA LIPMAN, PATRICIA LUDWICK, CECILE O'CONNOR, ELIZABETH SHEPHERD, SUZANNE TURNBULL
Kari / IRENE BALSER
The Ugly Boy / ALEX BRUCE
Herr von Eberkopf / MACON McCALMAN
Mr. Cotton / COLIN FOX
Mr. Ballon / DAVID RENTON
Servant / DAVID FERRY
Chief Eunuch / DON ALLISON
Slaves / GERALD BOWEN, DAVID FERRY
Thief / LIONEL SIMMONS
Receiver / DEAN HARRIS
Anitra / PATRICIA LUDWICK
Dancing Girls / GILLIAN HANNANT, NICOLA LIPMAN, CECILE O'CONNOR
Begriffenfeldt / PETER ELLIOTT
Keepers / DON ALLISON, R.D. REID
Fellah / LIONEL SIMMONS
Hussein / DAVID RENTON
Lunatics / IRENE BALSER, GERALD BOWEN, DAVID FERRY, GILLIAN HANNANT, NICOLA LIPMAN, PATRICIA LUDWICK, CECILE O'CONNOR, FLORENCE PATERSON, ELIZABETH SHEPHERD, ELIZABETH THOMSON, SUZANNE TURNBULL
A Ship's Captain / MACON McCALMAN
The Watch / DAVID FERRY
1st Mate / DON ALLISON
Bosun / R.D. REID
Cabin Boy / ALEX BRUCE
Cook / DEAN HARRIS
Strange Passenger / JERRY FRANKEN
Mourners / DON ALLISON, IRENE BALSER, GERALD BOWEN, ALEX BRUCE, DAVID FERRY, GILLIAN HANNANT, PATRICIA LUDWICK, CECILE O'CONNOR, R.D. REID, ELIZABETH SHEPHERD, LIONEL SIMMONS, SUZANNE TURNBULL
Representative of the Law / DAVID RENTON
Memories & Regrets / ALEX BRUCE, COLIN FOX, NICOLA LIPMAN, PATRICIA LUDWICK, CECILE O'CONNOR, ELIZABETH SHEPHERD
Button Moulder / PETER ELLIOTT
Thin Man / COLIN FOX
Churchgoers / THE COMPANY

AN ITALIAN STRAW HAT

by Eugene Labiche & Marc-Michel
text translated by Lynn and
Theodore Hoffman
lyrics by Michael Bawtree
music by Pierre Philippe
directed by Robert Sherrin
sets designed by Les Lawrence
costumes designed by Janet Logan
lighting by Robert C. Reinholdt
music director Barbara Spence

Felix / JERRY FRANKEN
Virginie / NICOLA LIPMAN
Uncle Vezinet / PETER ELLIOTT
Fadinard / COLIN FOX
Anais / IRENE BALSER
Emile Tavernier / DON ALLISON
Nonancourt / MACON McCALMAN
Helene / MARTI MARADEN
Bobin / R.D. REID
Clara / PATRICIA LUDWICK
Tardiveau / LIONEL SIMMONS
Wedding guests / ALEX BRUCE,
FLORENCE PATERSON
Achille de Rosalba / DEAN HARRIS
Baroness de Champigny / ELIZABETH
SHEPHERD
Servant / DAVID FERRY
Guests of the Baroness / GERALD BOWEN,
CECILE O'CONNOR, SUZANNE TURNBULL
Chambermaid / GILLIAN HANNANT
Beauperthuis / DAVID RENTON
Corporal / HEATH LAMBERTS
Soldiers / GERALD BOWEN, DAVID FERRY
Townspeople / GILLIAN HANNANT,
CECILE O'CONNOR, SUZANNE TURNBULL
Musicians / ADAM MUELLER, cello;
BARBARA SPENCE, piano; CHRISTOPHER
WILCOX, clarinet

▶

*Roger Rees (foreground) was little known when he played Marchbanks in Andrew Downie's production of **Candida** in 1973, but he has since become an international star of the English Royal Shakespeare Company. Comforting him is Joan Gregson in the title role, while her husband Reverend Morell (David Renton) looks on with concern.*

▼

Cutter and wardrobe supervisor Barbara Howatt discusses the cutting of a dress with seamstress Lynne Sorge.

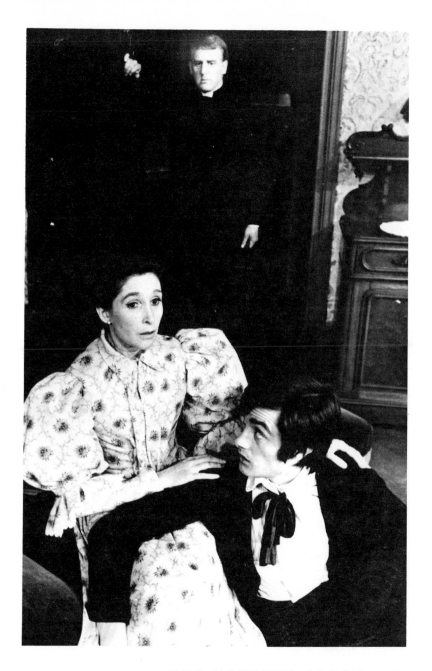

CANDIDA

by George Bernard Shaw
directed by Andrew Downie
designed by Maurice Strike
lighting by Richard Quigley

Prossy / FAITH WARD
Morell / DAVID RENTON
Lexy / ROBERT D. REID
Burgess / PATRICK BOXILL
Candida / JOAN GREGSON
Marchbanks / ROGER REES

SECOND STAGE

REVELATIONS

an adaptation of Ingmar
Bergman's "The Seventh Seal"
directed by Michael Mawson
music composed and directed
by Steven Freygood

Antonius Block / RICHARD DONAT
Jons / JERRY FRANKEN
Death / PETER ELLIOTT
Jof / GUY BANNERMAN
Mia / SUSAN HOGAN
Skat / TOM CAREW
A church painter / TOM CAREW
Steward / GUY BANNERMAN
Raval / PETER ELLIOTT
A girl / SUZANNE TURNBULL
Lisa / NICOLA LIPMAN
A monk / MICHAEL HOGAN
Tyan / PATRICIA LUDWICK
Plog / MICHAEL HOGAN
Karin / PATRICIA LUDWICK

THE COLLECTED WORKS OF BILLY THE KID

by Michael Ondaatje
directed by Michael Mawson
music by David Hellyer
performed by Jerry Franken
and Nicola Lipman

▶

Carpenters and stage hands putting the set together for **Joe Egg**.

▼

Bill and Jack Blackmore have worked as carpenters at Neptune for more than 25 years. Here they are assembling the walls for **Joe Egg** set.

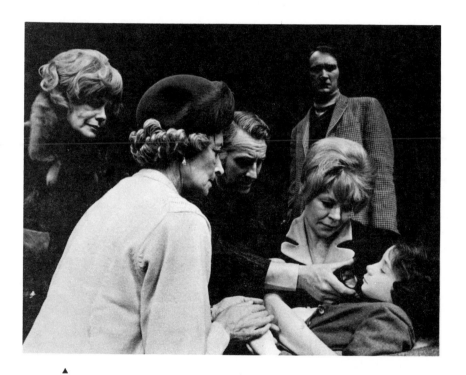

▲

Peter Nichols' moving tragi-comedy **A Day in the Death of Joe Egg** *examines the effect on parents of a child suffering from severe cerebral palsy: Irene Balser, Dora Dainton, David Renton, (mother) Ann Butler, (father at back) Colin Fox and (child) Elizabeth Thomson*

THE FOURSOME

by E.A. Whitehead
directed by Michael Mawson

Harry / NICK MANCUSO
Tim / RICHARD DONAT
Marie / SUZANNE TURNBULL
Bella / SUSAN LITTLE

PILK'S MADHOUSE

by Henry Pilk and Ken Campbell
directed by Michael Mawson
music by Steven Freygood

Cast:
PATRICIA LUDWICK, BLAIR BROWN,
PETER ELLIOTT, RICHARD DONAT,
LIONEL SIMMONS

THE SATYRICON

adapted from Petronius
montage by Michael Mawson
and Mark Young
design by Nina Huoslef and
Keith Turnbull
sound by Steven Freygood
slides by Sally Thompson

Asolto / DAVID MARRIAGE
Eumolpus / JOSEPH RUTTEN
Encolpio / IAN DEAKIN
Vernacchio / GEOFF LeBOUTILLIER
Giton / HANK WHITE
Quartilla / MARGOT SWEENY
Empress / JOAN ORENSTEIN
Trimalchio / GERRY O'BRIEN
Fortunata / SUSAN LITTLE
Captain / GEOFF LeBOUTILLIER
Lichas / WALTER BORDEN
Tryphaena / JOAN ORENSTEIN
Caesar / PETER BRADBURY
Proconsul / ROBERT HUGHES
Adrianne / PAT PHILLIPS
Dwarf / CLARENCE EVANS
Chrysis / AMY KLEIMAN
Oenetea / JOCELYN ST. DENIS
Felonius / GENESIUS

THE CABBAGETOWN PLAYERS

by David Tipe
directed by Robert D. Reid
stage manager Patricia Ney
set design by Geoff LeBoutillier
lighting design by Iain Joannes
costumes by Cathryn Miller

Diamond Cutters
Ben / DAVID RENTON
Jed / ROBERT D. REID
Girl / SUSAN LITTLE

The Travesty and the Fruit Fly
Hal / ROBERT D. REID
Princeton / DAVID RENTON

THE THREEPENNY OPERA

by Bertolt Brecht
original music by Kurt Weill
directed by Michael Mawson
music directed and arranged by
Steven Freygood
backdrops designed and painted
by Brian Porter

Ballad singer / JERRY FRANKEN
J.J. Peachum / RICHARD DONAT
Filch / LIONEL SIMMONS
Mrs. Peachum / FLORENCE PATERSON
Money Matthew / JERRY FRANKEN
MacHeath / TOM CAREW
Polly Peachum / BLAIR BROWN
Hook-finger Jacob / DON ALLISON,
IAN DEAKIN
Robert the Saw / CHARLIE P. ROBINSON
Ed / IAN DEAKIN
Wally the Weeper / KIRK INMAN
Jimmy the Second / E.J. REILLY
Reverend Kimball / LIONEL SIMMONS
Ginny Jenny / PATRICIA LUDWICK
Tiger Brown / PETER ELLIOT, DON ALLISON
Vixen Whore / MAGGIE THOMAS
Dolly / SUZANNE TURNBULL
Betty / CECILE O'CONNOR
Constable Smith / LIONEL SIMMONS
Lucy Brown / NICOLA LIPMAN
Musicians / MONIQUE GUSSET,
BLAINE JOLLIMORE, BAZIL RUSSELL

Colour of Dust opened the N.A.C. series the following year. R.D. Reid played a condemned man who had to be hanged nightly in this production, but on the Newfoundland tour at Grand Falls one night Reid remembers how "I blacked out very briefly and regained consciousness enough to realize that my eyes were open and the audience and I were looking at each other as I gently twirled about . . . The heaving bosom of my mourning girl never looked better as I was lowered on to it; but I knew I wasn't out of the woods just yet. The show must go on and rather than sit up and gasp in a few lungfuls of wind, I figured I could hang in (sorry) long enough to have them carry me off stage. A mistake. I woke up to the prodding foot of another actor and the collective urgings to *stop faking it!* . . . The conscientious stage manager, Chris Banks, had already stopped the show and asked the famous question, *Is there a doctor in the house?* I made the headlines in St. John's and Halifax. The next night and every night thereafter to the end of the run, I received a huge ovation on the completion of the *hanging.* None of my good friends on the show would talk to me after that." David Renton confesses, though, that "we were all shaken solid" by this incident.

Robert Sherrin still looks upon his time in Halifax with great pleasure as one of the most extraordinary and interesting periods of his life. These years were an exciting time for the theatre in Halifax. With two stages at Neptune and Pier One Theatre, founded by John Dunsworth and R.D. Reid, trying out many avant-garde works, there was a range and richness of theatre arts that has scarcely been matched since. Much work was also being done to encourage the interest of school children in the theatre. The Tritons, or Children of Neptune, was a group of young people who wanted to know more about its work. Several company members volunteered their time to discuss various aspects of theatre with them. David Renton, Jack Medley and Phyllis Malcolm Stewart worked with the young enthusiasts, sometimes to prepare them for National Theatre School auditions. The Tritons was an informal forerunner of Neptune Theatre School, to be founded by Tom Kerr in 1983.

In addition, at the request of Bob Sherrin, David Renton

▲

*The now famous hanging scene in the première production of Michael Cook's **Colour the Flesh the Colour of Dust**, which caused a sensation on tour in Newfoundland. Donald Meyers is releasing condemned man R.D. Reid from the rope, while bystanders show concern.*

FOREVER YOURS, MARIE-LOU

by Michel Tremblay
directed by Clarke Rogers
designed by Nancy Pankiw
lighting by Gary Clarke

Marie-Louise / JOAN ORENSTEIN
Leopold / JOSEPH RUTTEN
Carmen / PATRICIA LUDWICK
Manon / NICOLA LIPMAN

THE MARAT / SADE

by Peter Weiss
english version by Geoffrey Skelton
verse adapation by Adrian Mitchell
composed by R.C. Peaslee
directed by Michael Mawson
set by Trevor Parsons
lights by Gary Clarke
music directed by Steve Freygood

M. Coulmier / BRUCE ARMSTRONG
Mlle. Coulmier / FLORENCE GEORGE
Herald / JOSEPH RUTTEN
Cururucu Kokol / GERALD BOWEN
Rossignol / NICOLA LIPMAN
Jacques Roux / TERRY JUDD
Charlotte Corday / SUZANNE TURNBULL
Jean-Paul Marat / PETER ELLIOTT
Marquis de Sade / TOM CAREW
Simonne Evrard / JEAN BERGMANN
Duperret / PETER MUSHKAT
Mother Marie / JOAN ORENSTEIN
Avignon / LESLEY PRESTON
Charenton / JOHN DARTT
Reims / MORRIS WALKER
Calais / ANNE POLLETT
L'Isle / MARTHANNE WILLIAMSON
Nice / PAUL DAVIS
Musicians / STEVEN FREYGOOD, piano, organ;
CRAIG REINER, percussion; SALLY WRIGHT,
flute; CHRIS de ROSENROLL, trumpet

YOU'RE A GOOD MAN, CHARLIE BROWN

based on the comic strip "Peanuts"
by Charles M. Schultz
books, music and lyrics by Clark Gesner
directed by Grant Cowan
lighting by Bill Williams
music directed by Barbara Spence

Linus / DENI ALLAIRE
Snoopy / GRANT COWAN
Schroeder / MICHAEL JAMES
Patty / MARYLU MOYER
Lucy / DOROTHY POSTE
Charlie Brown / RICHARD WHELAN

ANDROCLES AND THE LION

by Aurand Harris (from Aesop)
directed by Tony Van Bridge
designed by Pat Flood

Androcles / GRANT COWAN
Lion / DONALD MEYERS
Isabella / MARTI MARADEN
Lelio / COLIN BERNHARDT
Pantalone / DAVID RENTON
Captain / DONALD Le GROS
Musician / JOHN BIRD

OF THE FIELDS, LATELY

by David French
directed by Bill Glassco
designed by Tiina Lipp
lighting by Bill Williams

Ben Mercer / TIM HENRY
Jacob Mercer / SEAN SULLIVAN
Mary Mercer / FLORENCE PATERSON
Wiff Roach / SANDY WEBSTER

▲
Playwright David French chose Florence Paterson to play Mary Mercer in Bill Glassco's production of **Of The Fields, Lately***. Also starring are the late Sean Sullivan as Jacob, Tim Henry as their son Ben, and Sandy Webster as friend Wiff Roach.*

organized a Student Theatre Company as a joint project of Neptune Theatre and the City of Halifax School Board. Thirty high-school (in the second year also some junior-high) students were given ten weeks' work, with rehearsals at King's College, a tour of high schools and a gala performance at Neptune, presenting revues which combined new works and established pieces: *Project 30* in 1973 and *Mind the Flower Pots* in 1974. There was still an attitude in some high schools that while it was acceptable for students to take time off for sports, to do so for drama and the arts was frivolous! The idea of a young company was abandoned during John Wood's tenure at Neptune. Wood preferred to send out young professionals to the schools, but the School Board withdrew its funding. A Young Neptune company was to be started by John Neville in 1979.

It was, of course, not all plain sailing. The building was still giving a number of problems. Peter Evans,who was president in the early seventies, had been involved with the building of Dalhousie Arts Centre. He could not help comparing the sophisticated equipment that was being installed for the use of Dalhousie Theatre Department with the poverty-stricken, outdated equipment at Neptune Theatre. All the sets at Neptune were still being flown from the ancient wooden structure that was there when the theatre was built. Some of the timbers in the fly-gallery had been pulled out from the wall and were dangerously pegged together. "How it didn't come down I'll never know," he says. New flies had to be built; a new lighting system to replace the first antiquated one and air-conditioning had to be installed.

Peter also found that he was not welcome when he dropped into a Neptune rehearsal then being held in the Dunn Theatre. The attitude was, "What the hell's he doing here? Your place is on the board and to raise money." Over the years much of that rift between artistic and management roles has been repaired. The board needs the business approach, he says, yet its members sometimes dismiss the artistic side. Peter's wife, Joan Gregson, agrees: "Yes, we need business people on the board, yes, we've got to sell the theatre like soap, but you've got to have a flair, a Barnum and Bailey approach to you, a love of doing spectacular things, taking risks. There is sometimes a need of expansiveness,

LOVE'S LABOUR'S LOST

by William Shakespeare
directed by Robert Sherrin
designed by Les Lawrence
lighting by Neil McLeod
music composed by Milan Kymlicka

Berowne / STUART WILSON
Longaville / COLIN BERNHARDT
Dumaine / RICHARD PARTINGTON
Ferdinand / ROBERT HALEY
Servant / RON MacINTYRE
Servant / ROBERT RODGER
Dull / MICHAEL LISCINSKY
Costard / DOUGLAS CHAMBERLAIN
Moth / ALEX BRUCE
Don Adriano de Amado / JOSEPH SHAW
Jaquenetta / NICOLA LIPMAN
Rosaline / CORIE SIMS
Maria / MARTI MARADEN
Katharine / JILL FRAPPIER
Princess of France / JOAN GREGSON
Boyet / DAVID RENTON
Marcade / JAY BOWEN
A Forester / JOHN DUNSWORTH
Sir Nathaniel / CHARLES HUDSON
Holofernes / BARRIE BALDARO

AFTER MAGRITTE

by Tom Stoppard
directed by Michael Mawson
set and costumes by Maurice Strike
lighting designed by Robert C. Reinholdt

Harris / JOHN HORTON
Thelma / JOAN GREGSON
Mother / FAITH WARD
Holmes / RICHARD PARTINGTON
Foot / DAVID RENTON

THE REAL INSPECTOR HOUND

by Tom Stoppard
directed by Michael Mawson
set and costumes by Maurice Strike
lighting by Robert C. Reinholdt

Moon / JOHN HORTON
Birdboot / BARRIE BALDARO
Mrs. Drudge / FAITH WARD
Simon / RICHARD PARTINGTON
Felicity / JILL FRAPPIER
Cynthia / JOAN GREGSON
Magnus / DAVID RENTON
Inspector Hound / PETER ELLIOTT

THE DEVIL'S DISCIPLE

by George Bernard Shaw
directed by Brian Murray
sets and costumes by Robert Doyle
lighting by Lynne Hyde

A Shaw Festival production
Mrs. Timothy Dudgeon / ELEANOR BEECROFT
Essie / KAREN AUSTIN
Christopher Dudgeon / HEATH LAMBERTS
Anthony Anderson / NORMAN WELSH
Judith / DOMINI BLYTHE
Lawyer Hawkins / PATRICK BOXILL
Mrs. William Dudgeon / JEANETTE ROMERIL
William Dudgeon / VINCENT COLE
Mrs. Titus Dudgeon / JOAN ORENSTEIN
Titus Dudgeon / KENNETH WICKES
Richard Dudgeon / ALAN SCARFE
A Sergeant / STUART KENT
Major Swindon / JAMES VALENTINE
General Burgoyne / TONY VAN BRIDGE
Rev. Mr. Brudenell / DREW RUSSELL
Soldiers, Officers, etc. / GILLIAN HANNANT,
BRIAN BISHOP, BILL CHANCELLOR, PETER
CROWE, ARTHUR GASS, JOHN MANOR-
HOUSE, BARRY MINSHULL, GREGORY
MORLEY, PETER MUSHKAT, OREST ULAN,
DAVID WINTERS

to say *Let's do it because it needs doing.*" This was to become the approach of the next artistic director, John Wood.

Sherrin comments on the extraordinary explosion of theatre at this time, with Neptune alone doing 15-17 productions a year. But the trouble with being an artistic director, he notes, is that there are only so many years when you can live under that kind of pressure. By the time he left in 1974 to join the CBC in Toronto it would have been overwhelming and it was time for somebody else to take over. But he left Neptune Theatre in a healthy condition for John Wood to take the helm.

▲

*"Marching on Parade": another chorus directed by Keith Turnbull.
This lively musical adaptation of* **The Good Soldier Schweik** *was set
in World War Two, Canada.*

THE GOOD SOLDIER SCHWEIK

*a free adaptation from the
novel by Jaroslav Hasek
directed by Keith Turnbull
original music and lyrics
composed by Phillip Schreibman
designed by Peter Wingate
lighting by Robert C. Reinholdt
assistant to the director Jackie Moriarty
music directed by Phillip Schreibman*

The Company:

NANCY BEATTY, JOHN BIRD,
JAY BOWEN, TOM CAREW,
DAVID FERRY, JERRY FRANKEN,
MICHAEL HOGAN, JAMES HURDLE
NICOLA LIPMAN, PATRICIA LUDWICK
DON MacQUARRIE, MICHAEL MAWSON
MINA ERIAN MINA, CECILE O'CONNOR
JOAN ORENSTEIN, DAVID RENTON
JOHN ROBY, JOCELYNE ST. DENIS
PHILLIP SCHREIBMAN, DEE VICTOR
SUZANNE TURNBULL

HARVEY

*by Mary Coyle Chase
directed by Michael Mawson
designed by Peter Wingate
lighting by Robert C. Reinholdt*

Myrtle Mae Simmons / NANCY BEATTY
Veta Louise Simmons / DEE VICTOR
Elwood P. Dowd / JAMES HURDLE
Miss Johnson / SUZANNE TURNBULL
Mrs. Ethel Chauvenet / JOAN ORENSTEIN
Ruth Kelly / NICOLA LIPMAN
Duane Wilson / MICHAEL HOGAN
Lyman Sanderson / DON MacQUARRIE
William R. Chumley / DAVID RENTON
Betty Chumley / FAITH WARD
Judge Omar Gaffney / WILLIAM FULTON
E.J. Lofgren / MINA ERIAN MINA

LA TURISTA

by Sam Shepard
directed by Lionel Simmons
set design by Brian Porter
lighting by Gary Clarke
stage manager Pat MacKenzie

Kent / RICHARD PARTINGTON
Salem / NICOLA LIPMAN
Witchdoctor / JOSEPH RUTTEN
Doc / JOSEPH RUTTEN
Boy / JAY BOWEN
Witchdoctor's Son / FRED PELLETIER

. . . AND ALL THE QUEEN'S MEN

a 'presentation' of the writings
and other art of men in Dorchester
Federal Maximum-Security Penitentiary
directed & edited by
Stephan Regina-Thon
lighting by Gary Clarke
rear-projections by Ernest Novaczek
written by Frank Guiney, Richard
Brannon, Robert E. Eby, Stafford Lake,
John MacDonald, Paul H. Thompson
Cast:
BRYAN MacPHEE, RON McINTYRE,
JOEL SAPP, JOAN ORENSTEIN,
DAVID RENTON
Musicians / LES ALLT, flute;
CHRIS deROSENROLE, trumpet;
STEVEN FREYGOOD, piano

▲
Another of many experimental Second Stage productions at Neptune:
The Marat/Sade *by Peter Weiss was directed by Michael Mawson in its tenth anniversary year.*

◄

Starring in Oscar Wilde's evergreen comedy of manners **The Importance of Being Earnest** *are Colin Fox, Fern Sloan, Madeleine Christie, Jack Medley and Denise Fergusson.*

►

The second Neptune production of the musical **The Fantasticks** *features Jeff Hyslop, Jack Northmore, Beth Ann Cole, Bob Ainslie, Bill Cole and Douglas Chamberlain.*

◄

In **The Matchmaker**, the Thornton Wilder comedy that later became the musical Hello Dolly!, are Brian McKay, Dean Regan, John Cripton, David Renton and Phyllis Malcolm Stewart.

►

The Neptune company which toured with Goldoni's **The Servant of Two Masters** played at the National Arts Centre, Ottawa. Douglas Chamberlain as Truffaldino is kneeling, while Tony Van Bridge as Dr. Lombardi stands behind him and the company looks on.

▼

Neptune Theatre when Arthur Miller's **The Price** was playing in 1972. The building was still giving problems.

four

JOHN WOOD

artistic director
1974 - 1977

November 1974-August 1975

GODSPELL

a musical based upon the
Gospel according to St. Matthew
conceived by John-Michael Tebelak
music and new lyrics by Stephen Schwartz
directed by John Wood
musical director Alan Laing
music conducted by Bob Quinn
lighting by Robert C. Reinholdt
set co-ordinator David Dague

Cast:
IRIS LYN ANGUS, MARC CONNORS (Jesus),
PAUL DAVIS, PAUL SHAW, JOANIE SIME,
P.M. HOWARD (John the Baptist/Judas),
MUGGSY SWEENY, SHARON LYSE TIMMINS,
JONATHAN WELSH, MURLETA WILLIAMS

"I WAS IN DAWSON CITY in the Yukon when I heard that I had become the artistic director of Neptune Theatre in Halifax at the other end of the country," recalls John Wood. "I determined then that the company I wanted to establish would eventually play in Dawson City. It did, but not while I was at Neptune. It happened five years later when we were at the National Arts Centre."

Wood comments on the difficult time people have accepting the idea of a theatre company: "an idea that is shared instinctively by a lot of people in different disciplines." Although Robert Sherrin had attempted to form such a group for Second Stage, it had not been possible to do so for the main stage. Wood was trying to re-establish at least some of the idea that Leon Major had promulgated at the beginning, by collecting a group of people who could work together artistically. He appointed three associate directors — Hamilton McClymont, Alan Laing, and David Renton — to act as a resource body and assist him in determining his artistic policy, with Laing as musical director. "Forming a company was what we set out to do, without knowing exactly how to do it."

One of Wood's first moves was to arrange for structural alterations, which reduced the thrust stage area to allow for an orchestra in the pit. The theatre was painted inside and out and expanded into an old wooden building on the corner of Sackville and Argyle Streets. Though the change was a distinct advantage for musicals, the intimacy of the apron stage and four seats were lost in the process. He had a new sound system designed and

▲

This musical updating of St. Matthew's Gospel, **Godspell**, featured Marc Connors (l.) as Jesus, with the entire company.

◄

"A document in madness" : Laertes (Brian McKay, c.), confronts his demented sister Ophelia (Marti Maraden), while Claudius (Michael Ball), Gertrude (Denise Fergusson) and Horatio (David Hemblen) look on in John Wood's production of **Hamlet**. Frank Maraden is also in attendance.

HAMLET

by William Shakespeare
directed by John Wood
music composed & conducted
by Alan Laing
designed by John Ferguson
lighting designed by Robert C. Reinholdt

Barnardo / RON MacINTYRE
Marcellus / GORDON CLAPP
Horatio / DAVID HEMBLEN
Hamlet / NEIL MUNRO
Claudius / MICHAEL BALL
Gertrude / DENISE FERGUSSON
Polonius / JOSEPH RUTTEN
Cornelius / LARRY LAMB
Laertes / BRIAN McKAY
Ophelia / MARTI MARADEN
Priest / GRAHAM WHITEHEAD
Osric / FRANK MARADEN
Reynaldo / GRAHAM WHITEHEAD
Rosencratz / JONATHAN WELSH
Guildenstern / TOM WOOD
Player King / DAVID RENTON
Player Queen / PAUL DAVIS
3rd Player / GRAHAM WHITEHEAD
4th Player / CHRISTOPHER PHILPOTTS
Fortinbras / GORDON CLAPP
Norwegian Captain / LARRY LAMB
Messenger / RON MacINTYRE
Sailor / CHRISTOPHER PHILPOTTS
Gravedigger / DAVID RENTON
Second Gravedigger / PAUL DAVIS
Stewards / RON MacINTYRE,
CHRISTOPHER PHILPOTTS

DUTCH UNCLE

by Simon Gray
directed by John Wood
designed by Jack Simon
lighting designed by Robert C. Reinholdt

Mr. Godboy / JACK MEDLEY
May Godboy / FLORENCE PATERSON
Eric Hoyden / BRIAN McKAY
Doris Hoyden / ZOË ALEXANDER
Inspector Hawkins / DAVID HEMBLEN
Hedderley / GORDON CLAPP

installed for *Hamlet.* He also obtained approval and financial backing for a separate sound room, though this was not installed until John Neville took over in 1978. "There was a wonderful feeling of adventure that year," he recalls."It was all new to us. None of us had ever launched something this important before ... We all wanted to *create* and *develop* together and share it: that's the feeling I remember — that and the stark terror."

Shortly before John Wood came to Neptune an attempt had been made to forge a link between the theatre and a penitentiary. In one of the final Second Stage plays in 1974, ... *And All the Queen's Men,* David Renton, Joan Orenstein and others, under the direction of Stephan Regina-Thon, had presented poetry and other art by men in Dorchester and other penitentiaries. Wood considers that one of the most important things that happened at this time was a growing relationship between Neptune and Springhill Penitentiary. A group of prisoners with guards and girlfriends often came to the Saturday matinees. Most of them were members of a drama group at the prison and a few were interested in trying to get into acting professionally. John gave one boy after he was released a small part in *Hamlet.* During the second year P.M. Howard gave a concert in Springhill. When he began to sing "Desperado" the entire audience stood, picked up their chairs, and raising them over their heads waved them to the song: they knew what it was about. Though Wood wasn't at the concert, it is his strongest memory of Neptune days: "I am moved every time somebody who was there tells me the story."

Wood remembers how in the fall of 1974 he was still one actor short for the opening production, *Godspell,* just before rehearsals started. He was talking to assistant stage manager Paul Shaw about the future of Neptune, and over a drink in *The Arrows* John asked Paul if he could sing: "He said *Yes,* so I asked him to be in *Godspell.* He said *Yes* — and the next morning I announced to the staff that we needed another A.S.M. because Paul was going into the show. From that point on nobody seemed surprised at surprises or changes. Paul Shaw is now the production stage manager for *Cats!*" The tour of *Godspell* got off to a good start, playing mostly in churches around the province: the "eclectic" group, including Marc Connors, now of The

Nylons fame, P.M. Howard, and Sharon Timmins, had "an exuberant time."

When John Wood first revealed the new season to the board, one member was very nervous about *Hamlet*. Wood thought the board would have "jumped up and down with great joy" at the proposal, but they didn't, and he feared one negative reaction might infect everyone. The season was approved, however. John still enthuses over Neil Munro's "extraordinary" Hamlet. Shortly after his Dawson City visit he asked Munro what he wanted to do and he said *"Hamlet — but I won't wear tights!"* At that moment Wood suddenly realized he had never done a play by Shakespeare — and he was starting with *Hamlet!* The company reheared in an unheated Keith's Brewery, with thick stone walls like Elsinore. "But it was an amazing experience," he says. "I've never been in quite that situation again where the creative energy from everyone was rampant . . . That's when I really knew what a company was and that there was one in Halifax."

This is how John recalls opening night: "No heat in the theatre. Everyone wrapped in furs for three and half hours. Hamlet in the shower. Hamlet picking his toes for *What a piece of work is a man.* Ophelia (Marti Maraden) soaking wet, water dripping from her black slip and hair, while she threatened the court with oversize scissors and the women in the house huddled in their fur coats. And Denise Fergusson as Gertrude sitting listening to Benny Goodman-style jazz (by Alan Laing) on a 1938 radio and regally walking off with an alcoholic determination to drink herself to death. My favourite image is Neil sitting in a large wicker chair, recently vacated by Gertrude, sipping tea from her cup and looking at tea leaves while he talked of bare bodkins and the future." In 1979 this same production was remounted in Ottawa and toured the country.

One of Wood's most significant contributions to Neptune was the staging of musicals: as he says, "Musicals are the happiest shows to do and I loved working with good actors who could also sing." Although *Jacques Brel* did not succeed with audiences it was one of his favourites: it had some "wonderful orchestrations" by Alan Laing and was affectingly performed by Brian McKay, P.M. Howard, Rita Howell, and — for the first time since those

YOU CAN'T TAKE IT WITH YOU

by Kaufman & Hart
directed by Donald Davis
costumes designed by Judy Peyton Ward
set designed by John Ferguson
lighting designed by Robert C. Reinholdt

Penelope Sycamore / RITA HOWELL
Essie / DENISE FERGUSSON
Rheba / MURLETA WILLIAMS
Paul Sycamore / DAVID RENTON
Mr. De Pinna / JOSEPH RUTTEN
Ed / TOM WOOD
Donald / ROBERT O'REE
Martin Vanderhof / JACK CRELEY
Alice / ROSEMARY DUNSMORE
Henderson / GORDON CLAPP
Tony Kirby / JONATHAN WELSH
Boris Kolenkhov / DAVID HEMBLEN
Gay Wellington / FLORENCE PATERSON
Mr. Kirby / GEORGE MURRAY
Mrs. Kirby / JOAN GREGSON
Three Men / MATTHEW DAVIS,
LARRY LAMB, GORDON CLAPP
Olga / JOAN ORENSTEIN

JACQUEL BREL IS ALIVE AND WELL AND LIVING IN PARIS

music by Jacques Brel
directed by John Wood with Alan Laing
designed by John Ferguson
lighting designed by Robert C. Reinholdt
music directed and conducted
by Alan Laing
choreographer Lynn McKay

A sailor / RORY DODD
A sailor / P.M. HOWARD
An old woman / RITA HOWELL
A whore / NICOLA LIPMAN
A sailor / BRIAN McKAY
Madame la Patronne / MARY McMURRAY
A girl / SHARON LYSE TIMMINS
Musicians / ALAN LAING, JOHN BIRD,
JOHN ROBY, JOEL ZEMEL

THE ADVENTURES
OF PINOCCHIO

adapted from the story by Carlo Collodi
directed by John Wood
music composed and conducted
by Alan Laing
designed by John Ferguson
lighting designed by Robert C. Reinholdt

Cast:
IRIS LYN ANGUS, GORDON CLAPP, PAUL
DAVIS, BRIAN McKAY, JACK MEDLEY,
DAVID RENTON, JOEL SAPP, MUGGSY
SWEENY, JONATHAN WELSH,
and MICHAEL BURGESS (Pinocchio)

Musicians / ALAN LAING, JOE SEALY, piano;
JOHN BIRD, drums, percussion; TERRY
FORSTER, bass

MY FAT FRIEND

by Charles Laurence
directed by David Brown
designed by Fred Allen
lighting designed by Robert C. Reinholdt

Henry / JACK MEDLEY
Vicky / ZOË ALEXANDER
James / BRIAN McKAY
Tom / DAVID HEMBLEN

13th SEASON

November 1975-April 1976

BRECHT ON BRECHT

by George Tabori
directed by David Renton
designed by Susan LePage
lighting designed by R.A. Elliott
musical director Monique Gusset

Cast:
GORDON CLAPP, DENISE FERGUSSON,
MONIQUE GUSSET, DAVID HEMBLEN,
JOAN ORENSTEIN

early years of Neptune — Mary McMurray. Neither *The Adventures of Pinocchio* (presented in collaboration with Dalhousie Arts Centre) nor *Dutch Uncle* was successful in that season, but *You Can't Take It With You* boasted fine performances from Jack Creley, Rita Howell and Tom Wood.

The next season opened with another of John Wood's favorite productions, Michael Ondaatje's *The Collected Works of Billy the Kid.* A chamber version of this play had previously been seen on Second Stage, but now Wood mounted it as a large-scale, main-stage work. He had previously directed the production very successfully at Stratford, but the magic was lost when it was revived for Neptune. The play was not at all well received when it went on a government-supported tour to the U.S. as a gift for the Bicentennial celebrations. When it opened at the Brooklyn Academy of Music the press was scathing and at one point there were thirteen people in the audience, including John Wood and his nine-year-old nephew; the run closed early and then the production went to Philadelphia with scarcely more success. But the company did get T-shirts with one press headline written across them: "Some imported trash"! The tour went to the N.A.C. in Ottawa where it was again controversial but better received; John still maintains, "It is one of the finest theatre pieces I have ever worked on."

Highlights of that second season included a beautifully elegant production of Wood's favorite Shaw play, *Misalliance,* with a magnificent set by Susan Benson; Gordon Pinsent starring with Florence Paterson in the première of his stage adaptation of his own novel, *John and the Missus;* a rare revival of George Kelly's hilarious satire on amateur dramatics, *The Torchbearers,* which Tony Randall *might* have directed long before John Neville brought him to Neptune; and *The Glass Menagerie,* in which John Wood *might* himself have played Tom if he hadn't got cold feet and hired R.H. Thomson instead!

The 1977 season opened with *King Lear* starring Eric Donkin. Peter Blais, an actor with the company, designed primitive costumes made from squares of jute. "I didn't know what they would look like until the actors arrived wearing them at rehearsal," recalls Wood. "But the effect was extraordinary and

▲

*A controversial Canadian view of an American legend: Michael Ondaatje's **The Collected Works of Billy the Kid**. Ivar Brogger, John Sweeney, Suzanne Ristic, David Renton, P.M. Howard (back), Neil Munro, Patricia Collins, Carole Galloway (front).*

THE COLLECTED WORKS OF BILLY THE KID

by Michael Ondaatje
directed by John Wood
music by Alan Laing
designed by John Ferguson
original lighting by Gil Weschler
interpreted for this production
by R.A. Elliott

Billy the Kid / NEIL MUNRO
Charlie Bowdre / JOHN SWEENEY
Tom O'Folliard / P.M. HOWARD
Angela Dickinson / PATRICIA COLLINS
Manuela Bowdre / SUZANNE RISTIC
Sallie Chisum / CAROLE GALLOWAY
John Chisum / DAVID RENTON
Pat Garrett / IVAR BROGGER

MISALLIANCE

by George Bernard Shaw
directed by John Wood
designed by Susan Benson
lighting designed by Michael Whitfield

John Tarleton jr. / STEVEN SUTHERLAND
Bentley Summerhays / PETER HUTT
Hypatia Tarleton / PATRICIA COLLINS
Mrs. Tarleton / SHEILA HANEY
Lord Summerhays / JACK MEDLEY
John Tarleton / ERIC DONKIN
Joseph Percival / DAVID HEMBLEN
Lina Szczepanowska / DENISE FERGUSSON
Julius Baker / FRANK MARADEN

THE GLASS MENAGERIE

by Tennessee Williams
directed by John Wood
designed by Jack Simon
designs executed by Susan LePage
incidental music by Alan Laing
lighting designed by R.A. Elliott

Amanda Wingfield / RITA HOWELL
Tom Wingfield / R.H. THOMSON
Laura Wingfield / CAROLE GALLOWAY
The Gentleman Caller / NEIL MUNRO

JOHN & THE MISSUS

by Gordon Pinsent
directed by Donald Davis
designed by Susan Benson,
with Michael Whitfield
music composed & performed
by Kenzie MacNeil

Sid Peddigrew / DOUGLAS CHAMBERLAIN
Holly Picard & Mrs. Sheppard / GAIL CLAPP
Ted Pratt & Tom Noble jr. / GORDON CLAPP
Faith / BRENDA DEVINE
Mr. Burridge & Raymond Burgess /
DAVID HEMBLEN
Jimmy Ludlow / PETER HUTT
Tom Ivany & Frank / LARRY LAMB
Rev. Wood & Alf Sheppard / RAYMOND
LANDRY
Fred Budgell / FRANK MARADEN
Matt / FRANK MOORE
Mrs. Crummy & Mrs. Noble / JOAN ORENSTEIN
The Missus / FLORENCE PATERSON
John Munn / GORDON PINSENT
Tom Noble / DAVID RENTON
Nish / CHUCK ROBINSON
Fudge / DENNIS THATCHER
Mrs. Burridge & Mrs. Margaret Burgess /
FAITH WARD
Townspeople / DOUGLAS AUGUSTUS GRANT,
MAGGIE GRICE, BOB MARTYN, MEREDITH
PUGSLEY, AMY NEWMAN

THE TORCHBEARERS

by George Kelly
directed by John Wood
designed by Robert Doyle
lighting designed by Donald Acaster

Frederick Ritter / DOUGLAS CHAMBERLAIN
Huxley Hossefrosse / DAVID HEMBLEN
Mr. Spindler / JACKSON DAVIES
Ralph Twiller / DAVID RENTON
Teddy Spearing / PETER BLAIS
Stage Manager / GORDON CLAPP
Paula Ritter / PATRICIA COLLINS
J. Duro Pampinelli / JOAN ORENSTEIN
Nelly Fell / RITA HOWELL
Florence McCrickett / BRENDA DEVINE
Clara Sheppard / JOAN GREGSON
Jenny / NICOLA LIPMAN

▶

George Kelly's parody of amateur dramatics, **The Torchbearers,**
shows off the talents of Joan Orenstein, Patricia Collins, David Hemblen,
Brenda Devine, Peter Blais and Rita Howell.

▲

Jack Medley, Denise Fergusson, Eric Donkin, Steven Sutherland,
Patricia Collins and David Hemblen in Susan Benson's elegant setting
of Shaw's Misalliance, directed with polish by John Wood.

▼

The première production of Gordon Pinsent's **John and the Missus**
in which the author (r.c.) in the title role gets rough with David Hemblen.
Also present are Gail Clapp, Kenzie MacNeil and Gordon Clapp.

KING LEAR

by William Shakespeare
directed by John Wood
music and sound by Alan Laing
set and props by John Ferguson
costumes designed by Peter Blais
lighting designed by Michael J. Whitfield

The Earl of Kent / DAVID RENTON
The Earl of Gloucester / MAX HELPMANN
Edmund / RODGER BARTON
King Lear / ERIC DONKIN
Goneril / PATRICIA GAGE
The Duke of Albany / FRANK MARADEN
Regan / DENISE FERGUSSON
The Duke of Cornwall / STEPHEN RUSSELL
Cordelia / JANET DOHERTY
The King of France / ABRAHAM GUENTHER
The Duke of Burgundy / GRAHAM WHITEHEAD
Edgar / RICHARD BLACKBURN
Oswald / CRAIG GARDNER
Servant / CHARLES FLETCHER
Knights / LEE J. CAMPBELL,
WILLIAM MERTON MALMO
Fool / RICHARD GREENBLATT
Servant / DON GOODSPEED
Second servant / ABRAHAM GUENTHER
An old man / LEE J. CAMPBELL
Messenger / TERRY DeWOLF
Doctor / GRAHAM WHITEHEAD
Herald / FRANK MacKAY
Servants, Knights, Soldiers /
TERRY DeWOLF, CHARLES FLETCHER,
FRANK MacKAY, GRAHAM WHITEHEAD,
DON GOODSPEED

▲

*The primitive costumes designed by Peter Blais for John Wood's production of **King Lear**: Eric Donkin as Lear is surrounded by Patricia Gage as Goneril, Frank Maraden as Albany, Stephen Russell as Cornwall, and Denise Fergusson as Regan.*

104 THE NEPTUNE STORY

ancient." John Ferguson's set contained a huge 12-foot square, beaten-gold wall map showing the division of the kingdom, which fell and became the stage after Lear's fateful decision. Frank MacKay made his debut as a singer in this production with his rendition of Alan Laing's music.

One big gun followed another. Wood describes getting the rights for such a new work as *Equus* as a "nightmare", but he persisted, and finally Peter Shaffer allowed the production of his play before it was in general release — perhaps because the playwright is Nicola Lipman's cousin. Wood copied John Dexter's definitive production with its stylized horses. The role of Dysart gave David Renton one of his best opportunities, and the production introduced an outstanding young performer in Richard Greenblatt as Alan. Wood does not remember any complaints about language or nudity, and was even invited to talk to the Unitarian church about the play. He feels audiences were sophisticated enough to delight in having the opportunity to see this much-discussed international success.

A return after many years to a short repertory season, including a tour of N.S. and P.E.I., was not an unqualified success. Best was W.O. Mitchell's new play *Back to Beulah,* with strong performances by Joan Orenstein, Rita Howell and Denise Fergusson; later this production was taken to the National Arts Centre with some success. The other plays, two musicals devised by John Wood and Alan Laing and an adaptation by Wood of Molière's *Scapin,* were less well received. But Wood's last productions at Neptune were among his best. *Gypsy* starring Rita Howell was arguably the most effective large-scale musical presentation ever seen on Neptune stage. John had been helping to mount a new play by a black Nova Scotian writer, but as this was not ready he used a mainly black cast, including two local performers, and led by internationally celebrated folk singer Odetta, for Paul Zindel's *The Effect of Gamma Rays on Man-in-the-Moon Marigolds.* Wood says that even though the black writer did not complete his script there was some resistance by certain members of the board: "One gentleman thought we'd have race riots at Neptune and shouldn't tempt fate. I was ashamed by the attitude and felt that indeed the time had come to leave." It

WILLIAM SCHWENCH AND ARTHUR WHO?

a party of the century with Gilbert and Sullivan conceived and directed by Alan Laing and John Wood arrangements and additional music by Alan Laing script and additional lyrics by John Wood designed by Robert Doyle lighting designed by R.A. Elliott

Director, Gilbert / DAVID RENTON
Rehearsal pianist, Sullivan / RICHARD GREENBLATT
with:
DENISE FERGUSSON, CRAIG GARDNER, RITA HOWELL, ALAN LAING, JOAN ORESTEIN, SHARRON TIMMINS

BACK TO BEULAH

by W.O. Mitchell directed by John Wood designed by Susan Benson lighting by R.A. Elliott

Harriet Waverly / JOAN ORENSTEIN
Joe Parsons / LEE J. CAMPBELL
Dr. Anders / JANET DOHERTY
Elizabeth Moffat / RITA HOWELL
Agnes Findlay / DENISE FERGUSSON
Dr. Wilson / CRAIG GARDNER
Detective Sproule / FRANK MacKAY

MA'S TRAVELLING CIRCUS & VAUDEVILLE SHOW

devised by Alan Laing and John Wood directed by John Wood music by Alan Laing designed by Sue LePage lighting by R.A. Elliott

Cast:
LEE J. CAMPBELL, JANET DOHERTY, CHARLES FLETCHER, CRAIG GARDNER, FRANK MacKAY, JILL ORENSTEIN, SHARRON TIMMINS

EQUUS

by Peter Shaffer
directed by John Wood
designed by John Ferguson
design of horse heads by Linda Whitney
sound by Alan Laing
movement by William Merton Malmo
lighting by Michael J. Whitfield

Martin Dysart / DAVID RENTON
Alan Strang / RICHARD GREENBLATT
Frank Strang / MAX HELPMANN
Dora Strang / JOAN GREGSON
Hesther Salomon / DENISE FERGUSSON
Jill Mason / MELDOY RYANE
Harry Dalton / RODGER BARTON
A horseman/Nugget / STEPHEN RUSSELL
A nurse / NICOLA LIPMAN
Horses / CHARLES FLETCHER, DON
GOODSPEED, ABRAHAM GUENTHER,
FRANK MacKAY, GRAHAM WHITEHEAD

THE EFFECT OF GAMMA RAYS ON MAN-IN-THE-MOON MARIGOLDS

by Paul Zindel
directed by John Wood
designed by Sue LePage
lighting designed by Robert C. Reinholdt

Tillie / MELANIE HENDERSON
Beatrice / ODETTA
Ruth / LORETTA GREENE
Nanny / JUNE BUNDY
Janice / SHARRON TIMMINS

took another eleven years for such prejudice to be finally broken down with *Shine Boy.*

A price had to be paid, however, for so many colourful and expensively mounted productions. By 1976 Neptune was announcing a deficit of $87,000. Government grants had been frozen; the city was taking back in taxes what it gave in grants. Little control was being kept over mounting costs. David Renton maintains that Wood was given a free mandate by the board to stage exciting, creative productions, and that if risks were to be taken the money would be found somewhere. Wood claims that the mounting deficit was due to the board's reluctance or inability to meet their fundraising goals. *Hamlet* ran $6,000 over budget, and overruns became regular.

The initial remedy in 1976 was for the first time to cut out a summer season and to allow the theatre to go dark for eight months. But the problem was more deeply rooted. Shortly after John Wood appointed three associate directors he added a fourth, Christopher Banks, to look after communications while Hamilton McClymont was responsible for administration. One explanation of the artistic director's carte blanche is that out of a proliferation of associate directors (when Wood resigned there were as many as seven) no one had the single authority to demand a restraining hand. Wood maintains that the associate directors were consultants who held honorary positions in recognition of their contributions. Murray Farr replaced McClymont for the 1977 season, but no one could stem the tide at this stage. The upgrading of the general manager's role was to become a prime objective of John Neville in 1978.

John Wood left Neptune Theatre in 1977 and accepted an appointment as director of the English theatre at the National Arts Centre. He felt the backing of the board erode as soon as a production was unsuccessful, an inevitable risk in the creative business of theatre. "They won't listen to me," he said. "They hire an artistic director and treat him like an employee." He advocated a much smaller board of about fifteen members who really believed in theatre and trusted the artistic director.

Despite all the troubles, John Wood maintains that "it was a

Peter Shaffer's international success **Equus**: Rodger Barton as the stable owner explains the grooming of horses to Alan Strang (Richard Greenblatt) while Jill Mason (Melody Ryane) watches. Two horses, with heads designed by Linda Whitney, can be seen in the background.

The first Neptune production to feature an almost entirely black cast: in this scene from **The Effect of Gamma Rays . . .** are Odetta, better known as a folk singer, and Loretta Greene.

GYPSY

book by Arthur Laurents
music by Jule Styne
lyrics by Stephen Sondheim
directed by John Wood
choreographed and musical numbers
staged by Joan Morton Lucas
musical direction by Roger Perkins
musical arrangements by Barbara Spence
sets and costumes by Robert Doyle
lighting designed by Robert C. Reinholdt

Louise (Gypsy Rose Lee) / BARBARA
BARSKY
June / LESLEY BALLANTYNE
Uncle Jocko / FRANK MacKAY
Georgie / CHARLES FLETCHER
Timmy / STEPHEN DOOKS
Balloon Girl / HEATHER MacIVOR
Baby Louise / KATHRYN BREAN
Baby June / MANDY MORRISON
Rose / RITA HOWELL
Chowsie I / TAI FU
Pop / LEE J. CAMPBELL
Newsboys / STEPHEN DOOKS, JIM SMITH,
JEFF LEWIS
Weber / ROSS SKELTON
Herbie / JAY DEVLIN
Louise / BARBARA BARSKY
June / LESLEY BALLANTYNE
Tulsa / CRAIG GARDNER
Yonkers / CHARLES FLETCHER
L.A. / IAN TYLER
Angie / MICHAEL CROSSMAN
Chowsie II / MANDI
Kringelein / LEE J. CAMPBELL
Mr. Goldstone / ROSS SKELTON
Lamb / STEWART
Waitress / PENNY EVANS
Miss Cratchitt / NICOLA LIPMAN
Agnes / SHARRON TIMMINS
Hollywood Blondes / PENNY EVANS,
LENORE ZANN, LAUREN LEE
Pastey / LEE J. CAMPBELL
Cigar / FRANK MacKAY
Tessie Tura / SHEENA LARKIN
Mazeppa / CAROLE GORDON
Electra / NICOLA LIPMAN
Phil / CHARLES FLETCHER
Bourgeon-Couchon / ROSS SKELTON
Caroline (the cow) / FRANK MacKAY,
LEE J. CAMPBELL

very special three years in most of our lives. We were allowed but not always encouraged to take risks. It couldn't have lasted a day longer than it did, and looking back on it now I am amazed at what was achieved — at the gall and arrogance we had in our desire to accomplish something for the Halifax audience and to make it proud of us; at the major triumphs and absolutely disastrous, outrageous failures the people of Halifax endured . . . That wonderful building must never be demolished. Build a new theatre — Halifax needs it badly — but continue to use the Neptune: our ghosts are still there."

▲

*Rita Howell, Denise Fergusson, Janet Doherty, Frank MacKay and Joan Orenstein in W.O. Mitchell's **Back to Beulah**.*

◄

*One of the more spectacular dance numbers from the Laurents- Styne musical **Gypsy**, directed by John Wood, with musical direction by Roger Perkins and design by Robert Doyle. The leading dancer is Lesley Ballantyne as June Havoc.*

SCAPIN

by Molière
adapted and directed by John Wood
designed by Sue LePage
Lighting designed by R.A. Elliott
music composed and performed
by John Bird

Carlo / FRANK MacKAY
Scapin / RICHARD GREENBLATT
Sylvester / CRAIG GARDNER
Octavio / LEE J. CAMPBELL
Hyacintha / SHARRON TIMMINS
Argante / JOAN ORENSTEIN
Geronte / DAVID RENTON
Leander / CHARLES FLETCHER
Nerina / JILL ORENSTEIN
Zerbinetta / JANET DOHERTY

five

DAVID RENTON

acting artistic director
1977 - 1978

November 1977-August 1978

ARMS AND THE MAN

by George Bernard Shaw
directed by David Renton
sets and costumes by Robert Doyle
lighting by R.A. Elliott

Raina Petkoff / NICOLA LIPMAN
Catherine Petkoff / FLORENCE PATERSON
Louka / MELODY RYANE
Captain Bluntschli / DAN MacDONALD
Russian Officer / STEN HORNBORG
Bulgarian Soldier / RAYMOND DOUCETTE
Nicola / JOHN DUNSWORTH
Major Petkoff / JOSEPH RUTTEN
Major Sergius Saranoff / DOUGLAS
CHAMBERLAIN

SAME TIME, NEXT YEAR

by Bernard Slade
directed by David Renton
costumes by Art Penson
lighting by Trevor Parsons

Doris / JOAN GREGSON
George / DAVID BROWN

SINCE JOHN NEVILLE, John Wood's successor, could not take over until May 1978, the board named David Renton acting artistic director. Renton does not blame Wood for the big deficit. The board had taken the line that money must be found for excellence, and risks had to be taken, but they didn't keep track of how "wild and wonderful" he was. Even so, it was difficult to understand how a quarter of a million dollars was spent in this period without the board's knowledge. Renton maintains that although some overruns were inevitable, the board should have avoided their repetition.

David Renton's mandate in the year he took control was to turn the situation around and make a profit. He did what he said he would do and realized a profit of $6,000. He said, "You don't have to run a theatre into the ground financially. You *can* be responsible and I was." On the other hand, "it is naïve to think you can operate a theatre without getting into some difficulties with overruns." Denise Rooney recalls that she joined Neptune as an accountant at this time, while Lynn Dickson took over for a year as general manager. Lynne worked with David in very difficult circumstances. Denise calls it a Catch-22 situation: if there is no money to promote shows, how do you get people to come to the theatre? Some accounts had not been paid for six or eight months, she says, and you had to indulge in some "creative chatter" on the phone to appease the creditors.

On the other hand Renton, aided by public relations directors Laura Bennet and Corinne Hartley-Robinson, took a very positive approach to promoting the quality of Neptune's

◄

One of Joan Gregson's "most fun" productions, which also toured Nova Scotia: with David Brown in Bernard Slade's **Same Time, Next Year**.

▼

Neptune's second production of Shaw's **Arms And The Man** shows off Robert Doyle's set and costume design: Dan MacDonald, Douglas Chamberlain, Florence Paterson, Nicola Lipman and Joseph Rutten.

THE SNOW QUEEN

adapted from Hans Christian Andersen
by Ray Whitley & Mark DeWolf
directed by David Renton
costumes and sets by Robert Doyle
lighting by R.A. Elliott
music composed & directed by John Roby
lyrics by Ray Whitley & Mark DeWolf
dance co-ordinator Douglas Chamberlain

Imp Perfect, M. Spider / DENI ALLAIRE
Herr Krohn, Robber Chief / BRUCE
ARMSTRONG
Narrator, Pedersen, Mr. Cones,
Klaus / BARRIE BALDARO
Kai, Crow, a Robber / JOHN BURKE
Imp Possible, Robber Girl / NICOLA LIPMAN
Granny, Snow Queen, Robber /
FLORENCE PATERSON
Gerda / MELODY RYANE
Sir George Antler, Mr. Hemlock / GREG
WANLESS

THE GINGERBREAD LADY

by Neil Simon
directed by William Davis
costumes and sets by Art Penson
lighting by Trevor Parsons

Jimmy Perry / GEORGE MERNER
Manuel / DENI ALLAIRE
Toby Landau / TOBY TARNOW
Evy Meara / MARY McMURRAY
Polly Meara / MELODY RYANE
Lou Tanner / DON ALLISON

product in attracting new subscribers. The public was being urged to be "Neptune Boosters" by wearing special buttons, and to see "Seven Super Shows" for only $30, while students and seniors could subscribe for half the regular subscription rate. As a result subscriptions exceeded 4,400 compared with 3,281 in the previous year. At this time also the fixed-interest mortgage that a group of interested citizens had previously guaranteed was now officially transferred to the Neptune Theatre Foundation, which finally owned its own building.

David Renton planned a new season with sound judgment to stabilize the uneasy situation, and to attract larger audiences without lowering artistic standards. Shaw and Ibsen were balanced with Slade and Simon. The season opened with Renton's own production of Shaw's *Arms and the Man,* with a strong cast led by Doug Chamberlain as Sergius — a role Renton had himself played in Neptune's first season, Nicola Lipman as Raina, Dan MacDonald as the "chocolate soldier", and Flo Paterson and Joseph Rutten leading the supporting players. Local authors Ray Whitley and Mark DeWolf wrote a colourful Christmas entertainment, *The Snow Queen.* Three actresses from Neptune's first company returned for leading roles: Diana Leblanc as Nora in Ibsen's *A Doll's House,* with Chuck Shamata co-starring as Torvald; Mary McMurray in Neil Simon's *The Gingerbread Lady;* and Joan Gregson starring with David Brown in *Same Time, Next Year.*

Bernard Slade's two-hander, directed by Renton, was the play chosen for the 1978 tour. Joan remembers it as one of the "most fun" productions she has ever done. On tour at the brand new "7.5" building in Port Hawkesbury she accidentally dropped a match outside the fireplace while lighting a fire at one performance, igniting some oily rags that had been left on stage. She was puzzled to see David Brown looking in alarm past her shoulders rather than at her, until they changed places and she realized she had nearly set fire to the theatre. Tour manager Bruce Blakemore recalls that they also played at Neil's Harbour, Cape Breton, for the first time on that tour: "I'm not sure who was more scared: us or the audience. Most of them had never seen live

▲

*Ibsen's **A Doll's House** before it becomes tragically divided: Faith Ward as the Nurse watches Nora (Diana Leblanc), hugging her children, played by Alix MacLean, Carey Gaul and Morgan Field.*

A DOLL'S HOUSE

by Henrik Ibsen
translated by Michael Meyer
directed by Bernard Hopkins
costumes and sets by Art Penson
lighting by Trevor Parsons

Nora / DIANA LEBLANC
Torvald / CHUCK SHAMATA
Nils Krogstad / DANIEL BUCCOS
Mrs. Linde / PAM ROGERS
Dr. Rank / DAVID RENTON
Nurse, Anne-Marie / FAITH WARD
Maid, Helen / NANCY MARSHALL
The Helmers' children / MORGAN FIELD
CAREY GAUL, ALIX MacLEAN
Pianist / MONIQUE GUSSET

▲

This Whitley-DeWolf adaptation of **The Snow Queen** *delighted its young audiences at Christmas: Bruce Armstrong, Greg Wanless, Florence Paterson, Melody Ryane, John Burke and Barrie Baldaro.*

theatre before, most of us were frightened they wouldn't like it. Needless to say, everyone had a wonderful time and Neptune continued to tour there for several years."

David Renton also restored a summer season with two Noël Coward shows, the revue *Oh Coward!* directed by Jack Creley, and two playlets from *Tonight at 8:30,* which included Renton starring with Joan Gregson in *Still Life.* New theatre director John Neville directed this production. Neptune's morale and credibility had been restored and Neville was able to take over the theatre when it was already moving towards solvency.

It had been stated in the annual meeting of the board and was "carved in stone" as far as David was concerned that he would continue for at least a year as John's first lieutenant: he was given the board's guarantee written in a press release in lieu of a contract. He believed then that the arrangement of sharing with Neville worked out by the board would have enabled him to continue both his association with Neptune and his contribution to the theatre and to the community. But it was not to be. Neville maintained that there was not enough money for two of them, though Renton considers it was rather that John was always one to "go it alone". Whatever the reason, many people were sorry to see David step down and have little to do with Neptune in the following years, as his service, perhaps in this year more than any other, was of inestimable value to the continuing well-being of Neptune Theatre.

OH COWARD!

devised by Roderick Cook
directed by Jack Creley
musical director Stephen Woodjetts
percussion by John Bird
lighting by Detlev Fuellbeck

Cast:
JACK CRELEY, ROD MENZIES,
SANDRA O'NEILL

TONIGHT AT 8:30

by Noël Coward
directed by John Neville
designed by Robert Doyle

Hands Across the Sea
Walters / LENORE ZANN
Lady Maureen Gilpin / FIONA REID
Commander Peter Gilpin / RAYMOND CLARKE
Lieut. Commander Alastair Corbett /
JOHN DUNSWORTH
Mrs. Wadhurst / FLORENCE PATERSON
Mr. Wadhurst / DAVID RENTON
Mr. Burnham / BRUCE ARMSTRONG
The Hon. Clare Wedderburn / JOAN GREGSON
Major Gosling / KEITH DINICOL

Still Life
Laura Jesson / JOAN GREGSON
Myrtle Bagot / FLORENCE PATERSON
Beryl Walters / FIONA REID
Stanley / BRUCE ARMSTRONG
Albert Godby / KEITH DINICOL
Alec Harvey / DAVID RENTON
Bill / JOHN DUNSWORTH
Johnnie / RAYMOND CLARKE
Mildred / LENORE ZANN
Dolly Messiter / FAITH WARD

six

JOHN NEVILLE

theatre director
1978 - 1983

OTHELLO

by William Shakespeare
directed by Tom Kerr
designed by Robert Doyle
songs composed by John Gray

Roderigo / BRIAN TAYLOR
Iago / ERIC SCHNEIDER
Brabantio / KEITH DINICOL
Othello / JOHN NEVILLE
Cassio / DAVID SCHURMANN
Duke of Venice / GRAHAM WHITEHEAD
First Senator / STEN HORNBORG
Second Senator / JOHN DUNSWORTH
Sailor / PERRY LEWIS
Messenger / TED WALLACE
Desdemona / GABRIELLE ROSE
Montano / WILLIAM WALLACE
First Gentleman / STEN HORNBORG
Second Gentleman / JOHN DUNSWORTH
Emilia / SUSAN WRIGHT
Bianca / NICOLA LIPMAN
Lodovico / KEITH DINICOL
Gratiano / GRAHAM WHITEHEAD
Senators, Messenger, Herald, Officer,
Sailors, Gentlemen / MATTHEW DAVIS,
KEITH DINICOL, BARRIE DUNN, JOHN
DUNSWORTH, STEN HORNBORG, PERRY
LEWIS, CHRISTOPHER THOMAS, TED
WALLACE, WILLIAM WALLACE

WHEN HE WAS TALKING to Peter Evans in 1977, John Wood was the first to suggest that John Neville might come to Neptune. As Peter recalls, "I kept it to myself a little while because I didn't believe him." Then he went to Jack Craig, at that time Neptune's president, and said, "*Neville's available.* There was a party down at Jack's place and they called Neville and said *Would you be available?* He said, *Yes.* That's how it happened." They explained the situation to Neville and negotiated a salary, much higher than had been paid to former artistic directors. They called Garnet Brown, then Minister of Culture, Recreation and Fitness, who said, "Get him and we'll find the money." The board was staggered, according to Evans.

Why would a classically trained actor of international eminence, who had also made a great name for himself as theatre director in Nottingham, England and Edmonton, Alberta, want to come to a small regional theatre in Halifax, Nova Scotia? "Almost all the things I have done in the last half of my career have been veering away from directions people expect me to take," explains Neville. When he arrived at Edmonton there was not one actor who lived there; now there is a large Equity base living there. "Everyone thought I was crazy to go there," he says, and they thought the same about the move to Halifax. But he tires of just being an actor. Like Major and Piller, he feels more comfortable when working for an easily identifiable community, which is not easy to do when you are based in London or New York. He is also attracted by a challenge, though he didn't look at it that way until it was pointed out to him.

▲

John Neville began his tenure by playing **Othello** and taking a Shakespeare play on tour in the province for the first time since Neptune's early days: here Desdemona (Gabrielle Rose) pledges herself to him while Iago (Eric Schneider) stands behind.

◄

Florence Paterson and David Schurmann "in splendid comic form" in Richard Ouzounian's production of Hugh Leonard's **The Au Pair Man**, designed by Arthur Penson.

The challenge of Neptune was enormous indeed. He inherited what he called "a disaster area". But he always explains that as a "working-class boy" he learned thrift early, in the days before there were credit cards. In order to implement this policy at Neptune he had to make many changes, the first being to establish amicable relations with the board and his colleagues. He speaks highly of president Jack Craig, who was a quiet, not brash, business man, but "dynamite on two legs, a wonderful man and a very dear friend." The board was behind him, "determined to lick this thing," to get it out of the way and "walk tall" again.

When the figures were added up, the deficit was in the region of $200,000; in 1977 the theatre had been on the point of closing for good. Neville considers that when the board hired as general manager Christopher Banks, who had previously worked in administration for both Sherrin and Wood, they had appointed the best man in the country for the job. He speaks of a wonderful professional and personal relationship with Banks, who through prudent management controlled a "tight ship", with many doing two jobs for the price of one: it can only be so if people believe in the product, if the spirit and morale are there. Banks said that Neville was the only artistic director he'd ever met who took an interest in administration and publicity, but as Neville asserts, "If we don't sell, we don't live."

What Neville did above all was to regularize a situation which was already becoming an accepted practice, that the artistic director and general manager were equal authorities responsible to the board. Now he established his role as theatre director: as *primus inter pares* in close consultation with his general manager he had the final responsibility for artistic policy modified by financial restraint. He saw his role as one of "benevolent dictator". Since 1978 Neptune has given theatre director and general manager equal billing. Late in 1980 Denise Rooney took over from Christopher Banks as general manager, and she remained in that position until September 1988. Neville has described how she grew into the job and how fortunate he was to have her there. She is a "very remarkable" person: "any crazy idea I have, somehow she seems to be able to make it work."

▲

John Neville brought noted comedy star Tony Randall to play Trigorin in his production of Chekhov's **The Sea Gull***; seated with Randall are Florence Paterson (Madame Arkadina) and Fiona Reid (Nina). Standing are Gillie Fenwick and David Schurmann. Robert Doyle designed this wooded set.*

THE SEA GULL

by Anton Chekhov
new translation by David French
directed by John Neville
designed by Robert Doyle

Irina Arkadina / FLORENCE PATERSON
Constantine Treplyov / BRENT CARVER
Peter Sorin / GILLIE FENWICK
Nina Zarechnaya / FIONA REID
Ilya Shamrayev / DAVID SCHURMANN
Polina / JOAN GREGSON
Masha / SUSAN WRIGHT
Boris Trigorin / TONY RANDALL
Yevgeny Dorn / DAVID RENTON
Semyon Medvedenko / KEITH DINICOL
Yakov / BRIAN TAYLOR
Cook / VAUGHAN LAFFIN
Maid / WANDA GRAHAM

THE RETURN OF A.J. RAFFLES

by Graham Greene
a co-production with Theatre New Brunswick at Rebecca Cohn auditorium
directed by Malcolm Black
designed by Arthur Penson
costumes by Hilary Corbett
lighting by Edsel Hilchie

A.J. Raffles / JOHN NEVILLE
Bunny / DAVID RENTON
Inspector Mackenzie / JACK NORTHMORE
'Mr. Portland' / ROLAND HEWGILL
Lord Alfred Douglas / IAN DEAKIN
The Marquess of Queensberry / ROBIN MARSHALL
A lady called Alice / DIANA KNIGHT
Lady's maid / ALICE HAMILTON
Mr. Smith / M.E. EVANS
Captain von Blixen / STEN HORNBORG

LUNCHTIME THEATRE

THE LOVER

by Harold Pinter
directed by Eric Schneider
designed by Bruce McKenna
lighting by Gary Clarke

Sarah / SUSAN WRIGHT
Richard / KEITH DINICOL
John / BARRIE DUNN

HEROES

by Ken Mitchell
directed by Andy McKim
lighting by Gary Clarke

Lois Lane / FERNE DOWNEY
Superman / BARRIE DUNN
Tonto / JOHN DUNSWORTH
The Lone Ranger / WILLIAM WALLACE

THE TYPISTS

by Murray Schisgal
directed by Andrew McKim
lighting by Gary Clarke

Sylvia Payton / JOAN GREGSON
Paul Cunningham / JOHN DUNSWORTH

DEAREST HOPE

in celebration of the
International Year of the Child
a recital taken from the book
Dearest Hope compiled by Sian James

Cast:
DOUGLAS CAMPBELL, NICOLA LIPMAN,
JOHN NEVILLE

Although everyone who works at Neptune has been quick to confirm the vital importance of Denise's role, she saw herself more as a "back-room girl" and shunned the limelight. Everyone knew her as "Mother Rooney"; even people her senior would say "Good morning, Mother" to her in the street. She had to be diplomatic, easy-going, understanding, sympathetic, yet her position of authority achieved universal respect. Her relations with the three theatre directors she worked with were based on mutual respect. She saw her job as a learning experience: it took four to six months to get to know a colleague well. "It's like a marriage," she explains. "Everything's going well until the first crisis — the first time you're late, the first time you burn the toast — how are you going to deal with that?" In building a close relationship they accepted that certain things are very much the artistic director's job, certain things the general manager's job. At times one might be more equal than the other.

Above all else the general manager's job is to keep a tight control on fiscal policy. But Neville realized from the beginning that restraint alone could not revive the theatre's fortunes. He had to restore the public's confidence in Neptune and as a result increase the subscription rate enormously. He began by making the people aware that the theatre belonged to them — not just in Halifax but in the whole of the province. Unlike previous artistic directors he was a regular performer and so kept himself in the public eye with a charisma that made him known everywhere he went: as Denise says, there wasn't a cab driver in Halifax who didn't know him. His first big gesture was to play the title role in *Othello* and tour with it throughout the province, the first time a Shakespeare play had toured since the time of Leon Major. "Neptune has a good Othello handy who works cheap," he said.

As president during part of John Neville's tenure Jacqueline Oland asserts how much respect the board had for him as an artist. He was certainly captain of the ship and ran the theatre his way. When a tough economic decision had to be made, such as the reduction of lunchtime theatre in 1983, he accepted the decision without bitterness. He expanded the idea of corporate sponsorships for productions, beginning with Maritime Tractors and Equipment sponsoring *Othello*. It took three years to get the message out to the business community. Neville reminds us, though, that sponsorships are a "tiny drop in the ocean". Productions like *Othello* or *Medea* cost about $80,000 each, and while sponsorships are welcome they cost the corporations only $5,000.

Jackie personally took much of the time-consuming load of this work off John's shoulders, with some help from board members. She recalls how newly established Petro Canada wanted to sponsor a Canadian play, but a few months later she had an apologetic call, "We've been asked to sponsor a play called *Filthy Rich* and we don't think that does our image any good!" A little later she was in New York for a *Cats* preview, talking to a senior executive in a major U.S. corporation. He said that it demonstrated the difference between American and Canadian attitudes towards business: if it was an American company they would say, "That's a great show for us — like the image — go for it!"

By the end of Neville's second year the deficit had been cut to $40,000. The number of subscriptions jumped to more than 6,000 by the third year, and to a high of about 9,500 by 1982-83. The provincial government helped by easing the amusement tax for one year. One other means of effecting economies was to attempt joint productions with Theatre New Brunswick. He collaborated with Malcolm Black, artistic director of T.N.B., on *The Return of A.J. Raffles,* which played with only moderate success in a larger auditorium, the Rebecca Cohn, in the summer of 1979. Neville says that the savings are not as much as one might think, and are certainly not half the cost of a single-theatre production because of transportation and other expenses. But it has the advantage that actors have more of a chance of living in the area: for example, some of the cast of Neptune's *The Sea Gull* were also in T.N.B.'s *Macbeth.*

Of all his considerable achievements at Neptune, Neville considers the school programme the most important. He had done much pioneering work taking the Edmonton Citadel-on-Wheels to rural schools and Indian reserves in northern Alberta.

17th SEASON
November 1979-April 1980

18 WHEELS

by John Gray
directed by Richard Ouzounian
designed by Guido Tondino
lighting by Gary Clarke
musical director John Gray

Vern / KEITH DINICOL
James / DENNY DOHERTY
Lloyd / ROSS DOUGLAS
Molly / WANDA WILKINSON
Sadie / SUSAN WRIGHT
Musicans / KEVIN HEAD, J.P. ELLIS, JOHN MacMILLAN

HOW THE OTHER HALF LOVES

by Alan Ayckbourn
directed by Leslie Yeo
designed by Arthur Penson
lighting by Gary Clarke

Fiona Foster / JOAN GREGSON
Teresa Phillips / NICOLA LIPMAN
Frank Foster / ERIC HOUSE
Bob Phillips / BARRIE DUNN
William Featherstone / KEITH DINICOL
Mary Featherstone / MIRIAM NEWHOUSE

THE MASTER BUILDER

by Henrik Ibsen
translated by Johan Fillinger
directed by Tony Randall
designed by Phillip Silver

Kaja Fosli / WANDA WILKINSON
Knut Brovik / ROBERT WALSH
Ragnar Brovik / IAN DEAKIN
Halvard Solness / JOHN NEVILLE
Aline Solness / ANN CASSON
Dr. Herdal / JOSEPH RUTTEN
Hilde Wangel / KATHY McKENNA

THE TAMING OF THE SHREW

by William Shakespeare
directed by Denise Coffey
designed by Robert Doyle

Christopher Sly / MAURICE EVANS
Vincentio of Pisa / BILL CARR
Signora Curtis / NICOLA LIPMAN
Tranio / BARRIE DUNN
Biondello / WALTER BORDEN
Ferdinanda / DONNA E. MacDONALD
Officer / DON A. MacDONALD
Lucentio / IAN DEAKIN
Baptista / JOSEPH RUTTEN
Gremio / JOHN DUNSWORTH
Hortensio / ROD MENZIES
Grumio / KEITH DINICOL
Petruchio / JOHN NEVILLE
Katherine / SUSAN WRIGHT
Bianca / WANDA WILKINSON
Three naughty waiters / PEPE,
GUISEPPE & VITO
The Piper / ALEX GRANT

BUTTERFLIES ARE FREE

by Leonard Gershe
directed by Andy McKim
designed by Robert Doyle
lighting by Gary Clarke

Don Baker / IAN DEAKIN
Jill Tanner / AMANDA HANCOX
Mrs. Baker / JOAN GREGSON
Ralph Austin / KEITH DINICOL

David Renton had always wanted to resume the student acting company from the days of Robert Sherrin, and he suggested to Neville creating a school touring company. Maritime Tel and Tel had offered a substantial grant for Drama in Education projects during Renton's directorship, but the board preferred to wait for Neville's arrival. Neville made Young Neptune a major part of his programme during his five years at the theatre.

He first called on the vast experience of Irene Watts from the Citadel-on-Wheels. Irene remembers arriving to find John checking paint on the boxes: "He was so vitally interested in any aspect of the tour, and always made time to come to rehearsals and see us on the road, indeed as did his wife Caroline . . . I remember one memorable day, actually Hallowe'en. There was a power cut due to bad weather; teachers went home for candles and flashlights and that was how we performed — in the basement in this spooky lighting!" Irene contributed several of her own original scripts, such as *Martha's Magic* and *Tales from Tolstoy.* Some plays, such as *Tomorrow Will Be Better,* were written by school children. For the first time two provincial government departments — Culture and Education — were giving grants for one project, so that one hundred fifty schools could be covered.

As the programme gathered momentum Neville gradually handed over management of the tours to Bill Carr, who had had much touring experience with Mermaid Theatre. The aim was threefold: to bring top-quality professional theatre into the schools throughout the province; to keep a regular programme going; and to encourage schools to start their own drama clubs. Even as funding was cut back, workshops for students and teachers continued. Bill Carr described it as "an act of love": if young people saw no theatre they developed no taste for it; their increasing knowledge raised their own standards and in turn those of the performers. Carr mentions students coming to mainstage productions and saying, "I saw you first when you toured the schools with Neptune." Each season requires several months' planning and complex integration both with mainstage productions and with school budgets, which are often not known long enough in advance for the planning needed. The demand

▲

The Young Neptune Company in live performance of **The Windigo***, by Dennis Foon, before a captive audience. The players are Walter Borden, Caitlyn Colquhoun, Barrie Dunn and Hans Böggild under John Neville's direction.*

▶

John Neville fostered Neptune's educational role by starting Young Neptune Touring Company. Here director Bill Carr is starting a rehearsal with company members Barrie Dunn, Cathy O'Connell, Caitlyn Colquhoun, Mark Latter, Walter Borden and Bayle Gorman.

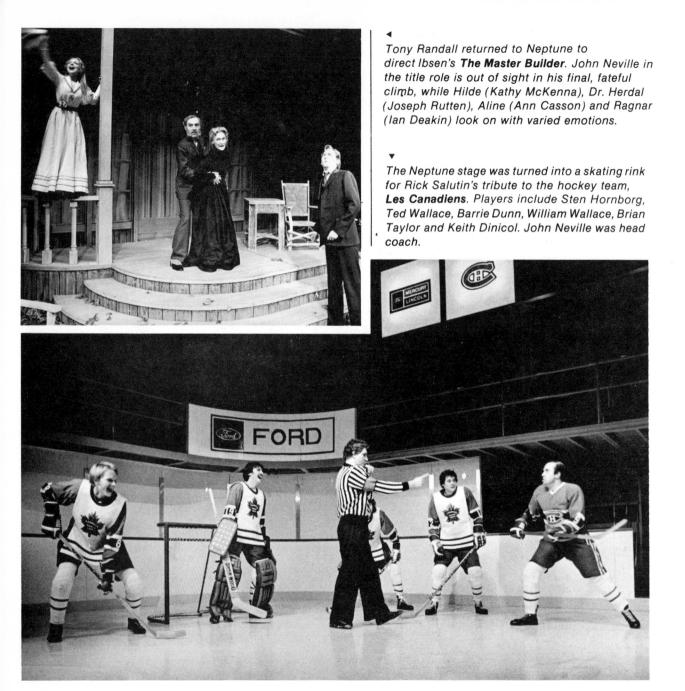

◄

Tony Randall returned to Neptune to direct Ibsen's **The Master Builder**. *John Neville in the title role is out of sight in his final, fateful climb, while Hilde (Kathy McKenna), Dr. Herdal (Joseph Rutten), Aline (Ann Casson) and Ragnar (Ian Deakin) look on with varied emotions.*

▼

The Neptune stage was turned into a skating rink for Rick Salutin's tribute to the hockey team, **Les Canadiens**. *Players include Sten Hornborg, Ted Wallace, Barrie Dunn, William Wallace, Brian Taylor and Keith Dinicol. John Neville was head coach.*

was such that requests from as many as ninety schools for performances or workshops had to be turned down in Neville's last season.

Neville always took a close personal interest in Young Neptune and in the people working for it. Walter Borden speaks highly of John and Caroline Neville's understanding of and sympathy for the problems of the black community, and of the help they gave to promoting and feeding the artistic side of their lives. There was a fear among the black community of going to public places such as Neptune or the Rebecca Cohn Auditorium, but John knew people and would bring them in. Walter says that after he'd done a performance the way he presented himself would reflect heavily on the community. When he was playing with Young Neptune the company often went into communities where people had never talked to a black person. A moving incident he recounts is the time at one high school when he was called "nigger" from the audience. "My fellow actors wanted to leave the stage — they just wanted to pack up and go," he recalls. "But we have to stay," Walter insisted. It was the practice to give a little talk to the audience before the performance; on this occasion Walter gave it, and he spoke about respect. "At the end of the show the young fellow who called the name came up and apologized."

One of Neville's major innovations, in the face of continuing lack of funding for a second stage, was the lunchtime theatre sponsored by the du Maurier Council for the Performing Arts. Helping to fill the ten-day gap required between productions, it offered some of the finest theatre seen at Neptune in recent years. It served several other purposes, including bringing in an entirely new audience of business people. Actors who might otherwise have little opportunity sometimes gave performances which outshone some of those in mainstage productions.

Cathy O'Connell and Timothy Webber were superb in Brian Friel's *Winners,* delicately orchestrated by Hans Böggild; these three youthful local artists, aided by John Dunsworth in a supporting role, brought a magical hour to the theatre. Equally

LUNCHTIME THEATRE

THE END OF THE BEGINNING

by Sean O'Casey
directed by Denise Coffey
assisted by Andy McKim
designed by Trevor Parsons
costumes by Lyn Kelly

Darry Berrill / DENNY DOHERTY
Barry Derrill / JOHN NEVILLE
Lizzie Berrill / DONNA E. MacDONALD

THE RUFFIAN ON THE STAIR

by Joe Orton
directed by David Renton
design co-ordinated by Lesley Preston
lighting by Gary K. Clarke

Joyce / JOAN GREGSON
Mike / TED BAIRSTOW
Wilson / BARRIE DUNN

THE WORKHOUSE WARD

by Lady Gregory
directed by Joseph Rutten
set designed by Lesley Preston
lighting by Gary K. Clarke

Mike McInerney / JOSEPH RUTTEN
Michael Miskell / AL FOSTER
Mrs. Donohoe / FLORA MONTGOMERY

THE DUMB WAITER

by Harold Pinter
directed by John Neville
set designed by Lesley Preston
lighting by Gary K. Clarke

Ben / KEITH DINICOL
Gus / IAN DEAKIN

THE TAMING OF THE SHREW

by William Shakespeare
directed by Dennis Coffey
designed by Robert Doyle
lighting by Gary K. Clarke

Christopher Sly / ROBIN MARSHALL
Vincentio of Pisa / BILL CARR
Signora Curtis / NICOLA LIPMAN
Tranio / BARRIE DUNN
Biondello / WALTER BORDEN
Ferdinanda / DONNA E. MacDONALD
Officer / DON A. MacDONALD
Lucentio / IAN DEAKIN
Baptista / JOSEPH RUTTEN
Gremio / JOHN DUNSWORTH
Hortensio / DAVID SCHURMANN
Grumio / DENNY DOHERTY
Petruchio / JOHN NEVILLE
Katherine / SUSAN WRIGHT
Bianca / WANDA WILKINSON
Stage Manager / DONALD BURDA
Three naughty waiters / PEPE,
GUISEPPE & VITO
The Piper / PETER MacNEILL

THE NIGHT OF THE IGUANA

by Tennessee Williams
directed by John Neville
set, costume and lighting
designed by Phillip Silver

Pancho / STUART NEMTIN
Maxine Faulk / NICOLA LIPMAN
Pedro / WALTER BORDEN
The Rev. T. Lawrence Shannon / ROLAND
HEWGILL
Hank / BILL CARR
Miss Judith Fellowes / WANDA WILKINSON
Hannah Jelkes / AMANDA HANCOX
Charlotte Goodall / CHRISTINA
JASTRZEMBSKA
Nonno (Jonathan Coffin) / ROBERT WALSH
Jake Latta / JOEL SAPP

▲

*Hannah (Amanda Hancox, r.) has brought her grandfather Nonno (Robert Walsh, c.) to a run-down Mexican hotel in Tennessee Wiliams' **The Night of the Iguana**, where she meets Maxine (Nicola Lipman) and Shannon (Roland Hewgill). Pedro (Walter Borden) and Pancho (Stuart Nemtin) look on. The atmospheric set is by Phillip Silver.*

moving was the beautifully detailed interplay of Cathy O'Connell and John Dunsworth in David Mamet's *Reunion,* directed by John Neville. Böggild's own evocation of east coast fishing life, *Salt Cod and Pork Scraps,* which also starred Timothy Webber, gave much pleasure, as did his production of O'Casey's *A Pound on Demand.* Even more successful was a sell-out production of the same author's hilarious *The End of the Beginning,* with John Neville and Denny Doherty as uproarious Irish yokels. Other delightful comedy duos included Nicola Lipman and David Brown in Shaw's *Village Wooing,* and Keith Dinicol and Susan Wright in Pinter's *The Lover.* Touches of the sinister-absurd were added with Orton's *Ruffian on the Stair,* Pinter's *The Dumbwaiter,* and Mrozek's chilling *Striptease.*

There were memorable performances in mainstage productions, too many to mention them all individually. John Neville frequently demonstrated the qualities that had made him such a distinguished actor: he was a majestic Othello, a suave King Magnus in Shaw's *The Apple Cart,* a gay barber playing so well with Douglas Campbell in Dyer's *Staircase,* a striking Solness in *The Master Builder,* or the smooth sophisticate in the Noël Coward role of Elyot in *Private Lives* opposite Amanda Hancox. Florence Paterson and David Schurmann were in splendid comic form in Richard Ouzounian's production of Leonard's *The Au Pair Man,* as were Eric House and Miriam Newhouse in the Ayckbourn *How the Other Half Loves* and *Absurd Person Singular,* both plays directed with flair by Leslie Yeo. Fiona Reid was a touching Nina in *The Sea Gull,* Joseph Rutten deliciously lascivious in Ostrovsky's *The Diary of a Scoundrel,* Joan Orenstein a regal Juno, Ann Casson a moving Aline Solness.

Neville managed to retain balanced programmes, not always making concessions to popular taste, and was at times daringly experimental. One of his boldest moves was to bring Tony Randall to Halifax, first to play Trigorin in *The Sea Gull* and then to direct *The Master Builder,* both modern classics which might not otherwise have been obvious audience draws. Later Randall returned to star in *The Diary of a Scoundrel* opposite Florence Paterson. He has continued to be an honorary

THE DIARY OF A SCOUNDREL

by Alexander Ostrovsky
English version by Rodney Ackland
directed by Tony Randall and John Neville
set, costumes and lighting by Phillip Silver
assistant designer Vivien Frow

Yegor / TONY RANDALL
Glafira / FLORENCE PATERSON
Neel / CHARLES IRVINE
Kleopatra / CHERYL WAGNER
Kroutitsky / JOSEPH RUTTEN
Ivan / DON ALLISON
Sofia / FAITH WARD
Mashenka / AMANDA HANCOX
Yegor / DONALD BURDA
Golutvin / BILL CARR
Maniefa / NICOLA LIPMAN
Sonya / BETTY BELMORE
Lubinka / BARBARA FULTON
Mamaev's manservant / CLIFF LEJEUNE
Grigori / JOHN DARTT

MUCH ADO ABOUT NOTHING

by William Shakespeare
directed by Denise Coffey
designed by Robert Doyle
lighting by Gary K. Clarke

Don Pedro / DAVID SCHURMANN
Don John / WALTER BORDEN
Claudio / BARRIE DUNN
Benedick / JOHN NEVILLE
Borachio / IAN DEAKIN
Conrade / DONALD BURDA
Leonato / JOSEPH RUTTEN
Antonio, Verges / JOHN DUNSWORTH
Hero / WANDA WILKINSON
Beatrice / SUSAN WRIGHT
Margaret / NICOLA LIPMAN
Ursula / DONNA E. MacDONALD
Dogberry / ROBIN MARSHALL
Balthasar / DENNY DOHERTY
Sexton, Friar Francis / BILL CARR
Watch 1 / ROY S. CAMERON
Watch 2 / RON WHEATLEY
Watch 3 / ROSS HARRINGTON

MEDEA

by Euripides
translated by Rex Warner
directed by Maurice E. Evans
and John Neville
sets and lighting by Peter Perina
costumes by Vivien Frow
choreography by Jeanne Robinson
music composed and orchestrated
by Stephen F. McKernan
musical director and
chorusmaster Rick Fox

Nurse / CHERYL WAGNER
Tutor / MAURICE E. EVANS
Medea / VICTORIA SNOW
Creon / BILL CARR
Jason / DONALD BURDA
Aegeus / JOSEPH RUTTEN
Messenger / WALTER BORDEN
Children / MATTHEW OLAND,
PATRICK OLAND
Chorus / JANET MacEWEN, BETTY BELMORE,
BILL CARR, PAT HENMAN, DEBBIE
PERROTT, DEBRA MEEKS, JIM MacSWAIN,
RON WHEATLEY, JEFF HUNTER
Dancers / JOHN BANNERMAN, BARB
FULTON, CLIFF LEJEUNE, LETA SMITH
Musicians / RICK FOX, DON PALMER,
SKIP BECKWITH, TIM CAHOON

THE FOURPOSTER

by Jan de Hartog
directed by John Neville
lighting by Gary K. Clarke
designed by Arthur Penson

Agnes / JOAN GREGSON
Michael / DAVID BROWN

▲
Joan Gregson repeats her success of Neptune's first season, **The Fourposter**, just eighteen years later, this time teamed with David Brown under John Neville's direction.

▼
Peter Perina's ingeniously striking set mirrors the Choruses of Corinthian singers and dancers surrounding **Medea** (Victoria Snow, third from left), in Euripides' tragedy. Modern incidental music was composed by Stephen F. McKernan.

◄
The wedding of Hero (Wanda Wilkinson) and Claudio (Barrie Dunn) by Friar Francis (Bill Carr) in **Much Ado About Nothing**. Guests include John Dunsworth as Antonio, Susan Wright as Beatrice, Joseph Rutten as Leonato, David Schurmann as Don Pedro, John Neville as Benedick, and Walter Borden as Don John.

LUNCHTIME THEATRE

VILLAGE WOOING

by George Bernard Shaw
directed by David Schurmann
designed by Lesley Preston
lighting by Gary K. Clarke

Z / NICOLA LIPMAN
A / DAVID BROWN
The Steward / MICHAEL LEWIS

LUNCH WITH TENNESSEE WILLIAMS

compiled and edited by John Neville
directed by Don Allison
set design by Phillip Silver
design co-ordination by Lesley Preston
lighting co-ordination by Darlene Dube

Cast:
NICOLA LIPMAN, BILL CARR,
CHERYL WAGNER, DAVID BULGER

SALT COD & PORK SCRAPS

written & directed by Hans Böggild
designed by Lesley Preston
lighting by Gary K. Clarke

Cast:
JOHN DUNSWORTH, DEBBIE PERROTT,
TIMOTHY WEBBER, NICOLA LIPMAN,
TONY QUINN

WINNERS

by Brian Friel
directed by Hans Böggild
designed by Lesley Preston
lighting by Gary K. Clarke

Mag / CATHY O'CONNELL
Joe / TIMOTHY WEBBER
Narrator / JOHN DUNSWORTH

STEP/DANCE

by Tom Gallant
directed by John Neville
set & costumes by Lesley Preston
lighting by Gary K. Clarke

Joe Sam / SEAN MULCAHY
Guitar / KENZIE MacNEIL
Jimmy Joe / MICHAEL ZELNIKER
Mary / FLORENCE PATERSON
Louise / CATHY O'CONNELL
Addy / NICOLA LIPMAN
Musician / MARTY RENO

ABSURD PERSON SINGULAR

by Alan Ayckbourn
directed by Leslie Yeo
set by Fred Allen
costumes by Vivien Frow

Jane / MIRIAM NEWHOUSE
Sidney / ERIC HOUSE
Ronald / VERNON CHAPMAN
Marion / FAITH WARD
Eva / AMANDA HANCOX
Geoffrey / DON ALLISON

EVER LOVING

by Margaret Hollingsworth
directed by Tom Kerr
set and lighting by Ted Roberts
costumes by Maxine Graham

Ruth Watson / ALISON MacLEOD
Dave O'Sullivan / KIM COATES
Diana Manning / JILL FRAPPIER
Paul Tomachuk / BILL CARR
Luce Maria Marini / NICOLA LIPMAN
Chuck Malecarne / RICK FOX

ambassador for Neptune. Denise Rooney says that he is still very generous, putting cheques in the mail for Neptune, even sending portions of royalties, and phoning twice a year to see how things are here.

At other times Neville would make a bold choice of play, such as Beckett's difficult *Endgame* in which he starred with Roland Hewgill. Hewgill recalls "those affronted clumping feet leaving at each performance!!" At the same time they were able to laugh at such demonstrations, and felt justified when people told them how much they enjoyed the performance: "It was worth doing," asserts Hewgill; "safe is not always best!" Maybe if a second stage had been available to Neville at that time, such a specialized piece might have gone down better than it did with the typical mainstage audience. Another interesting experiment was Neville's own production of Euripides' *Medea* with a spectacular set by Peter Perina and a modern rock score by Canadian composer Stephen McKernan.

If productions were not always to everyone's taste they were often strikingly original. Neville brought in Denise Coffey from England to direct *The Taming of the Shrew* and *Much Ado About Nothing* in repertory, revamped with local and modern references: the productions were very lively and amusing, even if purists missed some of the poetry. Phillip Silver designed a wonderfully atmospheric Mexican set for *The Night of the Iguana,* with Roland Hewgill as Shannon at one point standing in a downpour of real rain! Robert Ainslie, assisted by John Neville, proved that with *Guys and Dolls* he could mount a large-scale musical on that tiny stage as successfully as John Wood had done. Nor did Neville neglect Canadian plays: John Gray's *18 Wheels* in a lively production by Richard Ouzounian, Rick Salutin's *Les Canadiens,* which Neville himself directed, and Margaret Hollingsworth's *Ever Loving,* directed by Tom Kerr, were the most successful.

Other innovations of Neville's tenure included the instituting of an artist-in-residence. Tom Gallant was hired in 1981-82, and the production of his *Step Dance* made a move to restoring a policy which Leon Major had begun twenty years before. The

▲
Tom Gallant (front c.), Neptune's artist-in-residence 1981-82, wrote **Step/Dance** for the company. Also seated are director John Neville and Marty Reno. At the back are Cathy O'Connell, Sean Mulcahy, Nicola Lipman, Florence Paterson, Kenzie MacNeil and Michael Zelniker.

▶
Another popular lunch-time production was local actor/playwright Hans Böggild's evocation of Nova Scotian fishing life, **Salt Cod and Pork Scraps**, directed by the author: Tony Quinn, Timothy Webber, Debbie Perrott, Nicola Lipman and John Dunsworth.

PRIVATE LIVES

by Noël Coward
directed by Don Allison
sets by Arthur Penson
costumes by Vivien Frow
lighting by Gary K. Clarke

Sybil Chase / JILL FRAPPIER
Elyot Chase / JOHN NEVILLE
Victor Prynne / DON ALLISON
Amanda Prynne / AMANDA HANCOX
Louise / CATHY O'CONNELL

GUYS AND DOLLS

based on a story by Damon Runyon
book by Jo Swerling and Abe Burrows
music and lyrics by Frank Loesser
directed and choreographed by
Robert Ainslie
designed by Robert Doyle
lighting by Gary K. Clarke
musical director and
chorus master Rick Fox
assistant to the director John Neville

Nicely-Nicely Johnson / STAN LESK
Benny Southstreet / TOM GALLANT
Rusty Charlie / WALTER BORDEN
Sarah Brown / MARIE BARON
Arvide Abernathy / JOHN DUNSWORTH
Agatha / PATRICIA HENMAN
Harry the Horse / BILL CARR
Lieutenant Brannigan / DON ALLISON
Nathan Detroit / KEITH DINICOL
Angie the Ox / HANS BÖGGILD
Miss Adelaide / WANDA WILKINSON
Sky Masterson / VICTOR A. YOUNG
Mimi / PATRICIA HENMAN
General Cartwright / CAITLYN COLQUHOUN
Big Jule / BARRIE DUNN
Drunk / CLIFF LEJEUNE
Hot Box Waiter / PAUL RAVLO
M.C. / BILL CARR
Guys / ROB FRASER, C.E. BRUCE LANGILLE,
CLIFF LEJEUNE, PAUL RAVLO
Dolls / BARBARA FULTON, DIANE MOORE,
KIMBERLEY TIMLOCK, EWA JACHIMOWICZ
Musicians / RICK FOX, TIM CAHOON,
JOEL H. ZEMEL

▲

Some typically farcical confusions of family life in Ayckbourn's **Absurd Person Singular** *are hilariously displayed by Faith Ward, Amanda Hancox, Vernon Chapman, Miriam Newhouse and Eric House, under Leslie Yeo's direction.*

▼

Jill Frappier, John Neville, Amanda Hancox and Don Allison demonstrate the brittle wit and sophistication of Noël Coward in **Private Lives***.*

◄

The spectacular Frank Loesser musical **Guys and Dolls** *offered a challenge to director Robert Ainslie (front r.) and to assistant director John Neville and musical director Rick Fox (front l.), seen here with the entire company.*

THE NEPTUNE STORY **137**

ENDGAME

by Samuel Beckett
directed by Peter Froehlich
designed by Roy Robitschek

Clov / JOHN NEVILLE
Hamm / ROLAND HEWGILL
Nagg / KEITH DINICOL
Nell / PATRICIA HENMAN

•••••••••••••••••••••
⁞ LUNCHTIME THEATRE ⁞
•••••••••••••••••••••

COUNTING THE WAYS

by Edward Albee
directed by John Dunsworth
lighting by Gary K. Clarke

Cast:
IRIS QUINN and TOM GALLANT

STRIP-TEASE

by Slawomir Mrozek
directed by Hans Böggild
costumes by Bonnie Deakin
lighting by Carl Scott
Cast:
GARRISON CHRISJOHN,
JOHN DUNSWORTH / HANS BÖGGILD

CUTHBERT'S LAST STAND

a new musical première based on the short story The Third Person *by Henry James*
music and lyrics by Rick Fox
book by Dwayne Brenna
book revised by Victor A. Young
directed by Victor A. Young
musical director Rick Fox
set by Lesley Preston
costumes by Bonnie Deakin
lighting by Gary K. Clarke

Amy Frush / MARIE BARON
Susan Frush / FLORENCE PATERSON
Mr. Patton / DAVID RENTON

A POUND ON DEMAND

by Sean O'Casey
directed by Hans Böggild
stage manager Carol Chrisjohn
lighting by Gary K. Clarke

Girl / CAITLYN COLQUHOUN
Jerry / BILL CARR
Sammy / BARRIE DUNN
Woman / WALTER BORDEN
Policeman / JOHN NEVILLE

THE FLATTERING WORD

by George Kelly
directed by John Dunsworth
set by Lesley Preston
costumes by Bonnie Deakin
lighting by Gary K. Clarke

Mary Rigley / IRIS QUINN
The Rev. Loring Rigley / BILL CARR
Mrs. Zooker / NICOLA LIPMAN
Eugene Tesh / TOM GALLANT
Lena Zooker / SHANNA KELLY

20th SEASON

November 1982-May 1983

JUNO AND THE PAYCOCK

by Sean O'Casey
directed by Tom Kerr
set and costumes by Arthur Penson
lighting by Gary K. Clarke

Mary Boyle / CATHY O'CONNELL
Johnny Boyle / AARON FRY
Juno Boyle / JOAN ORENSTEIN
Jerry Devine / KIM COATES
"Captain" Jack Boyle / OWEN FORAN
"Joxer" Daley / SEAN MULCAHY
Coal Vendor's Boy / RON WHEATLEY
Charlie Bentham / DONALD BURDA
Mrs. Maisie Madigan / SHIRLEY DOUGLAS
Mrs. Tancred / PADDY ENGLISH
"Needle" Nugent / BILL CARR

twentieth season saw the tenure of a talented eighteen-year-old apprentice set designer, Andrew Murray, whose simple yet tasteful sets for *The Apple Cart* drew audience applause. Andrew, who has since gone on to design sets at Stratford, learned much from principal designer Arthur Penson. Other designers whose work was constantly impressive included Phillip Silver, Guido Tondino, Roy Robitschek, and the perennial Robert Doyle. The set that gave the most problems for the Blackmores was the one Fred Allen designed for *Absurd Person Singular*: three different kitchens were required, and at that time without having a turntable they had to build three separate sets.

Andrew recalls an amusing — and embarrassing — experience whenever a particular brand of gold-leaf paint is used in his presence: "After Neptune's fabulous carpenters, Jack and Bill Blackmore, had left for the day at 5:00, I was able to paint some scenery for my upcoming debut production of *The Apple Cart*. Around 7:00 I was startled when stage manager Carol Chrisjohn came bounding into the shop with a horrified look on her face. Unknown to me, for the past two hours I had been filling the entire theatre with incredibly potent paint fumes which awaited both actors and audience for the 8:00 curtain of the current production, *Filthy Rich!* It was a this point I realized that I was not feeling too well, but soon recovered enough to help in setting up fans and opening fire doors to air out the theatre. The ironic part of this story is the line in Act II of *Filthy Rich:* 'You know what life is? Life is a bad smell!' "

In 1981 John Neville, who achieved so much despite the constant problems of staging the plays, was calling the Neptune building a "slum". He was frustrated by the lack of facilities at the theatre, and having to use Keith Hall for rehearsals, props, costumes and storage. "Everyone was worn to shreds," trying to rehearse *Medea* with singers, dancers, actors and orchestra in several different places: "It was incredible it went on at all," he said. It was therefore hardly surprising that he campaigned endlessly for a new theatre, having been successful in building a new Citadel Theatre in Edmonton.

Peter Evans did the study for a combined Neptune Theatre

and Art Gallery of Nova Scotia complex on the Halifax waterfront. He would like to have seen a whole block including the CBC developed as a cultural centre on the waterfront. The theatre would have seated 850 people, and he maintains that the problem of operating costs could have been solved by bringing in other companies and arts organizations to share the stage. The existing theatre could still have been used as a second stage and as a conference centre. At a meeting at the Halifax Club in 1979 Evans and Neville met David MacDonald, Minister of Culture in the short-lived Joe Clark government. MacDonald made a commitment for the theatre/art gallery complex to go ahead on a cost-sharing basis. But when the Tory government was defeated, and Gerald Regan became the minister responsible, the plans stalled. The Waterfront Development Corporation didn't think the arts centre would bring the return they were looking for.

Evans says he will never forget the meeting at which the proposal was discussed, when John Neville came to the edge of the table and hit it hard, saying, "For Christ's sake, you can find a million reasons why it shouldn't happen. All you've got to do is say it's going to happen and it will happen." But his enthusiasm turned to frustration when the situation became confused by too many arguments. Denise Rooney says that the waterfront study made much sense, but nobody was prepared to come up with the private sector millions required in the cost sharing, and people started looking at alternatives. Canadian Actors' Equity calculates the size of the house on an A, B or C rating, and a theatre of 750-900 seats would have put Neptune into the A category, with a consequently astronomical jump in production costs and minimum salaries which artists can be paid.

Many people are still saddened that such an enterprising idea fell through, and that no ensuing government has had the courage to see that an arts building will attract far more people to the waterfront than office space. From this time Neville became embittered and labelled members of the provincial government as philistines. He did not leave because the plans for the new building failed — "I can do plays in an aircraft hanger," he said — but rather because Neptune was standing still. He maintained

THE WIZARD OF OZ

by Alfred Bradley
adapted from the story by L. Frank Baum
directed by Ronald Ulrich
sets and costumes by Arthur Penson
lighting by Gary K. Clarke

Uncle Henry / JOHN DUNSWORTH
Dorothy / SHERRY THOMSON
Aunt Em / NICOLA LIPMAN
The Good Witch of the North / CATHY O'CONNELL
The Scarecrow / STUART NEMTIN
The Tinman / DONALD BURDA
The Cowardly Lion / GARRISON CHRISJOHN
The Wicked Witch of the West / NICOLA LIPMAN
The Witch's Cat / WALTER BORDEN
The Queen of the Fieldmice / CATHY O'CONNELL
The Guardian of the Gates / JOHN DUNSWORTH
The Wizard of Oz / BILL CARR
Glinda / CATHY O'CONNELL

SPECIAL OCCASIONS

by Bernard Slade
directed by Ronald Ulrich
set and costumes by Arthur Penson
lighting by Gary K. Clarke

Amy Ruskin / SUSAN WRIGHT
Michael Ruskin / JOHN NEVILLE

FILTHY RICH

by George F. Walker
directed by Peter Froehlich
designed by Roy Robitschek

Tyrone M. Power / DONALD DAVIS
Jamie McLean / TONY NARDI
Ann Scott / KATE LYNCH
Susan Scott / SUSAN HOGAN
Police Detective Stackhouse / VICTOR ERTMANIS
Henry "the pig" Duvall / GEORGE MERNER
Fred Whittaker / DAVID INGRAHAM

THE APPLE CART

by Bernard Shaw
directed by John Neville and Tom Kerr
set and costumes by Andrew Murray
lighting by Gary K. Clarke

Pamphilius / OREST E. ULAN
Sempronius / AARON FRY
Boanerges / GEORGE MERNER
Magnus / JOHN NEVILLE
Joe Proteus / SEAN MULCAHY
Nicobar / DAVID SCHURMANN
Crassus / ROBERT WALSH
Pliny / DAVID RENTON
Balbus / JOHN DARTT
Lysistrata / JILL FRAPPIER
Amanda / JOAN GREGSON
Orinthia / LENORE ZANN
Jemima / PADDY ENGLISH
Mr. Vanhattan / DAVID BROWN

COMEBACK

by Ron Chudley
directed by Paddy English
designed by Arthur Penson
lighting by Gary K. Clarke

Miranda Stone / LAURA PRESS
Max Steinway / DON ALLISON
Dimitri Carusus / CHARLES KERR
Angele La Rue / JILL FRAPPIER

that professional theatre could not progress in the province until attitudes towards the arts changed, until in fact there was a "cultural revolution". He said at the time that it was a "typical attitude of politicians and bureaucrats" to renovate an old building for the art gallery and ignore the theatre. It is not only Neville who feels that the arts have a very low priority with both city and provincial governments!

John Neville spoke glowingly of the "wonderful team of people I shall miss sorely" when he finally handed over to Tom Kerr in 1983. He had fulfilled beyond anyone's expectations the five years that he had originally promised. He considered the fact that someone new was coming to be advantageous, healthy for the building and the whole situation. He paid tribute to the "fine artist" Tom Kerr, and held out hopes for the theatre's future under Tom's guidance. No one who knew John Neville will forget the impact he made on the theatrical and cultural life of Nova Scotia. He was the saviour of Neptune Theatre at one of its darkest economic hours. He gave the theatre a new artistic impetus and his many innovations brought a fresh quality and vigor to the cultural life of the community. We shall not readily forget what a privilege it was to have this world-renowned artist to lead us during these years.

▶

The happiness of the Boyle family (Joan
Orenstein, Cathy O'Connell, Aaron Fry and
Owen Foran) as Charlie Bentham (Donald
Burda) reads the will proves to be short-
lived in O'Casey's **Juno and the Paycock**,
directed by Tom Kerr in 1982.

▼

King Magnus (John Neville, seated c.)
surrounded by an unruly Cabinet (David
Schurmann, Robert Walsh, George Merner,
Joan Gregson, David Renton, John Dartt,
Sean Mulcahy and Jill Frappier in Bernard
Shaw's political extravaganza **The Apple
Cart**. Set design is by Andrew Murray.

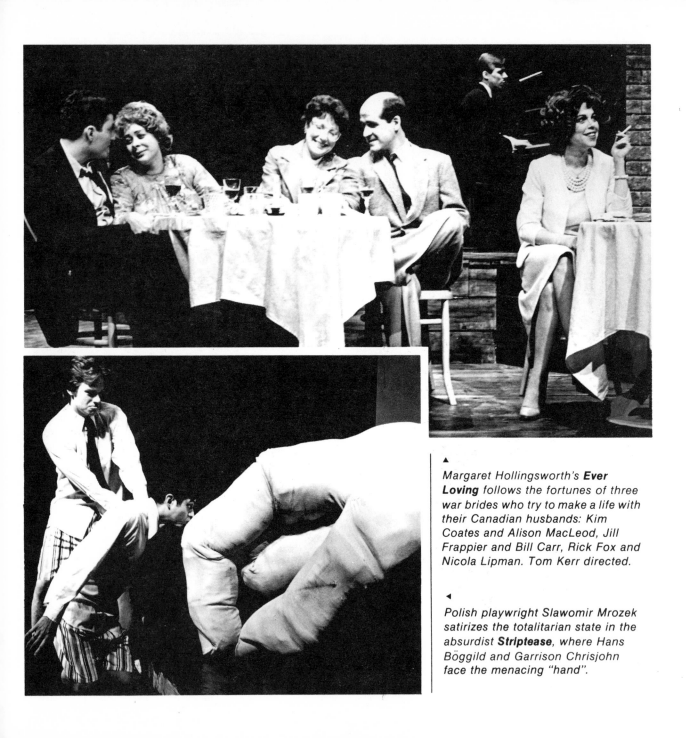

▲

Margaret Hollingsworth's **Ever Loving** follows the fortunes of three war brides who try to make a life with their Canadian husbands: Kim Coates and Alison MacLeod, Jill Frappier and Bill Carr, Rick Fox and Nicola Lipman. Tom Kerr directed.

◄

Polish playwright Slawomir Mrozek satirizes the totalitarian state in the absurdist **Striptease**, where Hans Böggild and Garrison Chrisjohn face the menacing "hand".

▲

Lunch-time theatre was a welcome innovation of John Neville's which brought in a different audience. Here Cathy O'Connell and John Dunsworth give a moving portrayal of a daughter-father relationship in David Mamet's Reunion.

THE GREEN CROW

*a feast of the life and
works of Sean O'Casey
by Sean Mulcahy
directed by Paddy English
designed by the company
stage manager Bayle Gorman
lighting by Carl Scott*

Cast:
CAITLYN COLQUHOUN, BARRIE DUNN,
JOAN GREGSON, DAVID RENTON,
SEAN MULCAHY

REUNION

*by David Mamet
directed and designed by
John Neville*

Carol Mindler / CATHY O'CONNELL
Bernie Cary / JOHN DUNSWORTH

THE PROPOSAL

*by Anton Chekhov
directed and designed by
David Schurmann
lighting by Gary K. Clarke*

Ivan Lomov / AARON FRY
Stephen Chubukov / GEORGE MERNER
Natasha Chubukov / CATHY O'CONNELL

seven

TOM KERR

theatre director
1983 - 1986

DEBUG & ENCORE

*an original musical celebration
of Neptune's twenty years
dialogue by John Gray
concept by Tom Kerr
music and lyrics by Rick Fox
book by John Gray
additional lyrics by Tom Kerr and
Susan Wright
directed by Tom Kerr
costumes by Robert Doyle
set and lighting by Stephen Degenstein
choreographed by Valerie Easton
musical director Scott Macmillan
with John Alphonse and his band*

Cast:
BILL CARR, STAN LESK, JAYNE LEWIS,
DAVID RENTON, DIANE STAPLEY, FAITH
WARD, WANDA WILKINSON, PATRICK
YOUNG

THE ARRIVAL OF TOM KERR as theatre director coincided with Neptune's twentieth anniversary. To celebrate this occasion Kerr conceived a musical revue *Debut and Encore,* which saluted Neptune's first twenty years with highlights of past musical productions; John Gray wrote the book, Rick Fox supplied music and lyrics, Robert Doyle designed the costumes, and set and lighting were by Stephen Degenstein. Among the performers were David Renton and Faith Ward. Tony Randall made a brief appearance on the opening night, June 23, and joined in the gala celebrations.

Tom Kerr had been Head of Drama at the University of Saskatchewan for seven years, and when he came Jackie Oland, president of the board, said, "We are confident that Mr. Kerr's enthusiasm, dedication and solid experience in all areas of the theatre, together with the exciting season he has planned for 1983-84, will ensure that Neptune's 21st season will be one of the most exciting in the history of the theatre." He straight away announced auditions so that he could meet members of the local acting community.

His plans for an opening production were certainly ambitious: Neptune became the first professional Canadian theatre company to mount a repertory production of *West Side Story* (directed by Tom Kerr) and *Romeo and Juliet* (under the direction of Alan Scarfe). The outstanding cast for both plays included Ian Deakin, Peggy Coffey, Jesse Collins, Susan Cuthbert, Kim Coates, Glen Cairns and Jerry Etienne. From

Shakespeare's **Romeo and Juliet**, directed by Alan Scarfe, ran in repertory with West Side Story: Peggy Coffey and Ian Deakin portray the "star-crossed lovers".

John Gray wrote **Debut and Encore** to celebrate Neptune's 20th anniversary: participating are Patrick Young, Wanda Wilkinson, Stan Lesk, Diane Stapley, David Renton, Faith Ward, Bill Carr and Jayne Lewis.

ROMEO AND JULIET

by William Shakespeare
directed by Alan Scarfe
set and costumes by Robert Doyle
lighting by Gary K. Clarke

Escalus / DON ALLISON
Paris / MAX REIMER
Page to Paris / JESSE COLLINS
Mercutio / MAURICE GODIN
Chief of the Prince's Watch / JOHN DUNSWORTH
Servants to the Watch / ROBERT DODDS, KIM STEBNER
Lord Capulet / GEORGE MERNER
Lady Capulet / SUSAN GATTONI
Juliet / PEGGY COFFEY
Angelica / WANDA WILKINSON
Tybalt / KIM COATES
Old Capulet / JOHN DUNSWORTH
Peter / STEPHEN McMULKIN
Sampson / ROBERT DODDS
Gregory / KIM STEBNER
Rosaline / SUSAN KYLE
Livia / SUSAN CUTHBERT
Helena / LINDA DAUPHINEE
Lord Montague / TONY JOHNSTONE
Lady Montague / SUSAN CUTHBERT
Romeo / IAN DEAKIN
Benvolio / GLEN CAIRNS
Abram / JESSE COLLINS
Balthasar / JERRY ETIENNE
Friar Laurence / ROBERT WALSH
Friar John / GLEN CAIRNS
An Apothecary / MAURICE GODIN
Simon Catling / JOHN DUNSWORTH
Hugh Rebeck / TONY JOHNSTONE
James Soundpost / JESSE COLLINS

THE SEA HORSE

by Edward J. Moore
directed by Tom Kerr
set, costumes & lighting by Ted Roberts

Gertie Blum / JANET WRIGHT
Harry Bales / JOHN NOVAK

---

that point Shakespeare and modern classical plays as well as musicals featured prominently in Kerr's programmes for the next three years.

For his production of *Twelfth Night,* in fact, Kerr combined Shakespeare with Gilbert and Sullivan, an unexpected unison which worked better than many people dared hope. A strong cast was led by David Schurmann as Malvolio, Amanda Hancox as Olivia and David Brown as Sir Toby. Included in the same season was a modern masterpiece, O'Neill's *A Moon for the Misbegotten,* firmly directed by Larry Lillo, and starring Janet Wright, Ron Halder and Sean Mulcahy in the demanding principal roles. Tom Kerr particularly remembers Janet's performance in this and in a much slighter play, *The Sea Horse;* he also recalls another virtuoso performance in another American classic, Wenna Shaw as Blanche Dubois playing opposite Kim Coates as Stanley in Tom's own production of *A Streetcar Named Desire;* Coates has since played the same role on Broadway!

In his second season Kerr mounted two major musicals in addition to a musical *Twelfth Night.* With the assistance of choreographer Grace MacDonald and a brilliant Master of Ceremonies in Maurice Godin he vividly recaptured the decadent life of 1930s Berlin in *Cabaret.* And John Gray's tribute to one of the most popular television shows ever seen in Canada, *Don Messer's Jubilee,* was sold out soon after it opened. This highly successful run was capped with a national tour, sparked by popular demand and interest across the country. The tour began in October 1985 after a two-week return engagement at Neptune Theatre, and ended in May 1986, though it cost Neptune dearly. Tom Kerr remembers Bill Carr leading the whole company in prayer before every Neptune performance: "I loved to join them; I found it beautiful and moving," Tom says. The third season also contained two musicals: Ann Mortifee's *Welcome to the Planet,* in which she starred as the singer with Louise Hoyt as choreographer/dancer; and the Webber-Rice *Evita,* directed by Richard Ouzounian, with Jayne Lewis as Eva Peron and Alfie Zappacosta as Che.

▲

*Leonard Bernstein's musical updating of Romeo and Juliet to modern New York depicts the rivalry between two gangs, The Jets and the Puerto Rican Sharks. In Tom Kerr's production of **West Side Story**, Jesse Collins, Stephen McMulkin, Maurice Godin, Kim Coates, Thierry Richard and Kim Stebner portray the Jets.*

WEST SIDE STORY

book by Arthur Laurents
music by Leonard Bernstein
lyrics by Stephen Sondheim
directed by Tom Kerr
choreography by Grace MacDonald
musical director Lloyd Nicholson
set and costumes by Robert Doyle
lighting by Gary K. Clarke

Riff / KIM STEBNER
Tony / JESSIE COLLINS
Action / KIM COATES
A-Rab / MAURICE GODIN
Diesel / THIERRY RICHARD
Baby John / STEPHEN McMULKIN
Bernardo / MAX REIMER
Maria / SUSAN CUTHBERT
Anita / SUSAN GATTONI
Chino / JERRY ETIENNE
Pepe / IAN DEAKIN
Indio / GLEN CAIRNS
Toro / ROBERT DODDS
Doc / ROBERT WALSH
Lt. Schrank / DON ALLISON
Graziella / KATHY MacLELLAN
Velma / LINDA KEIRSTEAD
Clarice / WANDA WILKINSON
Pauline / SARAH MILROY
Anybodys / SUSAN KYLE
Rosalia / PENELOPE EVANS
Consuelo / LINDA DAUPHINEE
Teresita / PEGGY COFFEY
Francisca / EWA JACHIMOWICZ
Officer Krupke / GEORG MERNER
Gladhand / JOHN DUNSWORTH
Musicians / LLOYD NICHOLSON, PAUL SIMONS, JOHN ALPHONSE, PAT KILBRIDE

MASS APPEAL

by Bill C. Davis
directed by Larry Lillo
set and costumes by Ted Roberts
lighting by Bob Elliott

Father Tim Parley / SEAN MULCAHY
Mark Dolson / JOHN MOFFAT

PRESENT LAUGHTER

by Noël Coward
directed by Tom Kerr
set designed by Jim Guedo
costumes by Vivien Frow
lighting by Carl R. Scott

Daphne Stillington / ALISON MacLEOD
Miss Erkison / DOROTHY WARD
Fred / BRIAN TAYLOR
Monica Reed / BARBARA CHILCOTT
Garry Essendine / ALAN SCARFE
Liz Essendine / JILL FRAPPIER
Roland Maule / GLEN CAIRNS
Henry Lyppiatt / JOHN DUNSWORTH
Morris Dixon / DON ALLISON
Joanne Lyppiatt / BARBARA MARCH
Lady Saltburn / FAITH WARD

YOU BETTER WATCH OUT
YOU BETTER NOT DIE

by John Gray
directed by Tom Kerr
set and costumes by Andrew Murray
lighting by David Ingraham

Desk Clerk / AARON FRY
Inspector Brewster / GEORGE MERNER
Harry Weed / EDWARD GREENHALGH
Edna Weed / JOAN ORENSTEIN
Chuck Swinton / STAN LESK
Ginny / WANDA WILKINSON
Julius McGee / ROBERT WALSH
Valet / TONY JOHNSTONE

LUNCHTIME THEATRE

HERRINGBONE

by Tom Cone
directed by Bob Paisley
musical director Paul Simons
lighting by Carl R. Scott

George Herringbone / FRANK MacKAY

▲
*Joanne (Barbara March) is only one of several people upset by Garry Essendine (Alan Scarfe) — possibly a self-portrayal of Noël Coward — in his play, **Present Laughter**. Looking on in dismay are Jill Frappier, Don Allison and John Dunsworth. Tom Kerr directed.*

The Gray and Mortifee plays were both world premières. Tom Kerr also directed other first productions, such as Tom MacDonnell's portrait of Second World War Halifax, *Victory*, with a cast led by Florence Paterson and David Brown, and John Gray's Christmas farce, *You Better Watch Out, You Better Not Die*, unmemorable as a play, but with some splendid comedy acting by Joan Orenstein and Edward Greenhalgh, and a fascinatingly ingenious set by Andrew Murray. Other productions of this period included Bill Davis' *Mass Appeal*, with Sean Mulcahy in fine form as the priest, the moving play about the problems of the deaf, *Children of a Lesser God*, and two Canadian plays, James Nichol's thriller *And When I Wake* and W.O. Mitchell's comedy *The Black Bonspiel of Wullie Mac-Crimmon*. Kerr also recalls especially the comedy playing of Alan Scarfe in Noël Coward's *Present Laughter* and the ensemble playing in Michael Frayn's backstage farce *Noises Off*. John Blackmore says that the set designed by Stephen Degenstein for the latter was particularly complicated, as it had to show a theatre stage both from front and back. The whole set was on casters: "We had two inches to spare on stage! And the crew had it down in twelve minutes!"

A memorable feature of the mainstage seasons was the Christmas plays for children. Jim Betts' *The Mystery of the Oak Island Treasure* proved very popular with young audiences, and above all Irene Watts' delightful staging of *A Christmas Carol* was possibly the best ever Christmas production at Neptune. According to Irene, "I remember Tom saying *We want a huge Christmas tree, choirs, a Dickensian Christmas*, and that's what we gave our audiences." The outstanding cast included David Brown, Sean Wright and Jerry Etienne. It was the late Maxim Mazumdar's first of several appearances at Neptune. As he recalls, "Ellen Horst and myself, as the warehouse owners, the Fezziwigs, were choreographed in a lively polka. Rehearsals for the dance had been fine, but at the opening public performance, the trapdoor set into the stage suddenly gave way as Ellen executed a particularly spectacular twirl. Down she went in a flurry of Victorian skirts dragging me in with her. It was quite the sight

NEXT

by Terrence McNally
directed by Don Allison
lighting by Carl Scott

Sgt. Thech / JOAN ORENSTEIN
Marion Cheever / DENNY DOHERTY

LAUNDRY & BOURBON

by James McLure
directed by Linda Moore
lighting by Carl R. Scott

Hattie Dealing / TRISHA LAMIE
Elizabeth Caulder / CATHY O'CONNELL
Amy Lee Fullernoy / IRIS QUINN

22nd SEASON

October 1984–April 1985

TWELFTH NIGHT

by William Shakespeare
music by William Schwenk Gilbert
and Arthur Seymour Sullivan
directed by Tom Kerr
musical director Lloyd Nicholson
set and lighting by Stephen Degenstein
costumes by Anne Elizabeth Dixon
musical arrangements by Lloyd Nicholson

Curio / JOHN BURKE
Fabian / JONATHAN WHITTAKER
Valentine / KERRY DOREY
Viola / VICTORIA SNOW
Sea Captain / JONATHAN WHITTAKER
Sailor / DAVID McKNIGHT
Duke Orsino / KIM COATES
Duke's Attendant / GLENN WHITE
Sir Toby / DAVID BROWN
Maria / ELLEN HORST
Sir Andrew / SIMON BRADBURY
Clown / BRUCE CLAYTON
Olivia / AMANDA HANCOX
Malvolio / DAVID SCHURMANN
Olivia's Attendant / LINDY MEADOWS
Antonio / DAVID McKNIGHT
Sebastian / GLEN CAIRNS

CABARET

book by Joe Masteroff
based on the play by John Van Druten
and stories by Christopher Isherwood
music by John Kander
lyrics by Fred Ebb
directed by Tom Kerr
choreography by Grace MacDonald
musical director Lloyd Nicholson
set and lighting by Stephen Degenstein

Master of ceremonies / MAURICE GODIN
Clifford Bradshaw / BRUCE CLAYTON
Ernst Ludwig / KERRY DOREY
Customs Officer / JONATHAN WHITTAKER
Fraulein Schneider / ELLEN HORST
Fraulein Kost / AMANDA HANCOX
Herr Schultz / DENNY DOHERTY
Telephone Girl / MARY LOU MARTIN
Max / KIM COATES
Sally Bowles / VICTORIA SNOW
Kit Kat Dancers:
Inga / LINDA DONNELLY-KEIRSTEAD
Heidi / MARY LOU MARTIN
Mausie / KATHRYN MacLELLAN
Christina / AMANDA HANCOX
Fritzy / LINDA ELLIOTT
Helga / JOHN BURKE
Sailors / DAVID McKNIGHT, GLEN CAIRNS
Taxi Man / DAVID McKNIGHT
Two ladies / KATHRYN MacLELLAN,
LINDA ELLIOTT
Gorilla / JOHN BURKE
Musicians / LLOYD NICHOLSON,
JOHN HOLLIS, JOHN ALPHONSE,
KAREN MacKAY, JOEL ZEMEL
Musical arrangements by Scott MacMillan
and Lloyd Nicholson

— me being dragged down by the Rubensesque Ms. Horst and landing with my rump sticking up at the balcony. The hilarity onstage and off threatened to bring the rest of our set down. Emerging rather shell-shocked, Ellen, in her most Dickensian tones, muttered, 'What the hell was that?' 'Well, dear,' came my rather feeble reply, 'it is a *very* old building.' We polkaed off as best we could to a great round of applause." My daughter, who was one of the Choristers in the production, remembers Maxim saying, "This building really is in need of repair!" Whichever version was right, each was also equally appropriate for Neptune Theatre! Once again Andrew Murray provided one of his several excellent sets of this period, this among his most imaginative.

An important innovation of Tom Kerr's tenure was the creation of a second stage for the first time since the early 1970s. The lunchtime theatre started by John Neville had been very successful at first but was becoming increasingly difficult to finance and mount between mainstage productions. There were three lunchtime productions in Kerr's first season — *Next* by Terrence McNally, *Herringbone* by Tom Cone, and *Laundry and Bourbon* by James McLure — and the final lunchtime presentation was *A Little Light Music* with Don Harron, Catherine McKinnon and Maxim Mazumdar in May 1986. But then an alternative space became available.

Glen Cairns, who ran Neptune North for Tom Kerr at this time, describes its beginnings in this way. It came about as a result of work on three different fronts: Tom Kerr had been looking for a way to revive Neptune's second stage since he arrived in Halifax; Eva Moore, Executive Director of the Nova Scotia Drama League, had been working hard for several years to create a new venue for theatre in the city; and Cairns himself had been running an alternative theatre company, Theatre Warehouse. Kerr and Cairns negotiated the merger of Neptune and Theatre Warehouse, agreeing that its purpose was to be in every way a challenging alternative to the main stage. In this way, through their close co-operation with Eva Moore, Neptune North came to be located in N.S.D.L.'s newly renovated Cunard Street Theatre in the city's north end.

▲

Among the ever-popular children's plays for Christmas was Jim Betts' **The Mystery of the Oak Island Treasure**. *Dr. Gunn (David Schurmann) excites the children (Andrew Sacamano and Sheva Carr) with his tale, while their mother (Cathy O'Connell) registers alarm.*

THE MYSTERY OF THE OAK ISLAND TREASURE

by Jim Betts
directed by Bob Paisley
costumes by Andrew Murray
set by Stephen Degenstein and
Andrew Murray
lighting by David Ingraham
sound by Melody Reed

Diana Hawkins / SHEVA CARR
Jason Hawkins / ANDREW SACAMANO
Joanna Hawkins / CATHY O'CONNELL
Dr. Robert Gunn / DAVID SCHURMANN
Captain Elijah Bones / DAVID BROWN
Scavenger John Timbers / KIM COATES
Seymour "Seadog" McWinkle / JONATHAN WHITTAKER

AND WHEN I WAKE

by James W. Nichol
directed by David Schurmann
set and costumes by Andrew Murray
lighting by Carl R. Scott

Miss Burns / RUTH OWEN
Marci Waters / JO ANN McINTYRE
Dawn Waters / SARAH DUNSWORTH
Terry Waters / KIM COATES
Wilson Kyle / RON HALDER
Danny / JOHN DARTT

NOISES OFF

by Michael Frayn
directed by Tom Kerr
assisted by Dorothy Ward
set design by Stephen Degenstein
lighting by David Ingraham
costumes by Sharrie-Ann Dial

Dotty Otley / JOAN GREGSON
Lloyd Dallas / DAVID BROWN
Garry Lejeune / GLEN CAIRNS
Brooke Ashton / LENORE ZANN
Poppy Norton-Taylor / CATHY O'CONNELL
Frederick Fellowes / BILL CARR
Belinda Blair / NICOLA LIPMAN
Tim Allgood / GLENN WHITE
Selsdon Mowbray / ROBERT WALSH

◀

John Gray's **Don Messer's Jubilee** was so popular it soon sold out at Neptune and subsequently toured the country. Helping to supply the nostalgia are Frank MacKay as Charlie Chamberlain and Jodie Friesen as Marg Osborne, while "The Islanders" in the background are flanked by two pairs of dancers.

▼

The decadence of Berlin night life is vividly portrayed in this dance number from **Cabaret**, based on Christopher Isherwood's stories of Germany in the 1930s. Maurice Godin (front centre) is Master of Ceremonies.

▲

*Phil Hogan (Sean Mulcahy) has his daughter Josie (Janet Wright) in his mind during Larry Lillo's production of Eugene O'Neill's **A Moon for the Misbegotten**.*

DON MESSER'S JUBILEE

written and composed by John Gray
directed by Tom Kerr
musical director John Gray
set and lighting by Stephen Degenstein
costumes by Andrew Murray
choreography by Linda Elliott

Rae Simmons / BILL CARR
The Islanders / PAUL SIMONS, DAVE HICKEY,
DON MOORE, JOHN FERGUSON
Charlie Chamberlain / FRANK MacKAY
Marg Osborne / JODIE FRIESEN
The Dancers / LINDA ELLIOTT, BOB PAISLEY,
KATHRYN MacLELLAN, ROY CAMERON

A MOON FOR
THE MISBEGOTTEN

by Eugene O'Neill
directed by Larry Lillo
set and costumes by Ted Roberts
lighting by Carl R. Scott

Josie Hogan / JANET WRIGHT
Mike Hogan / GLEN CAIRNS
Phil Hogan / SEAN MULCAHY
James Tyrone Jr. / RON HALDER
T. Stedman Harder / GARY VERMEIR

A CHRISTMAS CAROL
by Charles Dickens
adapted by Tom Kerr and Irene N. Watts
directed by Irene N. Watts
set design by Andrew Murray
lighting by David Ingraham
costumes by Sharrie Ann Dial

Town Crier / SHAWN WRIGHT
Charles Dickens, the Charitable Gentleman,
Mr. Fezziwig, Bell's Husband and Merchant II /
MAXIM MAZUMDAR
Bob Cratchit, Ghost of Christmas Past,
Merchant I / JERRY ETIENNE
Scrooge / DAVID BROWN
Jacob Marley, Ghost of Christmas Plenty,
young Scrooge and old Joe / DAVID McKNIGHT
Belle, Martha, Niece / PAMELA GERRAND
Mrs. Cratchit, Mrs. Fezziwig, laundress /
ELLEN HORST
Boy Scrooge, apprentice Scrooge, Peter Cratchit/
IAN PALMER
Belinda Cratchit, Child Ignorance /
BECKY CLARKE
Belinda Cratchit, Child Ignorance /
ROBYN PALMER
Tiny Tim, Child Want / OLIVER JUPP,
SIMON NAYLOR
Boy Caroler, apprentice Dick, boy who brings
turkey / JASON McINTOSH

The Choir: All Saints Cathedral
Junior Choir / MICHAEL COWIE,
KAREN FRANCIS, ROY FRANCIS,
ELIZABETH PIERCE, RACHEL PERKYNS,
ANDREW ROBSON, JESSICA ROGERS,
SARA ROGERS

As Cairns says, the first season was about ghettos: "the gay ghetto" in *Torch Song Trilogy,* with a brilliant virtuoso performance by Maxim Mazumdar; "the straight sexual ghetto" in *Sexual Perversity in Chicago;* and "the ghetto of poverty and cultural deprivation" in *Cold Comfort.* Cairns considers the photograph of Joe Rutten as Floyd in Jim Garrard's play, sitting alone on an army-style cot, rolling a cigarette, captures the essence of what he was trying to do with alternative theatre. He pays a high tribute to Rutten, "one of the finest actors in the country." He is critical of Richard Ouzounian's move of the second stage to the Dunn Theatre at Dalhousie University, saying that "it changed the basic premise of what the theatre was meant to be," but as we shall see in the next chapter, Ouzounian had little choice, because even while Kerr was theatre director, and even if the Cunard Street Theatre was filled, Neptune North was losing money. Kerr did compensate for a $12,000 loss on Neptune North with three extra mainstage performances, and considers the second stage should have been tried for at least three years to give it a chance to break even.

Kerr attached great importance to Neptune's continuing educational role. He retained John Neville's policy of appointing an artist-in-residence when the promising Nova Scotian playwright Cindy Cowan joined Neptune's staff in 1985. With the assistance of the Nova Scotia government he began an Apprentice Directors' Programme in 1983 to encourage professional training through on-the-job experience for potential directors. The first three successful candidates were Carol Chrisjohn, Michael Howell and Johanna Mercer. He brought Irene Watts back to revitalize the Young Neptune touring company, which performed her own play *The Rainstone* and Dennis Foon's *New Canadian Kid.* Then in successive seasons Carol Chrisjohn and Bob Paisley gained experience from directing the programme. Graduates were recruited from Dalhousie University's professional training programme.

Jennette White was one of the former Dalhousie students Tom Kerr picked to work with the young company. She describes how she played the role of the Bag Lady in Rex Deverell's *Melody*

▶
Among Neptune North's more experimental productions at Cunard Street Theatre was Jim Garrard's **Cold Comfort**. Director Glen Cairns considers that this picture of Joseph Rutten captures the essence of what he was trying to achieve with the alternative theatre.

▼
The curtain call for one of Neptune's warmest and most satisfying Christmas productions, **A Christmas Carol**. Among those taking a bow are (centre stage) Maxim Mazumdar as Dickens, Jerry Etienne as Bob Cratchit and David Brown as Scrooge. The revolving set was designed by Andrew Murray.

CHILDREN OF A LESSER GOD

by Mark Medoff
directed by Charles McFarland
apprentice director Martin Millerchip
set design by Andrew Murray
costumes by Sharrie Ann Dial
lighting by Bob Reinholt

Sarah Norman / MARY BETH BARBER
James Leeds / JOHN WRIGHT
Orin Dennis / DAVID McKNIGHT
Mr. Franklin / SUDSY CLARK
Mrs. Norman / JOAN GREGSON
Lydia / LORI DOLOMONT
Edna Klein / WANDA GRAHAM

EVITA

lyrics by Tim Rice
music by Andrew Lloyd Webber
directed by Richard Ouzounian
musical director Rick Fox
set and lighting by Stephen Degenstein
costumes by Janice Lindsay

Eva / JAYNE LEWIS
Che / ALFIE ZAPPACOSTA
Peron / RICHARD HURST
Peron's mistress / JANET MacEWEN
Magaldi / BLAINE PARKER
The Company:
JERRY ETIENNE, PAMELA GERRAND,
ELLEN HORST, DANIEL KASH,
LEE MacDOUGALL, JIM PETRIE,
JENNETTE WHITE, SHAWN WRIGHT,
CLARY CROFT, ROBERT FREDERICKSON,
MARY KELLY, MARY KNICKLE
Musicians / JOHN ALPHONSE, RICK FOX,
BOB HEWUS, SCOTT MACMILLAN, PAUL
SIMONS

▲
*Another popular musical of this period was the Webber-Rice **Evita**, based on the life of Eva Peron of Argentina. Jayne Lewis portrays Eva and Alfie Zappacosta (back right) Che Guevara. Between them is Jerry Etienne and in front are Blaine Parker and Lee MacDougall.*

Meets the Bag Lady. The Bag Lady is a strange character who asks the children "Will you be my friend?" At one school a child in a mentally disabled class who had a social problem and wouldn't talk or form an association with anybody was the only child to put up his hand and say, "I'll be your friend." He could identify with the Bag Lady because she was so different from everyone else. At another school a child with braces on both legs joined by a bar said the same: it made Jennette want to cry, but she had to go on with the play.

▲

*Jennette White, playing the title role in Rex Deverell's **Melody Meets The Bag Lady**, for school audiences, found the experience to be a particularly moving one: here she is with other Young Neptune players Nora Sheehan, Roy Cameron and Mike Balser.*

VICTORY

by Tom MacDonnell
directed by Tom Kerr
assisted by Glen Cairns
set and lighting by Stephen Degenstein
costumes by Hal Forbes
choral director & pianist Monique Gusset

George / DAVID BROWN
Nell / FLORENCE PATERSON
Andrew / GLENN N. WHITE
Maddie / JANET MacEWAN
Hup / LEE MacDOUGALL
Cully / JERRY ETIENNE
Ken / SHAWN WRIGHT
Allison / PAMELA GERRAND

WELCOME TO THE PLANET

by Ann Mortifee
directed by Tom Kerr
set and lighting by Stephen Degenstein
costumes by Sharrie-Ann Dial
sound created by Greg Pauker

Singer / ANN MORTIFEE
Dancer / LOUISE HOYT
Musicians / PAUL BURTON, TOM HAZLITT,
ROBBIE KING, BILL SAMPLE, RENE WORST

A STREETCAR NAMED DESIRE

by Tennessee Williams
directed by Tom Kerr
set and lighting by Ted Roberts
costumes by Hal Forbes

Stanley / KIM COATES
Stella / MARCIA KASH
Eunice / ELLEN HORST
Blanche / WENNA SHAW
Steve / DANIEL KASH
Pablo / WALTER BORDEN
Mitch / JERRY ETIENNE
Young Collector / MARK STEVENS
Doctor / MARTIN MILLERCHIP
Nurse / RUTH OWEN

THE BLACK BONSPIEL
OF WULLIE MacCRIMMON

by W.O. Mitchell
directed by Glen Cairns
set and costumes by Robert Doyle
lighting by David Ingraham

Charlie Brown / BILL CARR
Wullie MacCrimmon / DON HARRON
Clock / KELLY HANDEREK
O. Cloutie / MAXIM MAZUMDAR
Annie Brown / CATHERINE McKINNON
Judas Iscariot / MARTIN MILLERCHIP
Guy Fawkes / SCOTT OWEN
Malleable Charlie Brown / JOSEPH RUTTEN
Reverend Pringle / GLENN WHITE
Macbeth / SHAWN WRIGHT

● ● ● ● ● ● ● ● ● ● ● ● ● ●
NEPTUNE NORTH
at Cunard Street Theatre
● ● ● ● ● ● ● ● ● ● ● ● ● ●

TORCH SONG TRILOGY

by Harvey Fierstein
co-directed by Tom Kerr and Glen Cairns
lighting consultant David Ingraham
pianist Andrew Hains Gigeroff

Arnold / MAXIM MAZUMDAR
Ed / DAVID McKNIGHT
Lady Blues & Ma / ELLEN HORST
Laurel / PAM STEVENSON
Alan / GLEN CAIRNS
David / MARK STEVENS

COLD COMFORT

by Jim Garrard
directed by Glen Cairns
lighting by Chris Sprague
set design by Glen Cairns and
Kevin Moore

Floyd / JOSEPH RUTTEN
Dolores / GIZELE NOFTLE
Stephen / BOB PAISLEY

Another important innovation of Tom Kerr's was the foundation of Neptune Theatre School in 1983. Irene Watts first joined with Tom to set the school going, then by the second year classes were under the instruction of Dorothy Ward and Bob Paisley. "I strongly emphasize theatre training for young people as it is an activity that will enhance other areas of study and creativity," said Kerr in September 1984. "The fact that the school has doubled would indicate that it was needed in the community and it is being welcomed by both parent and student." Classes were offered in Story Theatre, Beginning Acting, and Adult and Professional Training, covering all aspects of basic stage technique. Each year the school has developed and it is still flourishing today.

Denise Rooney says that John Neville with his flamboyant manner was a difficult act to follow at Neptune, but Tom Kerr in his quieter way impressed everyone who met him with the high quality of his work and his constant help for people throughout the province. Eva Moore describes how on many occasions she called on Tom to work with the Nova Scotia Drama League: "There wasn't a chilly church hall he wouldn't go to as adjudicator," she says, "sometimes listening to and watching work that was of poor quality, but always being positive and encouraging." The bonds between Neptune and the N.S.D.L. were strongly reinforced at this time, and Tom also taught courses and gave workshops for the League. He taught speech at Dalhousie University Theatre Department, judged a beauty contest in Dartmouth, directed the musical comedy *I Do! I Do!* at Dartmouth Sportsplex in aid of the Dartmouth General Hospital, attended many functions for the Chamber of Commerce in his capacity as Neptune theatre director, and accommodated the Atlantic Theatre Conference at Neptune in 1985.

After the projected new waterfront Art Gallery of Nova Scotia/Neptune Theatre complex was put on hold, board president Jackie Oland went to Ottawa to talk to Gaston Blais of the Department of Communications. Blais returned the visit to Neptune at the time of Kerr's opening repertory. "If you tell me

▲

W.O. Mitchell's **The Black Bonspiel of Wullie McCrimmon** revealed many comic talents: directing operations is the late Maxim Mazumdar (second from left) as the devil disguised as O. Cloutie, leading astray the gullible Bill Carr, Kelly Handerek, Don Harron, Joseph Rutten and Glenn White.

▶

Another classic American drama, Tennessee Williams' **A Streetcar Named Desire**, shows Blanche Dubois (Wenna Shaw, centre) causing strife between her sister Stella (Marcia Kash) and brother-in-law Stanley (Kim Coates). Coates has since played this role on Broadway.

**SEXUAL PERVERSITY
IN CHICAGO**

*by David Mamet
directed with sound design by
Glen Cairns
light design by Kevin Moore*

Bernard / JOHN DARTT
Danny / PAUL D. SMITH
Joan / KATE ROSE
Deb / CATHY O'CONNELL

A SERMON

*by David Mamet
directed by Maxim Mazumdar*

Preacher / JERRY ETIENNE

LUNCHTIME THEATRE

A LITTLE LIGHT MUSIC

by Rene Taylor & Joseph Bologna

DON HARRON, MAXIM MAZUMDAR,
CATHERINE McKINNON

you're doing that I'll believe you," he said. "But I don't think it's possible to do it on that stage." Billy Joe MacLean, new provincial Minister of Culture, was very interested and extremely supportive, backed up by a solid deputy in Louis Stephen. Money was provided for Brian Arnott Associates/Novita Ltd. of Toronto to do a study which would consider three options: proceed with the waterfront plan; stay put on the present site and redevelop the existing building; or redevelop with the addition of a 200-seat second stage. Kerr said at the time that the waterfront plan was a wonderful idea, but the operating costs put it out of immediate range. He was surprised at the suggestions of renovations because of the inherent structural weaknesses of the existing building, but the second option was the cheapest and the most likely to materialize. In its twenty-sixth season Neptune is still awaiting a development plan for a newly renovated building.

When John Neville invited Tom Kerr to direct the Third Stage at Stratford in 1986 he left reluctantly, though what he was being offered was very important to him personally. "Neptune has been a highlight in my career," he said. "I think it is one of Canada's great theatres, in a marvellous city, and it is experiencing very exciting times. Currently there is a great potential for development in both the building and programmes offered by the theatre." At the time he left, the theatre was artistically strong, had had some record-breaking attendances, and had strengthened its place in the community with the educational programmes he established. He felt he had gained considerable audience trust, and had he stayed on "would have wished for a half season of an acting ensemble playing in rep.; perhaps a major Shakespeare, a *Peer Gynt* and a *Mother Courage* or *Cherry Orchard,* plus three new works." He was always seeking new ideas for a theatre he had grown to love.

eight

RICHARD OUZOUNIAN

artistic director
1986 - 1988

JOSEPH AND THE AMAZING TECHNICOLOR DREAMCOAT

by Andrew Lloyd Webber and Tim Rice
directed by Richard Ouzounian
musical director Rick Fox
choreographed by Valerie Moore
set and lighting by Stephen Degenstein
costumes by Patrick Clark

Benjamin / TROY ADAMS
Isaacher, Butler / DOUGLAS CARRIGAN
Judah / PATRICK COFFIN
Reuben / CLARY CROFT
Wife, Ismaelite / MELANIE DOANE
Napthali / PAUL EISEN
Joseph / STEVEN FOX
Wife, Ismaelite / RONALDA M. HUTTON
Mrs. Jacob / MARY KELLY
Levi / MAX MacDONALD
Gad / PETER T. MacDONALD
Narrator / FRANK MacKAY
Simeon, Baker / JIM PETRIE
Jacob, Potiphar / NICHOLAS RICE
Wife, Mrs. Potiphar / JENNETTE WHITE
Zebulon, Pharaoh / SHAWN WRIGHT
Musicians / RICK FOX, SCOTT MACMILLAN,
BRUCE JACOBS, JOHN ALPHONSE,
DON PALMER

WHEN RICHARD OUZOUNIAN replaced Tom Kerr as artistic director of Neptune Theatre he was no stranger to Halifax audiences. He had directed several plays at the theatre since 1978, and was well known across the country for his lively and original stagings. He seemed a natural choice to follow in the tradition set by his two predecessors of mounting imaginative productions yet at the same time co-ordinating with general manager Denise Rooney to maintain a responsible fiscal policy. Many people who have met Richard have commented on his sympathy and approachability; as Joan Gregson says, his phone number is even listed in the directory, so that you can talk to him at any time.

Ouzounian's first two seasons have exemplified his policy of giving opportunities to as many local performers as possible, while bringing in artists of national reputation to perform in or design selected plays. He began his tenure by following up his successful production of *Evita* the previous year with another Lloyd Webber-Rice musical, *Joseph and the Amazing Technicolor Dreamcoat*. In the programme Ouzounian said he wanted to start with a "bright, fresh, exciting show," but particularly to "make use of the large and varied bank of talent here in Nova Scotia. I am proud to tell you that fourteen of this show's sixteen cast members are from right here in the province." Rick Fox returned as musical director, and the lively and talented cast was led by Frank MacKay as the Narrator and Shawn Wright as the Elvis-like Pharaoh. In the other large-scale musical, *A Funny Thing Happened on the Way to the Forum,* Ouzounian

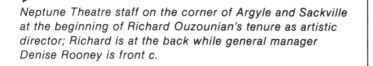

Neptune Theatre staff on the corner of Argyle and Sackville at the beginning of Richard Ouzounian's tenure as artistic director; Richard is at the back while general manager Denise Rooney is front c.

▼

Ouzounian's first production, the Webber-Rice **Joseph and the Amazing Technicolor Dreamcoat**, repeated his success with Evita. The brothers fail to recognize Joseph (Steven Fox, l.) when he puts them to the test in Egypt.

WHO'S AFRAID OF VIRGINIA WOOLF?

by Edward Albee
directed by Robin Phillips
set and costumes by Sue LePage
lighting by Louise Guinand

Martha / SUSAN WRIGHT
George / ALLAN GRAY
Honey / CAMILLE MITCHELL
Nick / KIMBLE HALL

SALT-WATER MOON

by David French
directed by Charles McFarland
set and costumes by Andrew Murray
lighting by David Ingraham

Mary Snow / CAROL SINCLAIR
Jacob Mercer / ROBB PATERSON
Musicians / SANDY MOORE, ROBB PATERSON

TARTUFFE

by Molière
adapted by Richard Ouzounian
directed by Richard Ouzounian
set by David Ingraham
lighting by Brian Pincott
costumes by Sharrie-Ann Dial

Orgon / RODGER BARTON
Tartuffe / WALTER BORDEN
Cleante / BILL CARR
Valere / DOUG CARRIGAN
Marianne / MELANIE DOANE
M. Loyal / JOHN DUNSWORTH
Officer / JOHN FULTON
Mme. Pernelle / JOAN GREGSON
Mountie / SCOTT OWEN
Damis / BRIAN PAUL
Dorine / JUDY SAVOY
Mountie / KEN SCHWARTZ
Elmire / DEBORAH TENNANT

cast himself in the lead role of Pseudolus, but on reflection wished he hadn't, as he was beset with laryngitis halfway through the run. The musical is far from the best Sondheim and needed the comic talents of a Zero Mostel or a Frankie Howerd to carry it. Yet many of the audience enjoyed the production, and these three musicals are among the top ten most attended shows in Neptune's history.

Richard's first two seasons have been light on classics or really absorbing straight plays. He did, however, invite renowned director Robin Phillips to direct Susan Wright and Allan Gray in Albee's searing comedy *Who's Afraid of Virginia Woolf?*. Purists may have questioned his own adaptation of Molière's famous comedy *Tartuffe,* updating it as a satire on North American politics, but it was surprisingly faithful to the original, even if Rodger Barton as Orgon and Walter Borden as Tartuffe did resemble Mulroney and Reagan respectively, if not always

▲
*In preparing his 1987 adaptation of Molière's **Tartuffe**,
Richard Ouzounian clearly has Canadian politics in mind.*

◄

Neptune's second production of Albee's **Who's Afraid of Virginia Woolf?** again brought strong performances — this time by Allan Gray, Camille Mitchell, Susan Wright and Kimble Hall under Robin Phillips' direction.

▼

Is that Ronald Reagan in the centre of this picture, being entertained in Ottawa by Mila and Brian Mulroney? Look again, and you will see that it is Tartuffe (Walter Borden) who is the guest of Elmire (Deborah Tennant) and Orgon (Rodger Barton) among the company in Richard Ouzounian's production of Molière's play, which was also seen on national television.

ALICE IN WONDERLAND

by Lewis Carroll
directed by Lorne Kennedy
set and costumes by Andrew Murray
lighting by David Ingraham

Alice / MELANIE DOANE
Her sister / JENNETTE WHITE
White Rabbit / BILL CARR
Caterpillar / SHAWN WRIGHT
Duchess / JENNETTE WHITE
Cook / SHAWN WRIGHT
Cheshire Cat / CAROLINE YEAGER
Mad Hatter / DOUGLAS CARRIGAN
March Hare / BILL CARR
Dormouse / JENNETTE WHITE
Tweedledee / JENNETTE WHITE
Tweedledum / SHAWN WRIGHT
Four / DOUGLAS CARRIGAN
Six / SHAWN WRIGHT
Queen of Hearts / CAROLINE YEAGER
Ten / JENNETTE WHITE
King of Hearts / BILL CARR

DRACULA

by Hamilton Deane and John Balderston
directed by Richard Ouzounian
set and costumes by Janice Lindsay
lighting by Peter McKinnon

Miss Wells / TRACY WAMBOLT
Jonathan Harker / ROBERT DODDS
Dr. Seward / HUGH CORSTON
Abraham Van Helsing / JOHN INNES
R.M. Renfield / ROBIN MOSSLEY
Butterworth / PAUL MacLEOD
Lucy Seward / CAROLINE YEAGER
Count Dracula / LORNE KENNEDY

respectfully. Judy Savoy gave a finely timed comic performance as Dorine, Ouzounian himself directed, and the production was a box-office hit which was turned into a nationally broadcast television drama. The twenty-fifth season ended with another evergreen comedy, Noël Coward's *Blithe Spirit.*

Another adaptation of Ouzounian's which proved very popular was *Barometer Rising,* from Hugh MacLennan's celebrated novel concerning the Halifax Explosion. Performed on the seventieth anniversary of this fateful incident, it proved a fitting tribute to one of Nova Scotia's and Canada's great writers, and a worthy and faithful version of the book. If it did not always work dramatically, it was often moving, made full use of an interesting set and lighting design by Stephen Degenstein, and again gave opportunities to several local performers, in a cast led by Ian Deakin and David Renton. Jennette White considers she has done her best work in that play, in the serious role of Aunt Maria, as a contrast to comedy and musical roles. She was able to talk to Hugh MacLennan, and enjoyed speaking the "beautiful language". She does remember, however, during the last week of the run, when the victims of the explosion were walking in a circle reciting, Paul MacLeod's line "the softer rumble of human traffic" came out as "the rumble of the softer people," and the cast had great difficulty retaining the serious tone of the play.

Ouzounian's tenure has been marked by productions of Canadian plays. In the first season we saw new works by two of Canada's most experienced playwrights: David French's third play about the Mercer family, *Salt Water Moon*; and Sharon Pollock's own production of her strong and partially autobiographical *Doc.* The relationship in the latter between the New Brunswick doctor and his daughter was poignant, moving, at times raw, yet always honest. Richard was therefore specially disturbed to receive threatening phone calls and vitriolic letters about the play. One example from a letter was, "I feel sorry for your wife and daughter if you are so sick a man as to think this is a good play." Ouzounian says that it gave no trouble in New Brunswick where everyone knows the doctor "and knows he talks worse than that!" He thinks the reaction is because some of us don't like to think that people talk so frankly in a family situation like our own, whereas a play like *Equus* would provoke less shock because its situation is more remote from our experiences. It was a fine production, the cast led by notable Canadian actors Goldie Semple and Michael Ball.

The Christmas plays have also continued. In 1986 *Alice in Wonderland* proved popular with audiences, who delighted especially in the imaginative sets and costumes designed by Andrew Murray. Six actors assumed a variety of roles, Sean Wright playing Tweedledum to Jennette Wright's Tweedledee, "like demented salt and pepper shakers" according to Sean. He had plenty of time to change costumes while Jennette at one point had a ten-second change, and used a dresser backstage to help her. Sean's job was to put a bathing cap inside out on her head in the dark and stuff her hair inside it. On one occasion the cap remained the right way out, and the audience, seeing the word "Speedo" blazoned across the cap, probably thought that Speedo was one of the sponsors. Jennette didn't know what Sean was giggling at and had a job holding her performance together. The following Christmas Bill Carr co-wrote with Stephen Naylor and starred in *Cinderella,* breaking tradition as an ugly stepbrother.

Two more new plays following *Barometer Rising* and *Cinderella* brought the number of world premières in one season to an unprecedented four. Neptune presented for one of the very few times since its early days a play written by an author living in Halifax: George Boyd's first play *Shine Boy* told the story of Halifax native George Dixon who rose to become the first black boxing world champion. Though this musical play had some rough edges it was a worthy effort and particularly important for the black community. Walter Borden, who gave one of the best performances as Geoff, Dixon's trainer, says that just as Neptune opened the doors for him to act it has done the same for Boyd as a playwright: "I feel very privileged to be in his work." He says that black people can come to the theatre and see for the first time what could be called "black theatre": theatre *about* the life of black people rather than just *for* black people.

The last world première came about by accident: the planned

DOC

by Sharon Pollock
original music by John Mills-Cockell
directed by Sharon Pollock
costumes by Hal Forbes
set and lighting by Stephen Degenstein

Ev / MICHAEL BALL
Bob / GOLDIE SEMPLE
Catherine / MARY-COLIN CHISHOLM
Katie / CAROL SINCLAIR
Oscar / LORNE KENNEDY

●●●●●●●●●●●●●●●●●●●●
● NEPTUNE NORTH ●
● at Cunard Street Theatre ●
●●●●●●●●●●●●●●●●●●●●

'NIGHT, MOTHER

by Marsha Norman
directed by Marcyanne Goldman
set and costumes by Lesley Preston
lighting and technical direction by
Chris Sprague

Thelma Cates / FLORENCE PATERSON
Jessie Cates / NICOLA LIPMAN

LA SAGOUINE

by Antonine Maillet
translation by Luis de Cespedes
directed by Linda Moore
set and costumes by Lesley Preston
lighting by Christopher G. Sprague

La Sagouine / JOAN ORENSTEIN

TALKING WITH

by Jane Martin
directed by Tracy Holmes
set and costumes by Catherine Phillips
lighting by Christopher G. Sprague
Cast:
JOAN GREGSON, JUDY SAVOY,
NICOLA LIPMAN, TRACY HOLMES,

The court of the Queen of Hearts in this Christmas adapation of **Alice in Wonderland** reveals some of the many quick costume changes required by performers Shawn Wright, Douglas Carrigan, Jennette White, Caroline Yeager and Bill Carr, while Melanie Doane (c.) as Alice looks on bemused.

The Chorus of Haligonians describe the effects of the Halifax Explosion in Richard Ouzounian's stage adaptation of Hugh MacLennan's novel **Barometer Rising**. Ian Deakin as Neil and Carol Sinclair as Penelope stand in front.

► Michael Ball (Ev), Goldie Semple (Bob), Mary-Colin Chisholm (Catherine) and Carol Sinclair (Katie) in Sharon Pollock's own production of her play, **Doc**. The character of Ev was modelled on her own father. The play caused threatening phone calls and vitriolic letters.

▼ Richard Ouzounian (c.) took the central role of Pseudolus in the Sondheim musical **A Funny Thing Happened on the Way to the Forum**. Valerie Moore directed, with designs by Patrick Clark.

25th SEASON

September 1987–May 1988

**A FUNNY THING HAPPENED
ON THE WAY TO THE FORUM**

book by Burt Shevelove and Larry Gelbart
music and lyrics by Stephen Sondheim
directed by Valerie Moore
set and costumes by Patrick Clark
lighting by Brian Pincott
musical director Paul Simons

Protean 2 / TROY ADAMS
Philia / ELIZABETH BEELER
Erronius / WALTER BORDEN
Protean 1 / DOUGLAS CARRIGAN
Senex / SUDSY CLARK
Hysterium / CLARY CROFT
Gymnasia / MELANIE DOANE
Femina / CHRISTINE GLEN
Geminae 1 / CAMILLE JAMES
Lycus / MAX MacDONALD
Miles Gloriosus / FRANK MacKAY
Pseudolus / RICHARD OUZOUNIAN
Vibrata / CAROLINE SCHILLER
Geminae 2 / CARRIE SPARKS
Protean 3 / RON WHEATLEY
Domina / JENNETTE WHITE
Hero / SHAWN WRIGHT
Musicians / JOHN ALPHONSE,
HOLLY ARSENAULT, PAUL SIMONS

production, Athol Fugard's *The Road to Mecca,* sadly disappeared from Halifax after a disagreement with Centaur Theatre of Montreal about what should have been a joint production, and with it those two sterling performers Joan Orenstein and Nicola Lipman. In its place Neptune offered *Olde Charlie Farquharson's Testament . . . And Magic Lantern Show,* with book and lyrics by Don Harron and Frank Peppiatt. The humour of Bill Carr's pre-performance ad-libbing with the audience and the wit of Lynn Johnston's cartoons could hardly make up for the high-school standard of humour of the show or its whisker-growing jokes, but the talents of Carr, Don Harron and Catherine McKinnon kept the audience amused.

Life has become a little easier for the Blackmores since the workshop and storage facility at Creighton Street was found in 1987. "Until then we had [scenery and props] in warehouses all over the city," says John. "Sometimes we save the whole set, hoping we can sell it to a theatre which hasn't got its own shop. We've been saving standard pieces, fireplaces, windows, doors; the rest we throw out or give away . . . The set I'm creating now — for *Blithe Spirit* — is as difficult as any to make, because it's realistic. It includes French doors, moulding, fireplaces and bookcases. Everything is practical. In a Noël Coward play we have to make everything look precisely right, to suit that character of the play. In 'kitchen sink' drama, on the other hand, you have to make everything look dirty and grungy. When you talk to the designer, you get a kind of feeling for the set he wants. On the average, it takes about three weeks to build a set. And we know the measurements of the Neptune stage, which isn't very big, by heart after all these years." Now he works at Creighton Street John misses meeting members of the cast.

Ouzounian was able to retain one season of Neptune North productions at Cunard Street. They were all plays for women: Florence Paterson and Nicola Lipman starred in Marsha Norman's *'Night, Mother*; Joan Gregson, Nicola Lipman, Judy Savoy and Tracy Holmes played in Jane Martin's *Talking With*; and Joan Orenstein gave a strong performance as an Acadian charwoman in Antoine Maillet's *La Sagouine*. As the Cunard

Street theatre became no longer economically viable, the only second stage production of the next season, Kent Stetson's *Warm Wind in China,* which concerned a victim of AIDS, attracted much attention and played to packed houses at the Dunn Theatre. Kent, who had been Neptune's playwright-in-residence, touched a nerve in the community and wrote a moving play on this sensitive subject. Eric Steiner's splendid direction drew fine performances from Timothy Webber, Peter Krantz, and — appropriately for Neptune's twenty-fifth season — Joan Gregson and David Renton reunited as the anguished parents.

Both the Young Neptune company and the Theatre School have continued to flourish. Irene Watts again directed the company, in its eighth year in 1986, in a touring repertoire that included *Story Book Theatre/The World of Pooh* for the youngest children and *Not So Dumb* by John Lazarus, about children with learning disabilities. Among the company were Robin Mossley, Gizele Noftle and Martin Surette. The next year Jennette White led the company of Troy Adams, Doug Carrigan, Melanie Doane and Camille James in a musical version of the King Arthur story by Richard Ouzounian and for older students *The Fitness Show* by Jim Biros and Peter Gibson.

Richard also asked Jennette to take over the Theatre School. He chose her because she had worked with the school's founder, Irene Watts, and had had much experience with young people as well as a sound record of administrative experience. She speaks highly of working with Richard, as he is full of life, says what he thinks and gives you the chance to try again when you make a mistake. He gives the theatre an essentially human quality and is always easy to talk to and seek advice from. In the school you can learn while having fun, she says. She cites in particular the 13 to 17-year-old performing class, whose last show, *Surviving the Thought,* was about youth suicide. A child of seven who was heard chanting the word "suicide" gave the theme for the play which the children wrote in groups; all knew of a friend or someone near who had committed suicide. In the course of the play the letters of the word "suicide" changed to those of "survive". The school offers classes not only for children but for

BAROMETER RISING

by Hugh MacLennan
adapted by Richard Ouzounian
directed by Richard Ouzounian
set and lighting by Stephen Degenstein
costumes by Hal Forbes

Mary, Mrs. Stevens, Nanny /
ELIZABETH BEELER
Evelyn, Sadie, Woman / BURGANDY CODE
Neil / IAN DEAKIN
Alec / LIONEL DOUCETTE
Alfred, Eliot, Captain, Soldier 2 /
JOHN DUNSWORTH
Jim, Policeman / MICHAEL KEATING
Roddie / ROBIN LINDSAY
Simon, corpse / JOHN LUNMAN
Soldier 1, officer / PAUL MacLEOD
Angus / GRAHAM McPHERSON
Geoffrey Wain / DAVID RENTON
Penelope / CAROL SINCLAIR
Maria, flower girl / JENNETTE WHITE

CINDERELLA

by Bill Carr and Steven Naylor
directed by Charles McFarland
musical director Steven Naylor
set and costumes by Patrick Clark
lighting by Brian Pincott

Cindy, Cinderella / ELIZABETH BEELER
Bruce, Bruscilda / BILL CARR
Luke, Lucretia / MAX MacDONALD
Martha, Fairy Godmother / JUDY SAVOY
Mother, Stepmother / JENNETTE WHITE
Paperboy, Page, Prince / SHAWN WRIGHT
Hamster / BEAST ZELLER
Musicians / STEVEN NAYLOR,
JOHN ALPHONSE, SCOTT MACMILLAN

◄

Shine Boy by Halifax playwright George Boyd was one of four world premières in the 1987-88 season. Playing here are John Dartt, Walter Borden, Caroline Schiller, Troy Adams, Douglas Carrigan, Dougie Richardson as boxing champion George Dixon, Camille James and Melanie Doane.

▼

Neptune celebrated the centenary of Conan Doyle's famous detective in 1987 with its production of **Sherlock Holmes and The Curse of The Sign of Four**: Joseph Rutten, Mary-Colin Chisholm, Graham MacPherson, Michael Keating, Maxim Mazumdar, Lionel Doucette and Paul MacLeod are in the tableau.

adults who are beginners or who would like to improve their skills. It is becoming one of Neptune's most valuable community services.

It is extraordinary how Richard Ouzounian has in the past two years frequently triumphed over adversity. He is the first to admit that performance standards have not always been as high as he would like to see. The explanation is not artistic but economic. Sometimes less experienced actors have been offered leading roles. While the Canadian Actors' Equity Association has given its members improved conditions and benefits over the years, it is sometimes difficult for theatre companies to finance productions with many Equity performers. The Association has gradually cut down the number of non-union players allowed in a production, and next year it will be as low as 20%. Even if an actor has only three lines, it becomes very expensive if he or she is a union member.

The season's playbill has demanded some compromises. When Ouzounian came to Neptune with high hopes he had been led to believe that there was no deficit. He soon found that there was a considerable accumulated deficit, partly from losses on the *Don Messer* tour and Neptune North. A change in the fiscal year revealed an accidental accounting error associated with provincial grants that had lain dormant for about twelve years; nobody is to blame for this unexpected item, but it has added to the total deficit. The grants from the three levels of government have been frozen for five to six years, while overheads and operating costs have risen astronomically. The financial support from the city is one of the lowest in the country: Neptune's budget is 75% of the Manitoba Theatre Centre's, yet the M.T.C. gets 600% from Winnipeg of what Neptune gets from Halifax.

To put on a two-character play for three and a half weeks costs about $55,000, whereas an eight-character play would cost another $25,000, while a big musical could be up to $100,000. For that reason it is economically impossible to stage many large-cast plays. At the same time Neptune must fill 86% of seats to break even: it is one of the highest rates in the country, compared with a 70-71% figure for the M.T.C., Vancouver Playhouse or Grand

SHERLOCK HOMES AND THE CURSE OF THE SIGN OF FOUR

by Dennis Rosa
directed by Richard Ouzounian
set and lighting by Stephen Degenstein
costumes by Hal Forbes

Mary Morstan / MARY-COLIN CHISHOLM
Inspector Lestrade / LIONEL DOUCETTE
Sherlock Holmes / MICHAEL KEATING
Wiggins / PAUL MacLEOD
Thaddeus Sholto / MAXIM MAZUMDAR
Dr. Watson / GRAHAM McPHERSON
Jonathan Small / JOSEPH RUTTEN

SHINE BOY

by George Boyd
music and lyrics by George Boyd
arrangements by Scott Macmillan
directed by Lorne Kennedy
set by William Chesney
costumes by Hal Forbes
lighting by Stephen Ross
musical director Scott Macmillan
choreography by Linda Elliott

Dizzy / TROY ADAMS
Kitty O'Rourke / ELIZABETH BEELER
Geoff / WALTER BORDEN
Elmer / LUCKY CAMPBELL
Porter / DOUGLAS CARRIGAN
Tommy O'Rourke / JOHN DARTT
Company Members / MELANIE DOANE,
CAMILLE JAMES
Sonny / LEONARD KANE
George Dixon / DOUGIE RICHARDSON
Rae / CAROLINE SCHILLER
Musicians / JOHN ALPHONSE, SCOTT
MACMILLAN, STEVEN NAYLOR, DANIEL
PARKER

OLDE CHARLIE FARQUHARSON'S TESTAMENT & MAGIC LANTERN SHOW

by Don Harron and Frank Peppiatt
music by Jimmy Dale
drawings by Lynn Johnston
directed by Frank Peppiatt
set by Mark Buntrock
lighting by David Ingraham
costumes by Patricia Walton

Orville Farquharson / BILL CARR
Charlie Farquharson / DON HARRON
Valeda Farquharson / CATHERINE McKINNON
Voice / CATHY O'CONNELL

BLITHE SPIRIT

by Noël Coward
directed by Richard Ouzounian
set and costumes by Janice Lindsay
lighting by Brian Pincott

Mrs. Bradman / MARY CLANCY
Madame Arcati / JOAN GREGSON
Edith / SHARON KLINE
Charles / BRIAN McKAY
Ruth / IRIS QUINN
Doctor Bradman / DAVID RENTON
Elvira / CAROLINE YEAGER

NEPTUNE NORTH

WARM WIND IN CHINA

by Kent Stetson
directed by Eric Steiner
set by Peter Perina
lighting by Bob Reinholdt
costumes by Patricia Walton

Slater / TIMOTHY WEBBER
Davis / PETER KRANTZ
Elna Slater / JOAN GREGSON
Jack Slater / DAVID RENTON

Theatre, London, Ontario. Those theatres have 250 more seats than Neptune, higher ticket prices, and better support from the province. Eighty-six percent is a *scary* figure, says Ouzounian. Yet a comparison with two other playhouses shows that in 1987-88 the Grand Theatre employed forty-one actors and three musicians, the M.T.C. fifty-three actors and no musicians, while Neptune employed sixty-four actors and ten musicians. Neptune also had more sets, including two multiple sets, than the other theatres.

Most theatres would think it wonderful, continues Ouzounian, if they achieved the 80% box office that Neptune did for *Who's Afraid of Virginia Woolf?* or the 82% for *Doc*. But each of those shows lost $15,000-$20,000. "If we achieve the 98% we did for *Joseph* or the 97% for *Dracula* people think we have plenty of money. But we don't. And yet I get letters to say why bother to do *Dracula*?" For the centenary of Sherlock Holmes in 1987 Richard wanted to do the original William Gillette play, with five sets and a cast of nineteen, and Nicholas Pennell to play Holmes. The budget estimate was that it would cost more than any musical that would break even at 94-95%. He had instead to use a script which cost less to stage, with less experienced actors in the leading roles, though the production was helped by the splendid supporting performances of Joseph Rutten and Maxim Mazumdar. Even if the theatre achieved a constant 100% box office it could not survive on that alone.

Ouzounian has also been criticized for moving the second stage from Cunard Street Theatre to the Dunn Theatre at Dalhousie University. But again it is not economically viable to run a professional theatre company in a 150-seat theatre, even if all seats are filled. There is an audience for second-stage plays, but not enough of them for productions to break even. *Warm Wind in China* achieved a modest profit of $450 at the Dunn with its 250 seats, but some of those were empty for the beginning of the run despite the enthusiasm at the end.

Such difficulties, of course, are not peculiar to Neptune. Artistic directors of all regional theatres face similar problems of rising operating costs and frozen grants. Richard Ouzounian's achievements in two short years have been many. He has been bold enough to take risks with several new works, giving more opportunities than ever before to local playwrights. He has given many Nova Scotian actors a chance to perform in the theatre. He has mounted some enjoyable productions which have attracted almost full houses and has helped to foster relations with the community by continuing Young Neptune and the Theatre School. Expectations are high for the twenty-fifth anniversary and the forthcoming season. Once again Neptune hopes to triumph over its problems to ensure the maintenance of the high standards it has achieved through the years.

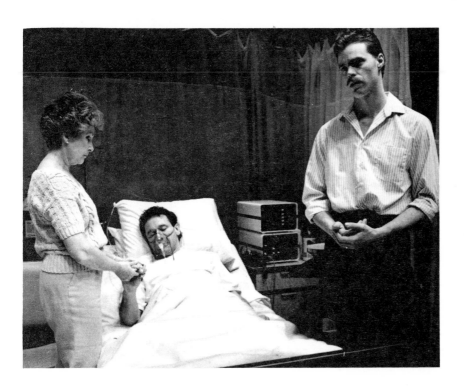

◄
Neptune North's final production, this time at the Dunn Theatre, was another world première, Kent Stetson's **Warm Wind In China**. *Eric Steiner's direction drew fine performances from Joan Gregson, Timothy Webber, Peter Krantz (seen here) and David Renton.*

The future of Neptune Theatre

ALLISTER BYRNE, president of the Neptune Theatre Foundation, finds that when his business takes him to Toronto, Winnipeg or Vancouver, one of his most delightful experiences is discovering how well Neptune Theatre is known across the country. Over twenty-five years it has grown from that initial bold experiment to become one of Canada's most highly prized and estimable theatres. The sample of tributes we are able to include at the end of this book testifies to the immense regard in which Neptune is held by the thousands of people who have worked for her as performers, directors, business managers, scenic and costume artists, stage managers, stagehands, carpenters, public relations officers, accountants, front-of-house and general office workers, and far from least board members and other volunteers who have given many hours of their time to help the theatre grow and prosper.

While artistic quality has fluctuated over the years, as it does in any comparable organization, the company has maintained on the whole a standard of excellence which is second to none for a regional theatre of its size. Some of the original vision of Leon Major has been fulfilled, even though it has proved impossible to maintain a year-round repertory company. Opportunities have frequently been given to playwrights, performers, and other artists from the province and the Atlantic region. The theatre has continued its touring tradition, even if far less expensive productions have to be toured nowadays than previously. Neptune has striven to prove that it is not a theatre just for a small audience in its capital city but that at least one mainstage production a year can be seen in some of the remotest parts of the province. At times the tour has been extended not only into Atlantic Canada but across the country. In recent years the Young Neptune company has gained strength and each year it

Costume sketch by Ken McBane
for **Charley's Aunt**, 1969

*Costume sketch by Robert Doyle, 1973, for **Peer Gynt***

visits schools throughout the province to stimulate the art of theatre among young people as an exciting and meaningful educational experience.

Neptune Theatre has striven to remove the elitist image that has dogged it since that gala opening, exciting as it was, on July 1, 1963. It is increasingly attempting to go further into the community to attract people from all walks of life, not just the wealthy and intellectuals. Richard Ouzounian continues the tradition of artistic directors who have sought to maintain a fine balancing line between popular, commercial entertainment and more intellectually stimulating fare. On several occasions a second stage has offered us more challenging and experimental drama, but it is constantly frustrated by economic problems and cannot survive without a more regular, consistent means of financial support. The popular lunchtime theatre started by John Neville is no longer economically viable. In spite of such difficulties there is a broader cross-section of the community attending the theatre today, many productions boast a higher than 90% attendance rate, and it is breaking down former barriers to reach out to such people as members of the black community, who may previously have been given the false impression that they were not welcome at arts organizations. Neptune's Theatre School, started by Tom Kerr, is still gaining strength and offering training in theatre not only to many young people but also to more mature members of the community.

Despite its continued excellence, Neptune Theatre is currently on hold. All arts organizations have to face the economic realities of their times. Never in its history has there been a limitless source of funding for the theatre. On many occasions there have been financial crises. In its early years the large-scale, exciting repertory seasons of Leon Major had to be guided by restraint, first by the controlling hands of Heinar Piller and John Hobday, who implemented the subscription campaigns and with the help of government grants managed to balance the books. Robert Sherrin maintained sound finances, but when John Wood mounted lavish and exciting productions restraint once again slipped away. John Neville's astute management

◂
These young performers are enjoying every minute of their Neptune Theatre School acting class. The "let's create" class for children aged 10-12 is one of many taught every year since 1983.

wiped out the large accumulated deficit, and he instituted a more fully responsible fiscal policy of high-quality artistic work modified by financial responsibility under the partnership of theatre director and general manager. In the latter role the ever-dependable Denise Rooney held the fort 1980-1988, in amicable association with Neville's successors Tom Kerr and Richard Ouzounian.

While the three levels of government have given continuous support to Neptune over twenty-five years, Al Byrne considers that the days are gone when the theatre can expect to rely so much on government handouts. For more than five years government grants have stood still while the theatre overheads have risen significantly. The twenty-fifth anniversary will be an opportunity for us to take stock of the situation. It is not the government's theatre, he says, not the board's, but the public's. The public, professions and businesses must join to support its theatre, as there is no other source of revenue. The box office has done its share, and ticket prices can be raised only so far. The rest is up to us.

The next three to five years will be very important in the life of Neptune. "We must continue to put on first-rate, top-quality theatre," says Byrne, "but at the same time we have to sell ourselves better. We have to come to the community and businesses and say, *We're here to serve you, in more ways than your just coming to the theatre six or eight times a season. This theatre makes a contribution to the community.*" Judging by his experiences of working for a national business company, Byrne knows that if employees are moving to Halifax, St. John's or Saint John, they will ask about schools and about the social life involving the arts. They know that a flourishing professional theatre company is an essential part of the community.

Many people will share my personal disappointment that the three levels of government and the private sector did not come together to make the Neptune Theatre/Art Gallery of Nova Scotia a reality, and to maintain a level of subsidy that could keep such an ambitious project going, even with the increased operating costs. It needed courage, determination and imagination to take such a bold step, and to create that wonderful building on the waterfront instead of soulless and often empty office blocks. Such a venture would have provided a major attraction to help bring more business to the city and to attract thousands more visitors every year. Its failure makes it even more imperative that the present aging building should be attractively restored and expanded with the purchase of adjacent property.

Byrne is conscious of treading warily, as all arts organizations equally need funding. Co-operation is needed between them, not rivalry. He has been working closely with the executive of Symphony Nova Scotia, and they agree that they need to be supportive of each other, as they are serving largely the same audiences, and are not in competition but partners.

The artistic growth of Neptune in the years to come is, in Byrne's view, dependent on four conditions:

(1) The physical aspects of the theatre need to be improved. If it is to progress it needs to expand its stage, seating, dressing room and lounge areas. Byrne considers that a 600-650 seat theatre would serve our needs for the next ten to fifteen years. The property on an adjacent site, at the back of the City Club building, has now been acquired by the City of Halifax, with funding support from the province. A task force, with representatives from the city and the province, is to be set up to study the best use of the property, ideally for arts-related activities. Neptune Theatre is one of several arts organizations that will have major input into the study. Both the provincial and city governments have been very supportive of Neptune's position.

(2) We have to *insist* that we retain a level of excellence on stage that rivals anywhere else in the country. This will mean maintaining Neptune's traditional qualities and not letting them slip.

(3) The theatre has to become even more involved in the community and to spend more time outside Halifax. One touring production is not enough. We have the responsibility to bring the best of the theatre to other parts of the province.

(4) We need to develop an endowment that the operating budget won't allow us. This would give us funding to improve the size and quality of mainstage productions and give us a second stage for more experimental work.

I would like to add a fifth condition. Neptune has for several years now done nothing for the multitude of visitors that flock to the province's capital city every summer. Denise Rooney maintains that a summer season *could* be run — and after all, Neptune began with summer seasons and ran them regularly for several years. One difficulty, apart from lack of additional funding and ever increasing operating costs, is that seasons have to be planned about three years in advance to fit in with programmes of tour operators. Bus tours move on after basic sites have been covered, but Neptune could provide an incentive to attract tourists while they are here. Denise warns us, though, that after a successful start *Debut and Encore* flagged badly when a summer run was attempted in 1983. Such an experience

Costume sketch by Robert Doyle, 1978, for **Othello**

▲

*Neptune Theatre's twenty-sixth season opened with Richard Ouzounian's production of Shakespeare's **A Midsummer Night's Dream**, last seen at the theatre in 1971. Titania (Caroline Yeager) caresses Bottom (Kelly Handerek).*

demands planning far ahead so that organized tours will take Neptune in as part of their regular activities.

Richard Ouzounian sees that his immediate goal is to present some high quality theatre in the 1988-89 year. Though in reality it will be Neptune's twenty-sixth season, the actual twenty-fifth anniversary date is July 1, 1988, so celebrations will continue in the following year. *A Midsummer Night's Dream,* the first Shakespearean production for four years, is balanced by Jerome Kilty's *Dear Liar,* a dramatization of G.B. Shaw's correspondence with Mrs. Patrick Campbell. Two award-winning Canadian plays are featured: Sharon Pollock's *Blood Relations* and Tom Wood's *B-Movie — the Play.* There is a world première — the musical *Take Twelve* by David Overton and John Arnold, and the season is capped by Ira Levin's long-running Broadway thriller, *Deathtrap.*

In spite of all the problems Neptune's character and strength have traditionally been founded on its will to survive, as it has survived for twenty-five years. But it is up to us, the public, to give it all the support we can. At the same time Neptune would like to feel it has the full backing of the government, even if it cannot be given much higher funding. If grants would increase annually just to cover the cost of living it would be a start. But above all, as John Neville said, "Attitudes have to change." Richard Ouzounian says that sometimes previous ministers of culture have shown comparatively little interest in Neptune. Now attitudes *are* changing. Both Richard Ouzounian and Allister Byrne speak highly of the support of the Hon. Brian Young when he was Minister of Tourism and Culture, and of his deputy, Bob Geraghty. There are high hopes that the Hon. Roland Thornhill, who took over Mr. Young's portfolio in December 1988, will continue this support.

In terms of operating costs for salaries and overheads there has been zero growth in funding for many years. Yet expenses such as salaries have grown enormously. Neptune is now big business in the city, with a payroll in excess of $1,000,000 annually. There is also constant competition to get the best actors and designers, and if they are found they have be paid according to their merit. When the government has been needed it has been supportive for essential repairs. For example, when in the winter of 1988 urgent roof and furnace repairs were required, the three levels of government combined to provide $150,000. But these are stop-gap measures. It will be an uphill battle for Neptune to keep up with rising costs and to overcome its deficit. Government funding, which was once over 75% of the total budget, is now less than 50%.

Unlike many theatres, however, Neptune has one great asset: it owns its building. The regularly increasing box-office returns, with a very high proportion of seats sold for every production, ensure that the company is doing everything in its power to overcome the obstacles that threaten the maintenance of highest professional standards. The way that members of the public can best help Neptune is in the first place to make sure that they support it by renewing or starting subscriptions: in that way Neptune can know in advance how much support it can depend on in planning its seasons. An additional means of support is a tax-deductible donation. May we all take this opportunity of the twenty-fifth anniversary celebrations for a concerted effort to see that Neptune remains one of Canada's best loved and most esteemed theatre companies.

Whatever efforts are made in this direction, Neptune needs to retain a strong leadership at the top. This book has reviewed the many varied qualities of successive artistic directors who have applied their creative imagination to fostering the theatre's progress. The Board's recent announcement that Tom Kerr will replace Richard Ouzounian as guest artistic director for one year recalls David Renton's successful year at standing in for John Neville until he was able to take over. But it also means that however successful Tom Kerr is Neptune Theatre will be marking time. The theatre could flounder if there is no artistic growth. The Board has a heavy responsibility to see that whoever is appointed to a more permanent position in 1990 possesses that rare combination of artistic vision and administrative skill to guide the theatre ahead to an even more prominent position than it holds today.

Tributes

from
representatives
of government

Hon. Alan R. Abraham
Lieutenant-Governor
1984-1988

As Honorary Patron of the Neptune Theatre Foundation, I am pleased to take this opportunity to extend best wishes on the occasion of Neptune's twenty-fifth anniversary.

Neptune has become one of the premier regional theatres in Canada during its quarter of a century operation and, during that time, has proven itself most beneficial to our community, not only by keeping the cultural life of Nova Scotia alive and well but also by using local talent for many and various skills.

Her Honour and I have attended and supported Neptune Theatre for many years and we extend best wishes to both performers and audiences for a 1988-89 season of pleasure and success.

Flora MacDonald
Federal Minister of Communication
1986-1988

I am pleased to congratulate the Neptune Theatre on its 25th anniversary. I would also like to take this opportunity to extend my warmest greetings to all the theatre lovers who will be attending the activities during this year of celebration.

The 25 years of the Neptune Theatre have witnessed a success which can be attributed to its dedicated workers, talented artists and supportive audiences.

As Minister responsible for arts and culture in Canada, I deeply appreciate the outstanding contribution the Neptune has made to helping the performing arts flourish in Nova Scotia. The influence of its cultural offerings, full of creativity and imagination, will surely support the development and growth of our Canadian cultural life and stimulate the public's appreciation of the vitality of the performing arts.

I would like to offer my best wishes to the Neptune Theatre for a very happy 25th anniversary. May your success continue for many years to come.

Stewart McInnes
M.P. for Halifax
1984-1988

My congratulations on this, the silver anniversary of Neptune Theatre. Since its inception in the summer of 1963, Neptune Theatre has been a credit to Halifax and to Nova Scotia. As well, I congratulate Richard Ouzounian and his staff for the past two years of exemplary production. The innovations introduced by Mr. Ouzounian plus the greater opportunities provided for local performers ably demonstrate a healthy theatre. And with the Young Neptune Players flourishing, more and more local talent should be available, not only for the parent company but for the growing number of local theatres around the province.

Again, my very sincere congratulations, and I wish Neptune well in its new season and for future decades.

Mary Clancy
M.P. for
Halifax, N.S.

It is a delight for me to be able to congratulate Neptune on its 25 years of theatrical endeavour. As a teen-ager, I delighted in the arrival of a permanent live theatre company in Halifax, and 25 years later my delight is no less.

I, of course, have a special place for Neptune since Richard Ouzounian invited me to take part in last season's *Blithe Spirit*. Being on stage in my own city with a company of the stature and professionalism of Neptune's was an experience that ranks very highly in my memory of treasured events.

While the future may seem perilous, as it often does for the arts endeavours, I know that Neptune will meet the challenge and thrive. Please be assured of my continuing support.

Hon. John M. Buchanan
Premier of
Nova Scotia

I take great pleasure in congratulating Neptune Theatre on 25 years of artistic excellence. As the dream of a first-rate professional theatre based in Halifax and serving all of Nova Scotia continues to unfold, we can all look forward to many more years of challenge and entertainment.

Neptune's international reptuation has been won by the hard work of hundreds of talented and dedicated artists, technicians, administrators and volunteers. The theatre's accomplishments are a source of pride to each and every one of us.

Over the years, Neptune has been an important source of opportunities for many talented Nova Scotian artists and technicians. Also, it has brought to our province some of Canada's most popular performers, who lived with us for a while and enriched our lives with their skills. Perhaps of greatest importance in the long term will be the chance Neptune has given to the province's playwrights to tell us stories that reflect our own lives and heritage.

To all those who have been a part of the extraordinary success of Neptune Theatre, I extend congratulations. May the second quarter century be just as rewarding.

Hon. Brian A. Young
Nova Scotia Minister of Tourism and Culture, 1987-1988

As Minister of Tourism and Culture, I would like to extend greetings and sincere congratulations to all those who have supported and worked with Neptune Theatre in its first twenty-five years. With dedication, vision and plain hard work, you have created an institution of which all Nova Scotians can be proud.

Through regional and national tours, Neptune has spread its influence far beyond its base in Halifax. The main-stage and school tours in Nova Scotia have brought the excellence of professional theatre to audiences and students in all parts of the province. Significant productions such as *Don Messer's Jubilee* by Truro's John Gray have delighted audiences from Neil's Harbour to the National Arts Centre.

Neptune has also met the challenge of keeping high quality theatre from all periods and styles before its audiences. From Sophocles' *Medea* to George Boyd's *Shine Boy,* the theatre has offered its supporters and artists the broadest spectrum of theatrical experience. Neptune's determination to present, over the years, everything from the classics to the latest local work has led to an extraordinary level of community support.

With loyal audiences, support from all three levels of government and the backing of the business and corporate communities, Neptune can look with confidence to the challenges ahead.

Vince MacLean

Leader of the
Opposition
Nova Scotia
Legislature

Congratulations to all associated with Neptune Theatre for 25 glorious years of theatre in Halifax. In that time, Neptune has become an artistic landmark, producing plays that reveal the depth of talent we have here in Nova Scotia and attracting talent from across Canada and around the world. I have enjoyed many Neptune productions over the years, and I look forward personally to enjoying many more. Once again, congratulations and best wishes for your next 25 years.

Alexa McDonough

Leader of the
Nova Scotia New
Democratic Party

Neptune Theatre's 25th anniversary is an occasion to remember twenty-five years of enlightenment, enjoyment and entertainment for thousands of Nova Scotians and visitors to our province.

Neptune has introduced so many — from school children to seniors — to the pleasure of theatre. It has offered opportunities for those with the talent to work in theatre — at the artistic level of writing, directing and performing, and at the administrative level of managing and promoting.

Neptune has helped Nova Scotians to discover and portray our own history and culture, adding to our sense of who we are. It has also exposed us to theatrical productions more universal in their expression, increasing our appreciation of human nature and our understanding of the human condition.

I hope to see the day when Neptune enjoys adequate, stable public funding within the context of a policy that sustains and fosters our Nova Scotia arts and culture.

May Neptune continue to challenge and delight us, and may it enjoy even greater success and prosperity during its next twenty-five years.

John Savage

Mayor of
Dartmouth, N.S.

The history of Neptune in Halifax is better told by people closer to the scene than myself, but one point I would like to emphasize is that Neptune belongs to the entire metropolitan area. I know that the citizens of Dartmouth join me in congratulating Neptune on 25 super years of enjoyable theatre. Criticism of professional theatre is always easy to find, but there is no doubt that the citizens of Dartmouth have enjoyed Neptune and continue to enjoy the performances on stage. We join with many others in congratulating Richard Ouzounian on the talent and ingenuity that he brings to Neptune, and we hope for many, many more years of successful theatre in metropolitan Halifax-Dartmouth. *Congratulations!*

Ron Wallace

Mayor of
Halifax, N.S.

On July 1st our Neptune Theatre will be 25 years old. This intimate little theatre in the heart of the downtown was born years before many of its patrons. For a quarter of a century Neptune has staged plays authored by such notables as Shakespeare to our own George Boyd. Outstanding directors and outstanding stage talent have filled the stage for the past 25 years. Neptune has earned a Canada-wide reputation for excellence. May the curtain soon rise on a restored Neptune with an expanded stage and attractive, spacious lounge. Neptune deserves attention, appreciation and strong support. *Happy Birthday, Neptune!*

Tributes

from
theatre artists,
administrators
and
volunteers

**David
Renton**

Leon Major's vision and grand design
for the first permament professional
year-round repertory company in
Canada has been and always will be my
ideal. I'm proud to have been a part of
this remarkable 25-year journey. I'm
looking forward to the year 2013 and
the 50th anniversary celebrations. At
79 I will be ready to repeat many of the
roles I played in my late twenties and
thirties. Perhaps I might realize an
ambition to play Lear at the character's
age of fourscore years. I intend to try
for it and hope the Neptune and its
supporters will be on the waterfront at
the Provincial Performing Arts Centre
to celebrate with me.

**Joan
Gregson**

Two years after I had received a Best
Actress Award in the Dominion Drama
Festival from adjudicator Leon Major,
he asked me to play in *The Fourposter*
with the new company he was starting at
Neptune Theatre. I was astounded and
delighted. My professional debut was in
Major Barbara, and I went on to play

many other parts. It has been a
tremendous experience to work with so
many and such gifted people over the
years. I have been thrilled to do so many
wonderful plays. It has opened up a
whole new life for me and a whole new
way of looking at things that I might
never have had.

**Deborah
Cass**

**Bernard
Behrens**

To my wife Deborah Cass and myself,
both founding members, Neptune
meant the opening of new theatrical
frontiers in Canada, and we are very
proud and happy to have been part of its
birth and struggle to survive. It also gave
us the opportunity to work steadily with
Leon Major, whom we greatly admire
and respect. We remember the good
and bad times, the happy, sad and angry
times. I do recall towards the end of the
second year our total exhaustion
because of the long endless hours of
commitment to make it work, but it is
nice to know that the belief we felt then
has been confirmed by the continuing
existence of Neptune.

**Mavor
Moore**

For me, Neptune was part of a memorable series of "launchings"—because my association with it was entirely before and during its opening season. I had already been associated with the launching of Toronto's New Play Society in the 40s, and in the 50s with CBC Television, the Canadian Theatre Centre and the National Theatre School—and was one of those strongly urging Leon Major to "take on" Neptune. I was delighted when he invited me to direct and perform in the first season, and greatly enjoyed this first stay in the Maritimes—especially, perhaps, working with the early board members.

**George
Sperdakos**

My Neptune Theatre experience encompassed the most glorious of personal and public services. The Neptune, the locale, the people, slugging it out at my craft, the joys and hardships, the pioneering aspect, all made me feel like a privileged adventurer. I was thrust into a vital microcosm, filled with divine opportunities. It was a chance to work with an excellent company of people, to stretch my skills with a wide variety of parts, to contact a curious new audience, to make friends with some grand people and to discover the best in myself. I owe those golden years, years I will never forget, to Neptune.

**Hon.
Robert
Stanfield**

The Neptune Theatre added a new dimension to life in Halifax 25 years ago: a real live professional theatre of high quality in our own town. Neptune was a bold and courageous venture by those who launched it. Many doubted its success. For me Neptune meant more enjoyment and additional pride in Halifax. Despite its quick artistic success, Neptune faced a financial challenge that would have overwhelmed the timid. A comparison with the established and successful Winnipeg theatre showed that Neptune was drawing to its box office as big a percentage of the population of Halifax-Dartmouth as the Winnipeg theatre was drawing in its city. But Winnipeg had twice the population to draw on and therefore twice the ticket sales. That difference indicated the extent of Neptune's challenge. I remember that we appointed Charlie Beazley, the most senior public servant in the province, to be a continuing liaison between the government and Neptune. This indicated the importance we attached to Neptune's survival and health. The theatre overcame its crises. I congratulate those who through 25 years have devoted the sweat and tears a theatre like Neptune demands. They have served Nova Scotia very well indeed. I hear the first 25 years are the hardest. Certainly they have been great years.

**Robert
Doyle**

Halifax at once made me welcome in 1963, and I grew to love the Maritimes, which have become my permanent home. Now as I look back at a very full lifetime of designing in this province, I can thank Neptune Theatre for the opportunity of establishing a very fruitful career, which has led me on to many of Canada's major repertory theatres. It all seems impossible now—however it was done—we never questioned the scale or the challenge of creating out of nothing. It has been interesting to watch the theatre grow over the past 25 years, witnessing the various directors come and go and working for many of them. Neptune has never taken a back seat to other regional theatres but has established itself as a good place to work, attracting talented performers, designers, directors and technicians from across Canada, the United States and England.

Mary McMurray

My first appearance at Neptune resulted from meeting Leon Major when I was engaged to sing for the Toronto Opera Company where he was directing *Rigoletto*. It was wonderful to be so secure with the first Neptune company. It was hard work learning one play in the morning, rehearsing another in the afternoon and playing a third in the evening. But it was three years of heaven working for Leon: he was very paternal, very protective, always positive and assessed people's abilities very well. We were working in a family, and treated one another like members of a family.

John Blackmore

My brother William and I have been the theatre's official carpenters and set makers from day one. Our first job was for *Major Barbara*, and we realized from the start that at Neptune the sets had to be just right. At the beginning we had

Leon Major and Bob Dexter, who had come in from Toronto and had worked in live theatre before. Apart from them, no one in props or wardrobe had much experience. We were lucky to have Bob Doyle. With his help and training as a set and costume designer, we managed. We construct the sets based on the designer's model, and we've built for all the main stage shows. We make realistic sets and symbolic ones. After 24 years in the cramped Neptune basement, we moved to the Creighton Street carpentry shop and set and props warehouse last August.

Ted Follows

My congratulations on the theatre's continuing success. I have a deep sense of pride and propriety in Neptune and will always feel that I am one of the small foundation stones on which the theatre was built and continues. Living in Halifax completed my Canadian education. It was an exciting three years, and the spell of our oldest province took a powerful hold on me. I still miss it to this day. In fact my former wife, Dawn, and I debated about staying on but decided as performers that there were other places and media to conquer. I don't regret our decision, but occasionally I long for that wet sea tang in the air.

Gary Krawford

I have fond memories of Halifax and the beautiful *new* Neptune Theatre. I was 21 and played many of the juvenile leads that season. We were a small repertory company, so I was given the opportunity to play some very challenging roles which would not have been available to me otherwise. Leon Major allowed me to do my first musical, *The Fantasticks*, at Neptune. One year later I was playing the same role in New York in the off-Broadway production. I am very happy that, 25 years later, the Neptune Theatre is still there and prospering.

Lloyd Newman

There are probably 20 people without whose contribution Neptune would never have begun and continued. I particularly remember three with whom I was closely associated during the earliest days and later during my tenure as Chairman of the Board. Halifax theatregoers can never repay their debt to Colonel Sidney C. Oland, Bob Strand and Charles Beazley Q.C., but we all know that it has taken many people, with their combined efforts, to sustain Neptune. These three are representative of the unnamed many. I thank them all.

David Brown

The success of Neptune Theatre has reflected a desire on the part of the citizenry of Halifax to enrich their cultural dimensions in what surely must be one of the most lively and colourful societies in North America. I shall always be grateful to the Neptune for providing me with a sound foundation upon which I've been able to pursue a very happy career in the theatre. Have a great 25th!

Peter Evans

It was wonderful to see a professional company opening in Halifax in 1963— the experience of a lifetime. The early days under Leon's direction held a very special sort of feeling. With Joan [Gregson] being so much involved and so good at what she does, it became a great thing in our lives. Once you are involved you get caught up in the emotional experience. Our kids got a lot out of the theatre. As president from 1973 to '74, I saw a whole different side of life: there is need for a business person to realize how hard people in theatre work; from my own point of view I got to understand just how hard their work is.

Ed Rubin

I have been involved with Neptune Theatre from its inception. Arthur Murphy invited me to go on the board because of my activities with Theatre Arts Guild. I attended many meetings and saw things come about; I am still an honorary board member. It was a wonderful dream, inspired by Colonel Sidney Oland, Dr. Arthur Murphy and Leon Major. A year after Neptune opened, I got up enough courage to say, "Leon, I'd like to have a go at it." Leon agreed, saying the difference between amateur and professional is a matter of attitude: it is the approach that makes all the difference. I called myself the "cameo kid," enjoying the work very much. I recalled the old cliché, "There are no small parts, only small actors." It was a lot of fun, but I took it all seriously. I have witnessed the growth of Neptune over the years—the highlights and frustrations. Neptune has been very much part of my life and my family's life. I love the theatre so much. I still love to be part of it. I was pleased to become chairman of the 25th Anniversary Committee when Tom Kerr asked me. The fact that Neptune has been here for 25 years is an achievement in itself; the fact that so many people have worked here is something to be very proud of.

Kurt Reis

I've directed many productions at the Neptune Theatre in the last 25 years. The first time I was there was for the 1964-65 season. It was a very special time for all of us. We were young, hopeful, dedicated and very certain that something new and exciting was happening here. It was a beginning, and we were part of it.

Ron Hastings

Being part of the theatrical community is a family experience. If this is so, Leon Major is my father and Neptune Theatre is where I grew up. My brothers and sisters were the ensemble players who jointly were involved in flexing muscles and spreading wings by interacting with a supportive and nurturing company. Whatever I do and wherever I go, Neptune and Halifax will always be my old neighborhood, thought of with great affection and appreciation.

Don Allison

Neptune Theatre is my *home* theatre, not only because I am a Nova Scotian, but also because my career was nurtured there from 1968 to 1973 when I had the great privilege of working with and learning from some of Canada's finest actors and directors. That cosy house with its friendly audiences has welcomed me *home* again and again for a total of 35 productions, so I look forward to our next reunion. Neptune, I wish you a heartfelt *Happy Birthday*!

Libby Day

My four years as the P.R. lady at Neptune coincided with an interesting transition period in the theatre's development. I think even the doomsayers were beginning to see that it was no longer a question of the theatre's *survival*—people were actually attending and enjoying the productions. We still had to struggle against the licentious reputation attached to the theatre. I was in fact once asked what a nice girl like me was doing working there, and what did my family think about it! I learned a lot about people, and about getting things done, and I have a lot of respect for the labour, paid and unpaid, and devotion which so many people gave to Neptune. It was very exciting. It was damned hard work—and the greatest possible fun.

Faith Ward

I started at Neptune in 1968 and did most of my work during Heinar Piller's period. Heinar was a particularly good director, who had a lot of energy. When I had difficulty over a costume in *The Boy Friend*, he said, "Faith, make it work for you." I learned from him that if a line won't go right, *you* have to make it work; you don't rely on the director to help you. The repertory system was very successful. It didn't get stale, kept you on your toes and demanded much more concentration than playing in stock. We managed with a revolve and multiple sets, even bringing in some from front of house. Sometimes we rehearsed in St. Paul's Church Hall, where the Five Fisherman restaurant is now. Sometimes we used the Schwartz building, made of solid wood impregnated with the most lovely scent of spices. We had to climb the wooden stairs to the top, and I thought, "My God, if there's a fire we'll never get out."

Patricia Ludwick

No one could have had a more wonderful introduction to professional theatre than I had at Neptune in the spring of 1969. My first week of rehearsals for *The Promise* took place in the director's house at Duncan's Cove, with the Atlantic at our feet and stacks of books to read around the fire. Over the next six months my love affair with Nova Scotia continued to blossom with a tour of the three Maritime Provinces, a summer of plays in repertory in one of Canada's most delightful theatres, and an experiment with theatre-in-the-round in the basement of King's College. After that, I was hooked: where else could I find such a community of artists, a city of such colour and vigour, and the chance to develop my craft for an audience so receptive? Neptune seemed to attract people full of energy, curiosity and, best of all, good humour. I remember the crew member who wore a kilt backstage; the box office worker who offered her own home to a group of bedraggled cyclists from Manhattan after selling them tickets to the show; the Polish seamen who came to the theatre whenever their ship was in port; the actors dressed as mermaids in the winning float at the Natal Day Parade; and the loyal fans from the Seahorse Tavern who never missed a show at the tiny Second Stage.

Richard Donat

Neptune Theatre meant steady employment for one season when I was young. It also meant that several of us were able to form a small group called Second Stage where we performed plays that could not be performed at Neptune. Here I had the opportunity of playing roles I would never have played otherwise, and my skill as an actor developed more quickly and interestingly. It was a wonderful time in those days, and I would like to extend my appreciation to Neptune, one of the loveliest theatres in the land.

D. Ray Pierce

I have fond memories of Neptune because it was my first professional company and because Nova Scotia was my home. It gave me a chance to come back from the States and earn a living in the area I knew best and where friends and friendly audiences were. In those days there was a flourishing career for the people at Neptune because Halifax was the headquarters of CBC-radio drama for the national network. My memories of Neptune are relatively fresh after 20 years. Without that experience I probably would never have gone on to do the directing, producing and arts management I have since accomplished in this community.

Roland Hewgill

I *loved* working at Neptune, and playing there was always a pleasure. I think the relationship from actor to audience is the best in the country—a wonderful feeling of intimacy which, sadly, new concrete blocks do not have. I have great affection for the place, the city of Halifax and *especially* the people. There have been so many moving, happy memories. One day I hope I'll play there again before God gathers me up!

Joseph Rutten

I had just completed my first four seasons at Stratford and was living in Toronto in 1966, when Leon Major invited me to come to Halifax. Since then, it has been my privilege to have acted in some dozen productions at Neptune Theatre, and in another four at Second Stage. The intimacy of Neptune and the gossamer but tangible weight of the accumulated theatrical vibrations are an actor's delight. None of the productions in which I have appeared has failed to bring me this wonderful communication with the audience. But I regret the passing of the ship's bell, which used to be rung at the start of every performance. It was a thrilling counterpart to the old three knocks with the staff or the firing of the gun at Stratford, lending a unique maritime flavour to the proceedings. Halifax without Neptune Theatre would be unthinkable. Long may they both live!

M. J. Walker

I first became actively involved with Neptune in the early 1970s, when I joined the now-defunct Tridents, the women's auxiliary of the theatre. I became chairman of that organization and joined the Board of Directors of the Foundation. I later became a member of the executive and in 1981 I was invited to become Honorary Vice-President and Life-Director. I have seen many changes in direction for the theatre under the leadership of various artistic directors who have been at the helm during my tenure, and I feel that these changes have kept the theatre so vibrant. I firmly believe that Neptune is an important component of the cultural life of this community, and I have been proud of my involvement with this great institution. Happy Birthday, Neptune!

Bruce Blakemore

The sense of smell is one of the strongest memory triggers we possess. I worked at Neptune as a stage and tour manager through the 1970s and early '80s, and sometimes when I encounter the gentle aroma of freshly cut pine I am transported back there. I entered the theatre from Argyle Street and my first impression was the smell of wood. The carpentry shop was at the bottom of the stairs leading up to the offices, and lumber was always stored in the stairwell. Another olfactory experience was provided by one of the rehearsal spaces. It was the old Schwartz spice warehouse on north Barrington Street, and the room at the back of the third floor where we rehearsed had been the cinnamon and nutmeg storage room. The old wood was permeated with those smells. It was wonderful—like working inside a cinnamon roll.

Nicola Lipman

I remember with tremendous warmth and clarity that period in the early '70s when Neptune's Second Stage first blossomed. This became a forum for new work and new artists, and those who ventured there were rarely disappointed. At the same time there was an equally vital and experimental theatre down on the waterfront called Pier One. The insistent rivalry but basic camaraderie that extended between these two theatres became a very attractive and magnetic force in the city, drawing many artists from all over the country to the region and providing a bonus and a challenge for audiences.

Ian Deakin

I am very proud to have been part of Neptune's history. As a student I watched many productions in the 1960s, never realizing that those actors I admired would later become my associates and friends. I recall the joy of joining the acting ranks at Second Stage, where we opened *Creeps* in a howling blizzard with an audience made up of the truly committed. My memories range from proposing to my wife Bonnie (who later headed Neptune's wardrobe department) between costume changes in the second intermission of *The Matchmaker* to clutching Juliet in my arms and speaking Shakespeare's immortal lines before a packed house. They also extend from the warmth of hospitality of those Nova Scotians who treated a visit by the Neptune company as a major annual event to the ghost who walks the catwalk in the theatre! Happy Birthday, Neptune. I know there will be many more.

Phillip Silver

During John Neville's directorship of Neptune, I had the pleasure of designing four very different productions: *Staircase, The Master Builder, The Night of the Iguana* and *The Diary of a Scoundrel*. All were challenging, but in retrospect, none more so than *Iguana*. The play demands a set depicting the outside of a run-down Mexican hotel nestled in a hillside jungle. Such a scene requires space, a virtue in limited supply at Neptune. The play also demands a tremendous tropical storm scene. I had done *Iguana* before in a larger theatre, but somehow the smaller space worked much better than I expected, and the visual result was very pleasing. As usual, the very capable technical staff solved the storm problems with ease. The Act I climax of John's production with that very fine actor Roland Hewgill standing centre stage in a great downpour, cursing the heavens amidst thunder, lightning, wind and rain, is a memory that will remain in my mind as typical of the fine theatre that is the Neptune tradition. It's an honour to be part of it!

Jackie Oland

The period when I was President of the Board was rather an exciting time. There was a lot of energy on the board and a sense of direction. We had people who were prepared to give their time and talents and we knew that the focus was to support the artistic director and general manager within the mandate of the board, to raise funds, lobby government and be as supportive as we could. It was not easy being president without having been on the executive, but Reigh Bustin was a solid treasurer, good friend and valued advisor, and Lloyd Newman was always very helpful. It was jolly hard work getting sponsorship for productions, but we had a good product to sell. I could not expect John Neville or Tom Kerr to do their work as theatre directors and also bear this additional burden.

Miriam Newhouse

A Westerner born and bred, I'd never been farther east than Toronto before I worked at Neptune. What an extraordinary change! To see sights far more beautiful and moving than the Rockies or the Pacific; to meet people with vitality and energy, with humour and guts unmatched in the West; to find a link between all that I was learning and all that I knew. Thanks, Neptune!

Tony Randall

Congratulations to Neptune! What a difference it made in my life! I had dreamed of doing the classics but the chance had never come. And then John Neville invited me to do *The Sea Gull*. It was a dream come true. My life has taken a new turn since then.

Sean Mulcahy

The Neptune Theatre meant five splendid roles over about three years. It possessed set construction and wardrobe departments that would be a credit to any theatre in the world. All this (during my visits) under the estimable leadership of John Neville and later Tom Kerr. Three of the plays I was in toured, and so Cape Breton entered my life— need one say more?! My visits invariably coincided with Remembrance Day and Halloween. Both celebrations were so

vastly different and both realized with such poignancy and pleasure by the people of Halifax.

John Dunsworth

My first hazy memories of Neptune were the parties that Leon Major threw when he stayed at my parents' home the first summer he was in Halifax. The only vivid memories I have of that time were the productions of *Ondine* and *The Fantasticks*. I was enthralled. In those early years, there were the Tridents— people who supported the Neptune and sold subscriptions. My mother Frances sold the most subscriptions two years running and won two trips to New York City. This is most impressive when you consider she was raising ten children at the time. When she was selling subscriptions her favourite line was "there's not a bad seat in the house." Over the years many wonderful local actors have appeared there, but the person I most connect with Neptune is David Renton. From character to fantastic character, he has always been a constant source of amazement. Never once in my wildest dreams did I imagine myself on stage there, but John Neville offered me many excellent roles; he even gave me my start as a professional director—albeit of lunchtime productions, but a start nevertheless.

Walter Borden

When John Neville found out I was an actor he said, "How would you like to play Biondello in *The Taming of the Shrew*?" I said, "I'd like that very much." From that point, I went into a series of things. Probably the most important was working with the Young Neptune Touring Company. It was very important to me. I couldn't just be Walter Borden, an actor; I had another role to play. It was sometimes trying, but I knew I had to do it: I had to be an ambassador for my community. For a long time I was the only professional black actor east of Montreal. *Shine Boy* has been a significant point in my life in Halifax; I can't think of a moment in all the 25 years I've worked in the province and the community that has been as poignant and special to me as the opening night of this play.

Denise Rooney

Neptune has been a great joy to me. Its high artistic standards evoke a sense of pride in anyone who has ever worked for this organization. In spite of fiscal restraints, we have grown and expanded over the past 25 years. That

development is living testimony to all of the former employees, artists, board members, donors and patrons who have made valuable contributions to Neptune. I thank you for your commitment, I thank Neptune for the enjoyment and opportunities it has given me, and I thank those who will come after us for the next 25 years. Happy Birthday, Neptune, and may you have many more!

Irene Watts

I worked with three artistic directors— Neville, Kerr and, very briefly, Ouzounian. Neville and I founded Young Neptune. I selected the season every year until this year (1987-8), usually contributing one original script. Our aim was to reach the widest possible community. Nothing stopped us! One of the best experiences was a collaboration with the Neptune Theatre School. *A Christmas Carol* cast several children from our classes, and I was fortunate to have the talents of the All Saints' Cathedral Junior Choir to help make this a truly magical Christmas. Tom Kerr and I collaborated on the script. It was under his tenure that we founded the school, and when I left in '86 there were classes for every age group, including a Heritage Class for senior citizens.

Kim Coates

Halifax and the Neptune Theatre are very special to me. My first professional show, *Ever Loving*, was done there. During the years 1982-86 I performed over ten plays at the Neptune and surrounding theatres. The city is literally my second home. The warmth of the people, Bud the Spud and Juicy Jane's sandwiches are things I'll never forget. Even though I'm from the Prairies, I feel a lot of my roots are spread around Argyle Street.

Glen Cairns

In 1985 Tom Kerr and I were able to revive the idea of a second stage for Neptune at the Cunard Street Theatre, the recently acquired facility of the Nova Scotia Drama League. We determined that the second stage should provide provocative programming which was rooted in the concept of "alternate" theatre and that it must never become a low-budget version of the main stage. *Cold Comfort* was at the aesthetic centre of the first season. Its inclusion represented the direction in which I wanted the theatre to move—towards the creation of indigenous work which would speak about who we are, as a distinctively Northern rather than an American or European people, in forms that better represented our identity than American or European naturalism or realism.

Andrew Murray

Neptune Theatre means a great deal to me. I arrived at Neptune's doors at the age of 19, under the invitation of John Neville, to fill the position of Artist-in-Residence for the 19th season. Mr. Neville and I had met several years earlier in my hometown of Antigonish, and he had promised that we would work together in the future. And so began a five-year and continuing relationship with the collection of buildings on the corner of Argyle and Sackville Streets. As apprentice and designer of many Neptune productions, I have met and worked with some of Canada's great theatrical personalities and have made many friends. Happy Birthday, Neptune!

Maxim Mazumdar

Neptune Theatre has given me more memorable stage opportunities than any other Canadian theatre company. I have had the chance to play the Devil, a fake Maharajah, a New York transvestite and to sing in a classy cabaret with the marvelously talented Don Harron, Catherine McKinnon and Paul Simons. Wonderful experiences all!

Jennette White

My memories of Neptune Theatre are varied, but all of them hold a special place in my thoughts and in my heart. There's the time when, being young and foolish, I and my fellow students at Dalhousie would touch the building reverently as we passed by, willing ourselves to work there one day. Then the day came when indeed I was asked by Tom Kerr to join the Young Neptune Touring Company. Later Richard Ouzounian gave me the opportunity to pass on my love of theatre by asking me to become Director of the Theatre

School, and he also encouraged me to write my first plays for children. These memories emphasize the realization that as a Nova Scotian who loves her work, I have been able to nurture my talent here, and indeed I have been nurtured myself in one of the best regional theatres in the country. May the next 25 to 100 years see the continued growth of a viable regional theatre, comparable to any in our country. *Happy Birthday, Neptune!*

Shawn Wright

I started at Neptune on a three-show contract—*A Christmas Carol, Victory* and *Evita.* Then I was called back for *The Black Bonspiel of Wullie MacCrimmon,* for which I had the chance to understudy Don Harron and take over from him for three performances. When I think of Neptune in my mind and my heart, it really was a professional coming-of-age for me. I enjoyed the exposure to new scripts: *Victory* and *Cinderalla.* I didn't realize how healthy the artistic environment is here. In larger centres the product is the thing—it is more commercial than artistic—but here the emphasis is on the individual rather than the whole machine. I like the Neptune audiences very much; they seem very open to being entertained, but it is not the same everywhere.

**Bruce
Klinger**
Neptune
General Manager
from November 1988

In 25 short years Neptune Theatre has become an institution in the City of Halifax and a wonderful asset to the Province of Nova Scotia. This fact is a great tribute to those staff, Board Members and performers who have worked so hard over the years to reach this point.

I have had the good fortune to know and work with a large number of the people who have contributed to the stature of this theatre and it has been a great honour to be associated with them.

As Neptune enters its next quarter-century the effort of all those who have put so many hours of their time to create this leading regional theatre will not be forgotten. The outlook for the next 25 years is bright indeed, thanks to those who have been a part of the first 25. Happy Birthday Neptune!

**Allister
Byrne**

My first experience with Neptune was as a theatregoer. When my friend Reigh Bustin, then president, invited me to join the board, I didn't know what was in store. It was an opportunity to see what was happening behind the scenes of the theatre, whereas I had only been six times a year to see the productions. A year later I took on the job of treasurer, and this got me up to full speed with regard to the operating of the theatre. The job really requires you to dissect the operations, not just chasing numbers around, but understanding how the theatre works and what its economics are. Last year the board asked me to assume the presidency. I have now moved to being up-front in planning a season with the artistic director and the board. It's been quite an experience. I've had no formal training in arts, yet I've found my life so much richer as a result of this work. It's a very important part of my life, and even now I spend about 20 hours a week on it.

**Beverly
West**

In mid-September of 1986, I took the weekend off and moved from the Charlottetown Festival in Prince Edward Island to assume the position of Public Relations Director at Neptune Theatre. That was just two short weeks before the opening of Richard Ouzounian's first season at Neptune Theatre. We are now in our third season, and during the past few years, I have had the opportunity of working with the people within the theatre, as well as the dedicated corporate and private citizens of Nova Scotia who have been an integral part of Neptune's growth over the past 25 years. It has been a great privilege to have worked with one of Canada's oldest professional theatres, with the dedicated staff and the many talented members of Canada's acting community. As Neptune looks forward to another quarter century, I wish it much success and prosperity. Happy 25th Anniversary, Neptune!

Index

(excluding playbills)

PHOTO CREDITS

Key: A - Dalhousie University Archives, Neptune Theatre Collection.

DOROTHY PERKYNS has had wide experience as teacher and journalist. Her articles have appeared in many periodicals, including *The Atlantic Advocate, Touring and Travel,* and *Canadian Churchman.* She has been a contributing editor of *Performing Arts in Canada* and theatre columnist for *Halifax* magazine. Her two books for children, *The Mystery of Hemlock Ravine* (1986) and *Rachel's Revolution* (1988) were both published by Lancelot Press.

BASIL DEAKIN was already a widely experienced journalist when he emigrated to Canada from England in 1963. During almost twenty-five years with *The Halifax Herald,* chiefly as drama critic, entertainment editor and associate editor, he maintained a close professional relationship with Neptune Theatre. Although retired since October 1987, he continues to write a twice-weekly column for *The Chronicle-Herald* and *The Mail-Star.*

DAVID RENTON's name, almost synonmous with Neptune, appears frequently in this book. He has played more than one hundred roles for Neptune, as well as appearing in other Canadian theatres, and is nationally known as a radio performer. He is highly regarded in the province as theatre director and drama education organizer and adviser.